About the Author

Katherine Livesey is a Young Adult Fantasy author living in the historic Northumberland countryside. She was born and raised in the wilds of Lancashire and spent much of her childhood running ragged across the moors or lost in a sea of books.

Katherine takes inspiration from folklore, fairy tales and the classics of the Fantasy genre, as well as the ever-changing but ever-present natural world that surrounds her home. When not writing, Katherine can usually be found knee-deep in mud walking her two Alaskan Huskies with her partner, baking up a storm in her little kitchen or watching an old favourite period drama.

katherinelivesey.co.uk

instagram.com/katherine.livesey
twitter.com/kliveseyauthor

Books by Katherine Livesey

Sisters of Shadow

Sisters of Moonlight

Sisters of Midnight

SISTERS OF MIDNIGHT

KATHERINE LIVESEY

One More Chapter
a division of HarperCollins*Publishers*
1 London Bridge Street
London SE1 9GF
www.harpercollins.co.uk
HarperCollins*Publishers*
1st Floor, Watermarque Building, Ringsend Road
Dublin 4, Ireland
This paperback edition 2022
1
First published in Great Britain
by HarperCollins*Publishers* 2022
Copyright © Katherine Livesey 2022
Map © Laura Hall
Katherine Livesey asserts the moral right to be identified
as the author of this work
A catalogue record of this book is available from the British Library

ISBN: 978-0-00-846774-6

This novel is entirely a work of fiction. The names, characters and incidents portrayed in it are the work of the author's imagination. Any resemblance to actual persons, living or dead, events or localities is entirely coincidental.

Printed and bound in the UK using 100% Renewable Electricity
by CPI Group (UK) Ltd

All rights reserved. No part of this publication may be reproduced, stored in a retrieval system, or transmitted, in any form or by any means, electronic, mechanical, photocopying, recording or otherwise, without the prior permission of the publishers.

*For Arron, you are my north star in the darkness.
Thank you for everything.*

Love is like the wild rose-briar,
Friendship like the holly-tree—
The holly is dark when the rose-briar blooms
But which will bloom most constantly?

— Emily Brontë, 'Love and Friendship'

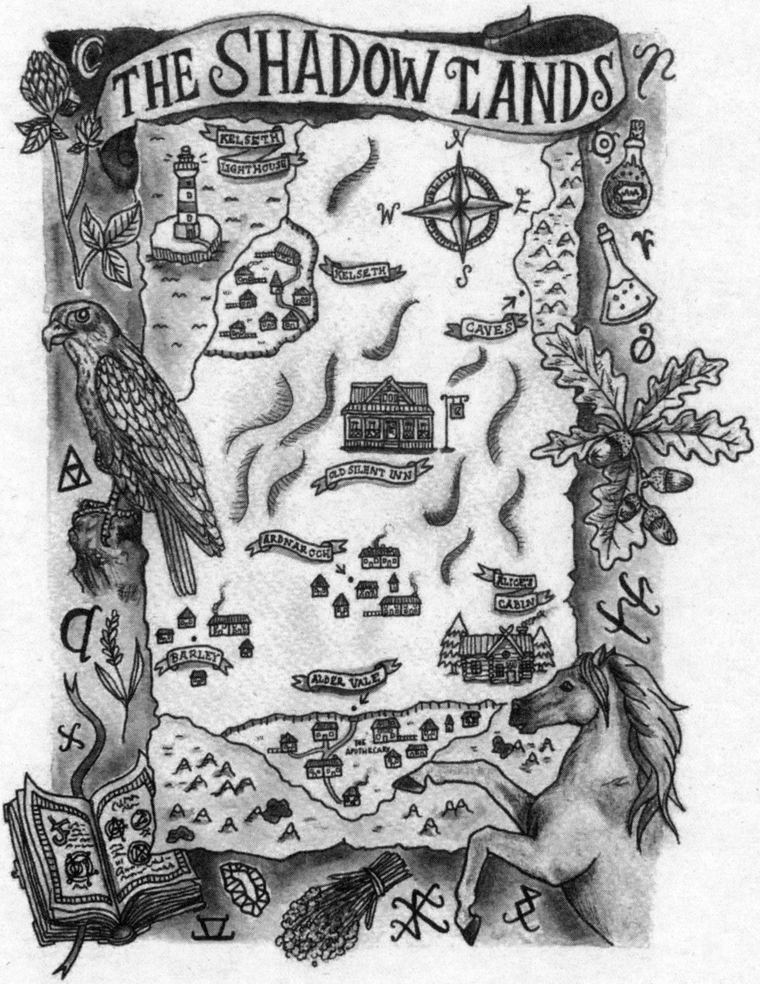
THE SHADOW LANDS
KELSETH LIGHTHOUSE
N
W
E
S
KELSETH
CAVES
OLD SILENT INN
ARDNAROCH
ALICE'S CABIN
BARLEY
ALDER VALE
THE APOTHECARY

Prologue

'The Shadow Sect must be eliminated.'

A strong, clipped voice echoed across a shadowy colourless hall. It was a grey, cavernous space, and looked as though all the colours had been washed away in a rainstorm, leaving only tones of light and dark grey: grey walls, grey vaulted ceiling, grey marble floor.

The windows dotted around the walls were tall and slender, letting in shafts of pale light that illuminated the crowd of golden-robed people listening to the speaker. Long black rectangular flags hung in rows from the ceiling, emblazoned with a golden tree encircled by a golden ring.

'Strength like theirs shouldn't exist. Their power is a plague. It's unnatural, unclean, unthinkable.' His voice reverberated around the room. The windows tremored in their frames with each syllable uttered. 'They are everything we stand against.' The man had wispy blonde hair and sharp violet eyes surrounded by deep crow's-feet wrinkles. The crowd were hanging on his every word, and he knew it. 'The Bloodletting at Oakencliff proved that we are not only capable of this, but that we will be revered for it; the people of the Shadow Lands need us to eliminate this threat, even if most of them don't know it yet. We will be their heroes. We will free them from this scourge.'

'Hear, hear!' a voice from the crowd shouted. Several others joined. 'Hear, hear!'

The man looked across the room at the mass of faces hanging on his every word. He knew that whatever he asked of them, whatever rule or law he put in place, they would follow, and they would execute. Ever since he had claimed the trust of the barons of Hythlund, he'd had the entire fiefdom at his disposal. This had been his greatest victory of all – so great, in fact, that for a while he had been contented to leave Oakencliff as the only cleansed village in the Shadow Lands. But that wasn't enough any longer. The Bloodletting had slowed the growth of the Shadow Sect, that was true, but he knew Hecate Winter well enough to know that she wasn't a woman who would be held down for long.

'Are you all clear on our plan?'

'Yes!' the crowd shouted in unison.

'Good.' His voice was amplified by the magic of a thin, brittle man who stood a few paces away, below the podium on which the speaker stood. Magic had its uses, for now. It would give them an edge in the fight against Hecate's cronies, an edge she wouldn't expect. Once the job was done, magic would be eliminated in all of its forms, but that was information he kept to himself for the time being. 'Just as we planned, our spy has been taken into the heart of their organisation; they see him as nothing but a weakling. It all played out exactly as we knew it would. He will continue to do our bidding, so long as we have this.' Two men in the same golden robes as the crowd dragged something – or rather someone – onto the podium. He was a young man, barely out of boyhood, with dark-brown curly hair and two large purple bruises bulging from both of his eyes. Blood ran in a delicate trickle from the corner of his mouth, and he could barely support himself. The robed men held him in a crooked, upright position.

'Tell them your name, boy,' the man demanded.

'W-w...' The boy stuttered. His jaw, too, was bruised and crooked. The man didn't seem to care. His struck the boy across the face, sending a tooth flying across the room.

'YOUR. NAME.'

'Wylf, sir. Wylf Leiflaed.'

'Wylf is rather a *favourite* of our spy. So long as he is here, with us, our spy will do exactly as we ask.'

'No...' the boy, Wylf, pleaded.

'Oh yes, my boy. We'll put you out of your misery soon enough, don't you worry.' His voice was venomous, and he held the crowd with his words of might and terror. They were both in awe and completely terrified of him, which was just how he liked it. With a flick of his wrist, the men dragged Wylf back out of sight. His cries echoed, then faded into silence.

'What of the traitor?' a voice shouted from the audience. 'What will you do with the traitor?'

A ripple of agreement passed through the crowd, as if the question had been plaguing them all.

'The traitor is under constant surveillance, and as we hoped, he has led us to the door of a castle that houses some of Hecate Winter's most promising allies. She will protect them, if they come under threat.'

'How do you know?' a rogue voice shouted.

'You dare question my knowledge?' the man on the podium growled. 'Question me again and you will suffer far worse a fate than any of our enemies.'

Silence filled the room once more.

'When Hecate comes to their aid, she will want them all back within her stronghold where she can best protect them. They will lead us straight to the Shadow Sect's door.' Cheers bubbled up through the crowd. The man paused a moment to soak in the reverence. 'Now, all we have to do is orchestrate a threatening, if not entirely devastating, attack, and they will take us straight to Hecate's hiding place. Once we've located their stronghold, we begin our final fight: we will take the Shadow Lands and rid them of this plague that calls themselves the Shadow Sect. Their evil will be stamped out, once and for all. Magic of their kind is a poison, and it must be eradicated. We must cleanse the world of their evil and build a golden future from the ashes.'

Jubilant shouts of victory filled the air. The man narrowed his eyes and stood up taller, bolstered by their loyalty. First the Shadow Sect, then the Shadow Lands. Fenn Crydlund and the Brotherhood of Light would destroy them all.

Chapter One

One moon cycle later

Thunder rumbled across the wide expanse of moorland and lightning streaked across the sky, illuminating Midnight Manor. Lily Knight, panic-stricken, cast her eyes around, trying to make sense of the scene through the tumult of snow hammering down from the blackness above. There was Jem Rafferty and his sister Grace, clinging to each other, faces etched with terror. Beside them, there were two curly-haired twins, Maeve and Brenna, clutching the hems of Jem and Grace's cloaks. On the floor, just inside the wrought-iron gates, were Cass and Morven, still retching from the intensity of whatever spell had been used to transport all of them from their home on the beach of Moonlight Castle, to here, leagues away, in the grounds of the manor house their mortal enemy called home. Morven's usually pristine mousy-coloured hair was dishevelled and Cass's white freckled skin looked completely devoid of colour.

A whooshing sound broke through the noise of the storm, and then another, and then another. Figures, hooded in golden cloaks, started to emerge from the darkness.

'SECURE THE GATES!' Lily heard someone yell.

It was Hecate Winter, the woman who had haunted them, destroyed their lighthouse, tortured Lily, and murdered their poor young ward, Glenn. She had *helped* them. With Lily's best friend, Alice Blackwell, at her side.

The figures in cloaks began their spectral chants once more, as they had at Moonlight Castle.

'Surrender to the Brotherhood.

Surrender to the Brotherhood.

Come into the light and

Surrender to the Brotherhood.'

Jem and Grace rushed forwards, pushing the huge, heavy gates to a close. Hecate's shouts continued, until people flooded out from the manor house with their arms outstretched, muttering spells and incantations as they went. The gates shimmered as the residents of Midnight Manor fortified it with their magic, until the golden-cloaked assailants were but shadows behind it.

Lily ran to join Jem, who had just taken several steps back from the gate, his eyes wide. The chanting was growing louder and more intense with each passing moment. Lily slipped her hands into Jem's and whispered, 'Are you all right?'

He squeezed her hand but didn't tear his eyes away from the men beyond the gate. Their shadowy figures were closer now, staring straight through the shimmering metal. The gate trembled in rhythm with the chants, but the shield didn't falter.

'HOW CAN THEY HAVE MAGIC?' Lily heard Grace yell, and wheeled around to see Alice muttering an incantation with Grace standing strong by her side, protecting her.

'I'll explain later!' Hecate shouted back. She was also focused with frightening intensity on the shield.

'Surrender to the Brotherhood.

Surrender to the Brotherhood.'

'I think it's working,' Jem turned to Lily, 'but we should stand back, just in case.'

Lily nodded and allowed more witches from inside Midnight Manor to take their place. They were surrounded now by dozens of people of varying ages, all focused on one target. Unflinching. Unrelenting.

A young man shouldered past Lily, catching her eye as he sauntered forward, throwing a careless grin in her direction. He wore a pristine deep-purple velvet suit, walked with a stick, and had thick hair that fell across one half of his face. There was something otherworldly about him, and Lily knew in an instant that he didn't belong in the Shadow Lands.

He walked directly at the gate, only stopping when his nose was pressed against the metal. The chanting faltered, then stopped. The boy appeared to be chuckling. He threw his arms wide open. 'Come and get me, then. If you're all as strong as you want folk to believe, come and get me and take me back to my dreadful father. Go on, do it.'

Lily realised he was taunting them, and it was working. The shield was visibly growing stronger, as if it were no longer met by resistance. Some of the cloaked figures even started to shout, instead of sticking to their uniform chanting.

'Farlan Aelfdene, your father will have your head on a platter for this, boy!' Lily heard one man shout.

'You freak!' another rejoindered. Very quickly, the men beyond the gate launched into a tirade, attacking the boy with their words.

Lily watched in awe as he continued to rile them up. He sauntered along the width of the gate like a bard on a stage, playing his audience. He even seemed to know some of them by name. Who was this boy? Why was he here?

The cloaked men started to disperse. Some of them backed away, disappearing into the darkness. Others vanished from the spots where they stood, as if they had suddenly become invisible. Only a few Brotherhood members remained, and they looked murderous.

This distraction, however, appeared to be exactly what Hecate and the rest of the Shadow Sect needed. An earth-shattering crack shattered through the storm and the shimmering gate turned solid silver, as though a curtain had just been flung across it.

'It's done!' Hecate cried, and slowly, each witch lowered their trembling arms. 'It's done. Well done, Farlan.' She sighed. 'But it's not over. Someone will have to keep watch on the gate for potential weaknesses. We'll sort a roster later, but for now, Ailsa, Rowenna, you have the first watch. I'll send someone to relieve you later. Everyone else, inside.'

Lily looked around for the rest of their group. Morven and Cass had the twins and were making their way towards Lily and Jem, but Grace was standing alone. She didn't have time to suggest to Jem that his sister might not be all right, as Alice was jogging towards them.

'I'm so glad you're not dead.' Alice sighed, tucking a gentle arm around Lily's waist and pulling her in for an awkward hug as they walked towards the manor. 'The vision, Hecate's vision, it was so real. I saw you dead on the floor, as clear as I see you now.'

'I wouldn't have let that happen, Alice,' Jem remarked, walking in step with the two friends. His voice sounded gravelly, and he spoke as if all hope and happiness had been driven from the world.

'Yes, but you left her alone there too, *Jem*.' Her mimicry of Jem's tone of voice cut through Lily. 'You couldn't protect her when you weren't by her side.' Alice's voice was as sharp as a dagger.

'How do you know I left her? What can you possibly understand about anything that has transpired these past few weeks? Anyway, there's no chance of our Lily being murdered in the future now, is there? I won't leave her side, and I wager neither will you. So…'

'So… I was talking to my friend. You were the one that butted in, remember?'

Lily stopped walking. 'Guys, can you stop it?'

Jem's face contorted. He looked tired and forlorn and Alice, too, had slumped shoulders and dark rings beneath her eyes.

'Sorry,' he muttered, letting out a long, steadying exhale. 'Alice,' he held out a hand.

Alice wavered but, seeing the pleading look in Lily's eyes, shook his outstretched hand. 'Jem.' She nodded.

'Is there somewhere private, quiet, where we can all talk? I can't lie and say that I'm comfortable residing in the home of my *mortal enemy*,' Jem rolled his eyes.

There he goes again, Lily thought, *somehow joking through the pain.*

'But,' Jem continued, 'it appears there are larger things at stake than my personal quest for revenge. So I need a counsel with you, with Morven and Cass and the girls, with Grace. We've got some things we need to figure out.'

Alice nodded. 'Follow me to the library.'

Chapter Two

Jem Rafferty gasped audibly as he walked into the library at Midnight Manor. It was like someone had taken his little bedroom and study space from the lighthouse and amplified it to fill a room ten times the size. The ceilings were vaulted with beautifully carved dark cherry wood. A second mezzanine floor wrapped around the room, and on both floors, from the stone slabs beneath their feet to the ceiling, were row upon row of books. A series of intricate cast-iron spiral staircases linked the lower and upper levels and wooden ladders on wheels stood tall and proud beside each bookcase.

Alice led the way through the library, followed diligently by Brenna and Maeve, and suspiciously by Cass and Morven. Grace lagged behind the group, dragging her feet. Jem wanted to keep up, to check in on his sister, but he couldn't help himself; he paused awe-struck, gazing around the warm majestic room, knowing full well that he resembled a codfish out of water.

Arched windows cut through the sea of books like a wave, reaching up to the ceiling at the far end of the room, but, as it was night-time, Jem didn't get to see the way the bright, warm sun illuminated the endless bookcases in its hazy and warm light. He admired the two perfectly neat rows of study tables that ran parallel to one another down the centre of the room, each one adorned with flickering lanterns that cast a cosy orange glow across the room and captured the dances of dust motes in their glow.

A gentle sneeze brought him back to himself and he looked around to where the sound had come from. It turned out he wasn't the only one of their party soaking in the general splendour of Midnight Manor's extraordinary library. Lily was a few steps behind him, trailing a finger along the spines of books on a shelf labelled 'Natural History' in exquisite gold paint delicately written on a panel at the top of the bookcase. The dust in the air had obviously tickled her nose; he watched as another sneeze slipped from her nose before she could stop it.

He stifled a smile and wandered over to her, letting his feet fall heavily so she would hear him coming. Lost in a sea of books, he didn't want to alarm her; there had been enough stress, mayhem, and fear recently to last them both a lifetime. The least he could do now was try to be conscientious.

'Hi,' he said, more awkwardly than he had expected. Why was he feeling nervous all of a sudden?

Lily turned around and looked up at him with a quizzical expression on her face. His stomach did an uncomfortable loop the loop. 'Why aren't you with the others?'

'Well, why aren't you?' Jem smirked.

'All right, good point.' She chuckled. 'I was, or rather, I am so overwhelmed by everything, that when I walked in here, it was a bit like walking into one of my forests. I felt a peace pass over me and I wasn't in a hurry to lose that feeling, so I hung back for a while, just to take it all in, y'know?'

Jem nodded. He knew more than he could express. 'Yep, I get it. I initiated this meeting and now all I want to do is run away. I miss when things were…' He paused, trying to find the right word.

'Simple?'

'Yeah, simple.' He exhaled.

'But, Jem, when things were simple, we didn't know each other. And even through all of this trauma and pain, I'll never regret getting into that rowing boat and coming to your island. Never.' She gave him a half-smile and blushed, no longer able to meet his eye.

'Jem! Lily!' Cass shouted from behind a door at the back of the room.

Jem chuckled and motioned for Lily to walk beside him to where Cass was standing looking dismayed. She linked his arm as they walked, and all he could think of was how nicely her arm fit in his.

Jem found himself in a reading room lit by a large candle-filled chandelier and the same warm glow of lanterns that permeated the main library. A large oval table filled the majority of the space, and everyone was either sitting or standing around it. He noticed that Alice and Grace couldn't have been further apart if they had tried, but he would think about how exactly he was going to fix that later. For now, they had more pressing issues.

'All right, everyone. We have once again found ourselves in a troubling situation, and once again we're somewhere unfamiliar. Only this time, we have Alice, who's been here before.'

'Yeah,' Morven chimed in, 'but this time we're also in a place where *Hecate Winter* lives. The murderer. How do we know who we can trust? Not to mention we don't have any belongings except the clothes on our backs.'

'Morven's right. We don't have anything here!' Cass grumbled.

Brenna put up her hand proudly as she responded, 'But we have each other, Cass! At least we're not all split up in different directions this time.'

'Thank you, Brenna!' Lily chirped up. 'Finally, some positivity. Yes, this situation isn't ideal.'

Morven glared at her.

'All right, it's less than ideal, but this is where we find ourselves. We have to pull up our bootstraps and work out exactly what we're going to do next.' Lily threw a reassuring smile at Morven, who didn't respond.

'Exactly! Which is why we're here right now. To work out what we're going to do next.' Jem was about to launch into a monologue in the hope that a plan would miraculously form itself as he spoke, but he was interrupted.

'In all honesty, I really think Hecate should be in here too.' It was Alice who spoke, and her voice was dark and quiet.

'You've got to be kidding me,' Grace shot back.

Jem wondered if that was the first time Grace had said anything to Alice since their fight outside the castle. He knew Grace felt – and rightfully so – that Alice had betrayed her by running back to Hecate after Jem and Lily had rescued them both from her in the first place. Grace could have handled almost anything – anything except that.

'She might have a point, Grace...' Lily mumbled.

'How can Hecate help anything? She kidnapped us, Alice. She's killed people right in front of our eyes. She's the reason we're all essentially homeless. And you want us to just let her swan on in here and welcome her with open arms?' Grace growled. 'You, of all people, should know better. Or, the old Alice would have.'

'Look,' Alice's voice sounded sharp and impatient. It

took all of Jem's self-control not to jump to his sister's defence; this was a battle she had to fight on her own. 'I know you're all of the same opinion and I'm not going to try and convince you otherwise. But this is bigger than the people in this room versus Hecate Winter. This is real oncoming war. The Brotherhood has taken every other fiefdom. The Shadow Lands are their final target. I had to rescue Farlan, the boy from earlier who mocked the men at the gate, from his stupid bloody mansion right on the border. The Brotherhood is seeping into our lands like a plague, stamping out magic, magic users, and anyone who consorts with us. They are the threat here, not Hecate. I'm not asking you to like her, but I'm asking you to listen. This war will be hard enough without us fighting within our own ranks.'

Silence fell. Alice, usually a quiet, spikey sort of person from Jem's limited experience, had given a speech he himself would have been proud to deliver. The intensity was clear in her emerald eyes and her knuckles, which she rested against the table, were white as snow.

'She killed Glenn,' a small voice piped up. Brenna.

'I know,' Alice whispered, not looking up.

'She destroyed everything.' Cass's voice was raspy and broken.

'I know that, too.'

Jem surprised himself with the words that slipped out of his mouth, but from the moment he spoke them, he knew they were right. 'I agree... with Alice. I hate Hecate as much as all of you, if not more. There hasn't been a day since Glenn died that I haven't imagined how it would feel to wring that woman's neck.' He exhaled. 'But, if it's as bad as she says it is, then we have to look beyond ourselves. When Grace and I caught a ship in Oakencliff, they were celebrating something called... something called...' He scratched his head.

'The Bloodletting,' Grace murmured. 'The day the Brotherhood wiped out the Shadow Sect from the town. It's celebrated, revered as a great victory. Hecate's followers are the only significant group still practising magic, which makes them the prime target. Wipe out Hecate and the Shadow Lands will cease to be as we know it. If we let them take control, everything will change, and every single one of us will be murdered as traitors, whether we have magic or not. We're here in the Shadow Sect's stronghold, which makes us the enemy. No one is going to listen to a bunch of kids declaring their innocence. We're outsiders – we always have been. No one's coming to our aid. I, too, as much as it pains me, have to say that Alice has a point. Hecate should be involved – for no other reason than that we should know what she's planning, and what that means for us.'

A smile tugged at the corner of Alice's lips.

'But that doesn't mean I've forgiven you, so stop looking so damn smug,' Grace snapped. '*I haven't forgiven you.*'

Alice's eyes dropped to the table again, any hint of a smile wiped from her face.

Chapter Three

The oak door of the reading room was flung open with such force that the flames danced a jig in the lanterns.

'I see you've all finally come to your senses.' Hecate's velvet voice reverberated around the room as she sauntered into the room in her usual elegant jewel-coloured dress, her hands weighed down with a myriad of heavy rings. Any sign or indication that she had lost her cool demeanour outside by the gates when the Brotherhood attacked had disappeared entirely and she had reassumed her air of cold, sultry devilishness.

Lily watched as Jem tried not to let his hatred take over him, but she could see the flicker of rage flare in his eyes. She was confident that gaining Hecate's trust and reaching some kind of understanding with her was essential for their survival, but it was almost impossible for her to see past the traumas that Hecate had caused in all of their lives. Lily herself had been tortured brutally by Hecate's hand, and although that had been the catalyst for releasing her magic, this new version of Lily was more scarred and damaged. Sitting in that room in Midnight Manor, she knew which version of herself she preferred.

Behind Hecate followed the young man from the gates, the one who had provoked the Brotherhood. *What was his name*, Lily thought, narrowing her eyes, *Farran? Fallon?*

Hecate gestured for the boy to take a seat. He looked embarrassed, with a red face and his eyes trailing along the floor. Hecate didn't notice. She looked around the room, an eagle surveying the landscape for its next kill. 'So, why exactly have I been summoned? Or did you all just want to drink tea and gossip?'

'Stop!' Grace shot out of her chair, ramming her fists onto the table. 'Stop making light of this.'

'Are you threatening me, Rafferty?' Hecate's eyes had darkened, and Lily shivered. This woman was terrifying, no matter what Alice said. They could all be dead at the flick of her wrist anyway, Brotherhood or no Brotherhood.

Grace stood her ground, looking directly into Hecate's eyes. Lily was sure she saw a warmth rise to Alice's cheeks at Grace's courage and defiance. 'Why is he here?'

This wasn't the direction Lily had expected the conversation to go.

'Why does it matter?' Hecate narrowed her eyes.

Grace growled. 'Because we don't know him, we don't

trust him. It was hard enough to agree to let you in the room, but he's a total stranger. I don't even know his name.'

Murmurs of agreement rippled around the small room. It seemed that Grace had said what they were all thinking.

'He's here because I asked him to be here. He's the closest thing we have to an insider; he knows how the Brotherhood thinks.' Hecate shrugged.

'Well...' The boy's face was caught somewhere between a smirk and a frown. 'That's generous. I left Hythlund, the world beyond, when I was a child. So everything I know is historic. Things could be different.'

'He's an Aelfdene. They're a very significant family across the border. His father is a baron...' Hecate trailed off. 'Well, that's not my story to tell. But Farlan needs us, and we need him. It makes sense for him to be in the same conversations that I am. If you don't like that, then I will leave this room. And then you can all get out of my house and figure out what you're going to do next without anywhere to live. Your choice.' She leaned back on the wall with a passive look on her face. Her impossibly long fingernails tapped against the wooden panelling.

There was silence for a few moments. *The boy is a baron's son?* Lily didn't feel like that piece of information made him any easier to trust.

After a few more moments, Grace broke the silence. 'Tell us what the plan is. Tell us what we need to do. Keep it simple,' she snapped.

Hecate held her hands up in faux surrender. 'You're no

fun anymore, Rafferty. Blackwell's made you soft, but she herself has remained hard and true, steadfast without the betrayal of emotion, unbent by the yearnings of her heart. You could learn something from her. That is, of course, if you can bear to look her in the eye.'

'All right, now stop it.' It was Jem's turn to pipe up. 'This isn't helpful in any way. We asked you here because Alice convinced us that you're on our side – or rather, that we're all on the same side versus another common enemy. Please refrain from any more games.'

Hecate rolled her eyes and winked at Alice, who looked straight back down at the table without reacting. 'Fine. The Brotherhood, as you know, aren't satisfied with the fact that they've wiped out magic across the entire world. No, they want to entirely wipe it out here, too. They've already claimed Oakencliff, a village on the coast where I had a lovely little stronghold when I was first starting up. I lost too many witches to count when the Brotherhood decided to claim the village as their own. But, strangely, that village seemed to satisfy them for a while.

'I've had scouts keep eyes on their movements around the border, which is how I knew we needed to claim Farlan before he could be used as some kind of strange bait or example for the rest of the land. He's also incredibly clever, with a touch of magic himself. That's if you can see past his flouncy arrogance.'

'Hey!' Farlan looked affronted, but Lily caught him

throwing a wink at Alice who chuckled gently at a joke no one else seemed privy to.

'Anyway, I have since found out that the Brotherhood is under new ruling. Their latest leader, Fenn Crydlund, is as bad as they come: nasty, cruel, like everything they say I am but far, far worse. Now, the thing with Fenn is that, somehow, he's managing to recruit *witches* through unknown techniques. He's bringing them into the Brotherhood, indoctrinating them so that they think there are 'good' witches and 'bad' witches, which is why they're able to perform magic yet still consider us the bad guys. I imagine his plan is to wipe out the witches within the Brotherhood once we're all dead and buried... Who knows, but that explains why they were able to track us from the castle and magically appear outside our gates.'

'But who's training them? There can't be hundreds of untrained witches just wandering the Shadow Lands with full control of their power, waiting to be found?' The question had escaped Lily's lips before she had a chance to overthink it.

Jem nodded in agreement. 'Exactly. You tortured Lily to extract her magic, and from what I've heard from Grace, that's not uncommon.'

'Ah, see, that's where I really do have to hold my very beautiful hands up and admit this one might be my fault.'

'What? Why?' Alice finally looked up from the table, confusion evident in her features.

'Some witches have been too volatile, too untrustworthy

to continue on with the Shadow Sect; others have wronged me or another witch so badly that they didn't deserve a place in our ranks anymore.'

'So you kicked them out?' Alice and Grace said simultaneously. Both of them looked up at each other in surprise.

'Yes, I kicked them out. I thought they'd skulk on back to their homes and carry on with their lives as if nothing had happened, but it turns out I essentially created an army of witches with me as their common enemy without even realising. All Fenn had to do was find them and win them over, which I imagine didn't take much.' Hecate perched on the edge of one of the crooked wooden seats that surrounded the table, drumming her black fingernails on the tabletop. 'So yes, I gave Fenn the perfect weapons, and he's figured out how to use them... and now our entire mission is at stake.'

Cass, who had been sitting uncharacteristically quietly on a chair on the left side of the table, perked up. 'Mission? What mission?'

'See, this is why you've all always thought I was a cruel, miserable old hag stealing children for my own delight!' Hecate's mannerisms were getting more enthusiastic and eccentric by the minute. Her arms were flailing everywhere as she spoke and her bracelets jangling on her wrists made the sound of wind gusting through Lily's favourite windchime in the apothecary. 'I have always had a mission;

I haven't been existing all this time completely bent on revenge and nothing else.'

'Haven't you?' Grace squawked.

'No, Rafferty sibling number one, I haven't.' She winked at Jem, who visibly recoiled, and continued. 'My mission has always been to create a safe haven for witches of all ages and creeds, but primarily children.'

Jem's eyes widened.

'Yes, Rafferty sibling number two, our goals are rather similar. I want to turn Midnight Manor into a school of sorts. When the Brotherhood comes, their ideology will come with them. Soon the people who are ambivalent towards magic users will fear us, and those who already fear us will hate us. That kind of ideology is hard to fight – much harder than the Brotherhood itself. So I want to create a place where those with magic can come. A place to learn, to find other lost souls, to create a community of witches who are stronger because they have their own kind around them. And I don't want to build it to create an army, I just don't want another child going through the trauma that I went through. No one else will go through that if I can help it.'

Grace rolled her eyes. 'But right now, you *are* building an army.'

'All right, all right. Yes, right now I'm building an army. But one utopian day, we won't be under immediate threat of siege by Fenn and his cronies, and then I can focus on actually turning this place into something worthwhile. Is that enough for you?' With the last word she stood up, her chair slamming violently against the floor with an ear-splitting crash. 'Have I satisfied you now?'

Alice ignored Hecate's last question. 'So what do we have to do?'

'It's obvious, isn't it?' Morven said. 'We have to find out what the Brotherhood is planning, so we can prepare ourselves. We cannot fight that which we don't know.'

'Correct, young girl who's name I am yet to learn.' Hecate continued, 'We need to infiltrate them. Quite frankly, you four,' she pointed at Morven, Cass, Brenna and Maeve, 'are too young to go infiltrating anywhere right now. I sense magic in both of the young girls, so you will need to stay here to see if we can unlock something in you. Grace, Alice, that means you will need to guide them, to help them, otherwise the ordeal may be too much for all of them to bear.'

'Don't touch them,' Jem growled.

'Don't worry, I'm sure your lovely sister will prevent anything from happening to them. Farlan, you too need tuition in this area, and I don't want you out of my sight. You can tag along with them – they'll help you.'

Farlan didn't look too thrilled at the prospect, but had clearly learned when he could get away with talking back. Now wasn't one of those times.

'But you two,' she waved a sharpened fingernail between Jem and Lily, 'you two will go on this trip. If Rafferty sibling number two has half the brains of his sister, he will figure out a way to get the two of you past their security. And you, Knight, have the distinct advantage of being a direct relation of an ex-member of the Brotherhood. All you have to do is say you ran away from him and came to where you really belong. Convince them you want to repair the damage your uncle did.'

'They'll murder her on the spot,' hissed Alice. 'This is madness!'

'Ah, well, if they're clever, no one will touch either of them. If they're stupid… well, that's on them.' Hecate shrugged as if she was talking about whether or not she wanted marmalade on her toast.

Jem ran a hand through his long russet hair, frowning. 'It's not a terrible idea.'

Lily glanced at him standing by her side. In any other circumstance, she would have jumped at the chance to spend some time with Jem, even though the thought made her stomach contract uncomfortably. But infiltrating the Brotherhood? It sounded stupid – impossible even. Did she have the courage?

As if Morven had heard her thoughts, the girl said, 'Lily, you're the bravest person here. I hate to say it, but Hecate's right – this may be our only chance to get this information, our only chance to arm ourselves against whatever their plans are. Once upon a time, you slung a bag over your shoulder and a cloak around yourself and stepped out into the unknown to rescue Alice. This is just the next, and hopefully final, step on that journey. You could save us all.'

'Alice, I might be forced to get rid of you as my right-hand woman! This young girl has all the spirit I'm after. What's your name, child?' Lily presumed Hecate was joking, but the rage in Alice's eyes told a different story.

'Morven.'

'Good. A strong name. I'll keep an eye on you.' Hecate winked, a troubling glint in her eye. Lily didn't like this one bit.

Looking around the room, Lily saw the people she loved the most, the people she would do anything in the world for. Jem reached out and held her hand tightly, and she turned to look up at him, scanning his face for any sign of fear or trepidation. Instead, she saw fierce determination. Once again, Jem Rafferty was willing to go to the ends of the earth for these children, and she realised it would be an honour to go there by his side, regardless of the outcome.

'All right,' she said, not taking her eyes from Jem, 'we'll do it.'

Chapter Four

After the meeting, they all found bedrooms in the dark and shadowy north wing of the manor, where Alice and Hecate also had rooms. Lily had spent a while pacing back and forth in front of a large window, her boots echoing on the old wooden floor. Her mind was filled with worst-case scenarios, disasters, and nightmares. The flickering candle on the windowsill cast strange, ghostly shadows on the peeling, faded floral wallpaper on the walls.

On her thousandth circuit around the room, something outside the window caught her eye. It was the middle of the night, so there was no way anyone should have been up and about. Lily dashed over to the window and pressed her face to the glass. Sure enough, a cloaked figure was wandering across the grounds towards what Lily presumed was the gardens; she could see the outline of a large glasshouse and rows of pristine hedges in the moonlight.

The storm of earlier on had thankfully subsided, but her window was still covered in a build-up of snowflakes that meant getting a solid idea of who was out there was difficult. The figure stopped for a moment, plucked a leaf from the hedge, and lifted it to their face. The hood of the cloak fell down and revealed waist-length inky-black hair. *Alice.*

Lily threw her cloak on over her ivory nightgown and stepped into her boots, quickly getting frustrated by the laces. She swore, and settled on only fastening them halfway, at the ankle, before grabbing the candlestick and dashing out of the bedroom door. She picked her way through the labyrinthine corridors of the manor and flung open the huge front door, trying her best to close it swiftly, but quietly, behind her.

Her cloak fluttering in her wake, she ran across the snow-covered grass. It was slushy and horrible underfoot, as the storm had covered the already frozen ground with another layer of frozen sludge. She was careful not to slip as she ran, keeping her eyes on the distant shadow of Alice so she didn't lose her friend.

Before long, she was close enough to risk shouting out Alice's name without fear that everyone in the manor would hear her. At the sound of Lily's voice, Alice whipped around, at first frowning and then, catching sight of Lily, her face softened into a relief-filled smile.

'Lily?' She held her own candle up to her eyeline. 'Lily, is that you?'

'Yes!' Lily choked, out of breath from all the running. Soon enough, she found herself face to face with Alice, shivering in the cold night air.

'What are you doing?!' Alice's eyes were full of concern.

'I couldn't sleep,' Lily panted. 'I saw you... from the window.' Now her teeth were chattering. 'I thought... you could use the company.' She stopped and tried to catch her breath.

'Come on, the greenhouse will be warmer. We light fires in there to keep the air warm for the plants at this time of year.'

Lily didn't need telling twice. She followed Alice around the garden and into the glasshouse Lily had just been able to make out from her bedroom window. It was much larger now she was down on the ground, with great cast-iron cresting along the spine of the roof and pieces of glass larger than she had ever seen before. It made her think of the windows in the apothecary, where she had hung shards of sea glass to refract the sunbeams as they shone in with the early morning sunlight.

The greenhouse was grand. She stepped in through the glass door and found herself enveloped in warm, humid air. The smell was like her forests in the middle of summer; if she closed her eyes, she could almost forget that it was only just past midwinter outside. That is, she could have forgotten had her hands not been chunks of ice themselves.

The greenhouse was illuminated by a shaft of silverish moonlight. Alice, presumably unsatisfied with the current light levels, flicked her wrists upwards and sent sparks flying from her fingertips like shooting stars. In mere moments, they were surrounded by what looked like thousands of glimmering fireflies which emitted swathes of golden glowing light. As they moved through the greenhouse, the twinkling lights followed them, moved with them, like their own personal lanterns.

Alice led her wordlessly down a red-bricked pathway that snaked through a variety of familiar and very unfamiliar plants until she reached a small wooden table and chairs, hidden at the very back by unusual plants with huge fan-like leaves that she didn't recognise.

'Come, sit.' Alice gestured to the chairs and Lily did as she asked, feeling strangely formal. She placed her candlestick on the tired-looking table, and noticed that the wax had dripped down onto the brass handle like little teardrops.

Alice sat down with her, shifting her chair to sit closer to Lily's, then she took both of Lily's cold hands in her own warm ones.

'Why couldn't you sleep?' Alice asked.

Lily pulled her hands back from Alice's and let them rest in her lap. 'Why do you think?' Her instant response came out harsher than she had intended, and she blushed. 'Sorry, I'm just a bit overwhelmed... again.' She looked down at her hands and tried to resist the urge to pick at them, an urge that always came over her when things were difficult or stressful. She imagined what Jem would say if he saw her hurting herself like that, and then swiftly sat on her hands. Now that they were hidden beneath her cloak and her nightgown, perhaps she'd have the strength to resist.

'Of course.' Alice lifted Lily's chin with an affectionate hand. 'You don't have to hide from me, Lil.'

'How can I not? I don't know who you are anymore, or who I am. So much has changed since those days in your cabin; we're both entirely different people.' The words were flowing out of her like rain from a hurricane. 'I can't remember how to be Alice and Lily anymore. I can't find it within me to feel like the Sisters of Shadow.' Lily braced herself for her best friend's usual, spikey remark in response to her honesty, but it never came.

'I understand.' Alice looked past Lily into nothingness, but didn't look down. She wasn't hiding herself any longer. 'I've been the catalyst of every inch of that change, and I'm sorry. Truly, genuinely sorry. I've made some decisions that are hard to justify, especially to you. You've always made me want to be the very best version of myself, but I always felt like I was missing the essential piece of who I was. I found that, with Hecate, and I know that's absolutely awful for you to hear, because all you know of her is evil.' She sighed. 'I'm not denying that she's done horrendous things, and I'm not trying to say she's a good person. But I am saying that she nurtured the power in me that I always, always wanted. She's shown me a future where I don't have to be the exiled stranger living in the forest away from prying eyes; she's given me a future, Lily, a future of my own making. I'm not that strange little witch-girl anymore, devoid of power and devoid of love.' She spat, and Lily knew she was picturing Orla and the other Alder Vale bullies who had made Alice's life there a total misery.

'I'm not here to judge you, Alice, I promise. I'm just lost... so very lost.' Lily's voice crackled and broke, betraying her emotions.

Alice moved her chair even closer, so the two of them were as close as they could be. 'I know. I'm sorry. Look, when you get back from this trip, I really do promise that I'll teach you to use your magic. I'll teach you everything you want to know and I'll help you find your way back to yourself, even if that version of Lily is different to who you once were. We all change and evolve through life, and we have to learn to lean in to that tide. I'm living proof of that. But you will always be the same Lily who wanted to fly up into the tree to sit with the little songbird on a branch. Keep hold of that.'

Lily nodded, deep in thought. 'It feels strange to be leaving you again.'

'This will be the last time. I promise.' Alice rested her head on Lily's shoulder. 'If I could come with you this time, I would. But I have people to protect here. I want to prove myself to your friends because all they know of me is betrayal and that's not who I am.' She exhaled slowly, carefully. 'Anyway, you'll be much safer with Jem by your side. And happier too, I'd wager.' Lily felt Alice nudge her shoulder gently.

'I could never be happier than when I'm with you, Ali. But... I suppose it's a different kind of happiness with Jem.'

'Exactly.'

'And you have to promise me that by the time I'm back, you and Grace will be back to normal. She's good for you – I can see that, clear as day, even in the limited time we've spent together. Everything you've attributed to Hecate, I think you should consider attributing to Grace too. Who really gave you purpose and strength whilst you were stuck in that horrible cave lair? Because I know for a fact that day to day, it wasn't Hecate. Remember who Grace was to you, Alice, and get her back. She is the only person alive that I would trust to protect you as I have tried to over the years.'

Alice sniffled, so Lily knew to stop talking. Silence was what her friend needed the most – comfortable, friendly, compassionate silence.

A while passed, the two friends holding on to one another in a gentle but fierce embrace. Lily had relaxed into the warm humidity of the greenhouse and envied Alice's ability to spend time every day in this beautiful secret slice of paradise. She yawned, the tiredness rumbling through her entire body. Tomorrow – or rather, later that day – she would have to venture out again on the final mission to save everything she cared for.

But now, it was time for bed.

Chapter Five

Jem Rafferty couldn't sleep. Or rather, he hadn't slept. As he was pacing for the hundredth time that night, he noticed a flicker of sunlight on the horizon, far in the distance. Sunlight. That meant it was already morning and time for him and Lily to leave.

He already couldn't bear the thought of leaving the children so soon after returning with Grace, but the alternative options weren't worth thinking about either; he had to do this, and he was glad to do it with Lily by his side. The children would, at least, have Grace this time, and there were more people in the manor to keep an eye on them, even if he didn't know anyone here enough to trust them.

A swift, quiet knocking on his door roused him from his thoughts and brought him back to himself. He quickly glanced in the mirror hanging on the wall to ensure he didn't look too much of a fright in case it was Lily on the other side of the door. Alas, he realised, the rings under his eyes and the shadow of stubble on his cheeks weren't going to go away anytime soon, and his hair was scraped back into its usual knot. He didn't look hideous, per se, just like a much more exhausted version of Tired Jem. Lily had seen him looking far worse, he was sure.

He wandered over to the door and prised it open.

'Hi, can we come in?' It wasn't Lily at all. A nervous-looking Morven and Cass were standing on the other side of the threshold. One look at their faces betrayed the fact that they, too, hadn't done much sleeping overnight.

He pulled open the door and gestured for them to enter. He looked around at his room with fresh eyes as they walked in, and realised he probably should have considered using his sleeplessness to tidy up a bit. He didn't have any belongings, due to their swift exit from the castle, and yet somehow the room was still a mess. His duvet was strewn across the windowsill where he had sat earlier in the night, trying to read by moonlight a book on natural history he had taken from the library, to no avail. His boots were star-crossed lovers, at opposite ends of the room, and his candle had burned so far down that it was sitting miserably in a pool of its own wax, wax which had dribbled almost all across the top of the dresser.

Cass and Morven perched on the end of the bed, and

Jem took himself to the windowsill, where he sat on his soft duvet and tried to look relaxed and knowledgeable. 'What can I do for you?' he asked.

'We've been thinking...' Cass began.

'Yeah, both of us have been thinking...'

'All right,' Jem pushed, 'what have you been thinking about?'

'I think – or rather *we* think,' Morven stuttered, 'that we've been cooped up a bit too much.'

'Cooped up?' Jem was confused. Where was this going?

'Cooped up, yeah,' Cass repeated. He was wringing his hands together as if he was really nervous.

'You're going to have to come out and say whatever you're here to say, guys, because you're making me nervous.'

'We've decided we're going to leave for a while, but... we wanted to be useful. We don't just want to go and never come back, we just want to get away, learn about life, experience things a bit.'

Jem closed his eyes and exhaled deeply. He wasn't their father; he had no right to prevent them from doing what they wanted. 'All right. What's your plan?'

'Well that's the thing, Jem,' Morven said. 'We don't have one. We were hoping you would have an idea as to how we could be useful. Not in the war, of course, but after. What can we do to make things easier once this is all over?'

Jem pulled his hair from its knot, allowing it to cascade

in a waterfall down his back. Running a hand through it, he sighed. 'We can't go back to the castle, that much is certain.' He looked out of the window to the sludgy snow that covered the grounds of the manor. *What will we need when this is over?* 'We need a home. Somewhere safe and dependable, somewhere we don't need to leave again, if we don't want to. You could go in search of that, if you wanted to? That way you'll always have a home to come back to. Even if the two of you decide your time with us is over and you want to venture out into the world for good, you'll know where to find us.'

Cass nodded, looking to his sister for a cue. Jem always enjoyed their company as their sibling dynamic was so different from what he and Grace had. The fierce love was the same, but Cass and Morven rarely seemed to disagree; they went through life permanently on the same page.

Morven spoke next. 'That sounds reasonable. A place to call home, not just for us, but for the children who come after us; a sanctuary of sorts.' She nodded. 'Yeah, I like that idea.'

'The thing is though, Jem,' Cass began, sounding nervous, 'I'd quite like to see the world beyond, too. All we've ever known is the Shadow Lands, and that's all right, but it would be nice to know what else is out there. We spend so much of our time fearing it, discussing it. I'd like to come back to you with real useful knowledge of what it's like.'

Jem felt his throat constrict. *The world beyond?* He tried to clear his throat before talking, hoping the panic wasn't showing in his face. 'I can't stop you from doing anything, Cass – I'm not your parent. I can only guide you towards what I think is right. Leaving the Shadow Lands is a dangerous business from what I've heard. It's a different place, so different that they'll know you're not from there the moment you cross the border. I don't know how you'll be treated, or what you'll see. The experience could change you for ever. Are you ready for that?'

Morven took Cass's hand. 'We are. The knowledge we gain might be useful in the future, and you've always said there's no such thing as knowing too much.'

Jem cursed his previous self. He couldn't argue with that. 'All right. Promise me you'll be careful? And promise me, too, that you'll come back. You don't have to stay, but it would be a great weight off my mind to know you're safe and well. That's all I ask.'

'Of course we will. We'll come back with a plan for where we will all live, brimming with new knowledge and exciting stories. You've had enough adventure lately, Jem, it's our turn now.' Cass puffed up his chest, looking every inch the man he was growing into.

'I just look forward to the day when adventure is no longer a regular word in my vocabulary. I'm ready to be an old man in a comfy chair by a fire, where adventure is just something that happened to me a long time ago.' He leaned back against the window, the cold of the glass seeping through his shirt and chilling his shoulders. 'I'm so tired.'

Cass and Morven wandered over and placed a kiss each on Jem's frowning forehead. He felt his features relax as he looked up at the two people in front of him: no longer children but not quite adults. If they were his only legacy, he knew he would still have succeeded.

Chapter Six

The sun was no longer peeping but roaring over the horizon line, casting its great sanguine light over the endless swathes of heather-strewn snow-topped moorland surrounding Midnight Manor. It was as though the sun knew its radiance would be short-lived, because the clouds began to gather fiercely across the sky, smothering the warm light with their cold, grey blanket.

Lily left her room with the sunlight glowing through her window, but by the time she had reached the oak front door, great big raindrops had started to fall. The snow was starting to disappear, leaving behind a miserable, water-logged landscape that even her trusty leather boots would struggle to keep out.

All of her belongings had been left at the castle, but after their conversation in the greenhouse, Alice had taken her to a room filled with clothes, bags, extra layers and anything else she could have possibly needed. Apparently, when setting up the manor for the purpose of providing shelter for witches, she had prioritised conjuring up everything a person who had nothing could require. Lily had chosen to forego dresses; she had got used to the convenience of movement that trousers could provide, even if she didn't feel as much like herself when wearing them. She had found a pair of soft woollen leggings and a long-sleeved tunic to wear as underlayers, and then for over the top, a pair of thick woven trousers, a buttoned-down flax shirt, a thick fisherman's jumper in her favourite shade of deep forest green, and a woollen shawl which she wrapped over her shoulders, crossed over her front and then tied in a knot at the small of her back. She knew these layers would be sufficient to keep her warm, no matter what the unpredictable weather threw at them, and Alice had gifted her a pair of cream mittens, softer than anything she had ever owned, which she stored in her rucksack.

She had struggled to find a pack that suited her as much as her trusty bag that she had brought all the way from Alder Vale, but after a little searching, Alice found her a leather pack with two shoulder straps that she could easily carry on her back. Because it was so much roomier than her previous bag, Lily bundled in a simple brown dress with pretty leather fastenings down the forearms and on either side of her waist. She had a vague idea that perhaps a visit to Alf would be necessary and if she were to avoid the worst of the gossip, she thought a dress would help. She couldn't deny she was tempted to strut across the village green in form-fitting trousers with an unknown man by her side, purely to see Orla McHail and Jemima Darroch's faces, but after laughing so hard her cheeks hurt with Alice, they had both decided it was better not to risk tormenting them. Not this time, anyway.

Just before she and Alice had left the clothes room, Alice had pressed a gift into Lily's hands: a small wicker basket with a lid, made in such a way that a leather belt could be woven through it, so it could be fastened around her waist. 'For foraging,' Alice had said. 'You should have somewhere to keep the things you find where they won't get lost or broken. The last thing you want is a squished mushroom rotting away in the bottom of your pack before you've had a chance to eat it.' Her friend had grinned, but Lily had noticed the tears swimming in her eyes.

'Did you make this?' Lily had asked, her own throat constricting with the threat of overflowing emotion.

Alice had nodded. 'I made this last time I was here,' Alice had explained, 'when I was missing you.'

Lily had embraced Alice and felt like her heart might explode from her chest. Alice had then pressed a makeshift purse into Lily's hand – her final gift. Lily pulled the drawstrings apart and looked inside to find it filled to the brim with gold coins. She hadn't known what to say, so she had pulled her best friend into an enveloping hug once more.

Lily stepped out of the front door, allowing the lovely

memory to wash over her. She took a few steps forward, so she was no longer shielded from the weather in the doorway and turned her face to the sky. She allowed a few silent tears to fall down her cheeks, mixing with the increasingly heavy rain. In the distance, she could hear the familiar lament of a robin hidden in the hedgerows somewhere, and its simple song filled her with hope and peace. She breathed in and out slowly, deliberately, her eyes closed, surrendering to the rain.

'What are you doing, you strange creature?' A voice, strange and acerbic, brought her back to earth.

Lily whirled around, feeling vulnerable and attacked. Standing in the doorway was the boy, Farlan, in his velvet suit, expensive shoes, and long black cane. He was smiling, but in a peculiar, sardonic way, as if he were moments from bursting into laughter at her expense. Her seething expression seemed to derail him slightly, and she watched as he, almost nervously, pushed his hair from his face. Beneath the sheath of blonde hair was a painful-looking scar where his eye should have been. 'Who are you? And I mean, really, who are you?' she asked. 'And, more importantly, don't you have something better to be doing than tormenting me?'

He held out a hand, but didn't move closer to her. Tentatively, she walked forward and shook it firmly once, before retracting her own hand so sharply that it caused him to raise an eyebrow. 'As you know, I'm Farlan Aelfdene, son of the Baron of Aelfdene who is the right-hand man to the very charming, increasingly murderous Fenn Crydlund, I am a fugitive of Hecate Winter, lover of fine wines and piano concertos, bored out of my bloody brains. It's a pleasure to formally meet you. And you are?'

'Lily Knight.'

'That's it? But I gave you all sorts of interesting information about me! Come on, try harder.' He smirked and raised his eyebrow again.

Is he flirting with me? she wondered. She'd never been flirted with before, not unless you counted Frank, the boy that helped at the apothecary, who had been obsessed with her purely because she was the only female who had communicated with him that wasn't his mother or one of his sisters. 'All right,' she said. 'I'm Lily Knight, niece of apothecary-owner and disgraced member of the Brotherhood, Alfryd Knight.' She paused, satisfied with his dramatic jaw-drop. 'Best friend of Hecate Winter's right-hand woman, witch, devourer of books, lover of the natural world. It's a pleasure.' She held out her hand this time, allowing him to shake it properly.

'Lily?' Jem's voice reverberated around the entrance hall of the manor, and she dropped Farlan's hand faster than if it had been a burning hot bun straight from the oven. She blushed and took a step back, forgetting that there was a small ledge up to the front door of the manor, and went sprawling backwards onto the soggy ground. She landed with an almighty thump, but her full backpack prevented her from becoming winded. 'Lily?' Jem asked again, joining Farlan at the door.

Lily watched as Jem glanced at Farlan with confusion evident in his eyes, before he saw her on her back, scrambling to get to her feet. Jem looked between Farlan and Lily, but didn't say anything further for a moment.

'Sorry, Jem,' Lily choked, finally finding her way back to her feet again. 'I tripped.'

Farlan grinned at Jem. 'These girls, I just can't stop them from swooning at the sight of me. It's really rather inconvenient.'

Lily felt her cheeks burning. 'I did *not* swoon,' she growled.

'Sounds like exactly the kind of thing a woman hopelessly in love would say after she had swooned at the feet of a man, don't you think?' He nudged Jem, who still hadn't spoken. Lily noticed his jaw was clenched, along with his fists.

'We need to be leaving, Lily. Are you ready to go?' Jem managed, through gritted teeth.

Lily brushed herself off. 'Ye-yes, yes, I'm ready when you are.' *Good grief, this is embarrassing.*

'Right,' Jem said. 'Alice is waiting. Let's go.' He squeezed himself past Farlan, who didn't make an effort to move out of the way, and walked straight past Lily, who had to practically jog to keep up.

One last glance behind her revealed a chuckling Farlan, clearly very pleased with himself. *Twit*, Lily thought to herself. She hoped her cheeks had returned to their normal colour as she skipped a few more steps before she dropped into pace next to Jem. 'Where are we going?'

Jem swallowed. 'Alice is meeting us in the gardens. Apparently there's an alternative exit which means we won't have to remove the spells on the front gate.' He fell back into silence, looking straight ahead.

Lily's mind was reeling. They were about to head off on a journey together and things felt more awkward than ever before. 'Sorry about him,' she said.

He waved a hand, still not looking at her. 'No matter. We've got more important things to worry about.'

'I wasn't flirting with him,' Lily said before she could stop herself. The words hung in the air, the heavy raindrops refusing to wash them away.

'I never said you were, Lil.'

'All right. But I wasn't. You don't need to worry about him.' She could feel the prickling of heat on her neck as her annoyance grew. Why was *she* in trouble for something some stupid boy had done?

'I'm not worried.'

This didn't come out very convincingly at all. All the thunder had left his voice. He ran a hand through his hair and she knew he was suddenly as nervous as she was.

'Well, fine. All right. Whatever.' She shrugged, trying not to let it bother her. Why was he acting so weird? Could it be... jealousy? She blushed, her eyes widening as she stared pointedly at the floor as she walked.

They picked their way through the garden along a path that was lined with a carpet of snowdrops. Lily found herself wishing that someone else could be accompanying them on this journey, because whatever this stirring feeling was in the pit of her stomach, it was becoming inconveniently hard to ignore.

'Hi, you two,' Alice said. Lily looked up to see her friend frowning. 'Everything all right?'

'Yeah,' and 'Fine,' Jem and Lily said in unison.

Alice narrowed her eyes, looking from one of them to the other.

'Well, whatever it is, you'd better sort it out sooner rather than later. You won't be able to hide anything from each other on this kind of journey, believe me. Secrecy kills. So sort it out.'

Lily was about to comment on how it was ironic for Alice to be giving her and Jem relationship advice when she and Grace couldn't sort things out, but then caught herself. *Relationship advice? Me and Jem? What am I thinking?*

'Anyway, Lily, you forgot your cloak.' Alice handed her a heavy emerald mass of material.

She took off her bag, fastened the mantle around her shoulders, and instantly felt comforted. She slung the bag back over her shoulders and smiled. 'Thanks. Shall we go?'

The three of them, Alice leading the way, walked towards a dark corner of the gardens. As they approached, Lily noticed a hidden archway concealed by layers of moss and ivy cut into the outer stone wall of the manor's land.

When they reached it, Alice pushed with her shoulder against the wall in the centre of the archway and a heavy door swung slowly inwards. Beyond it was a short stone passageway.

'Through here. Push on the door at the other side. I've already cast the spell to unlock it. Whistle one short, sharp sound once you're through and the door is closed again, and I'll reset the spell. That whistle will then work to reopen this door when you need to come back through.'

Jem and Lily nodded.

'Finally, let me cast a protection spell on you both. It won't make you impervious to danger, but it should go some way to preventing you from getting yourselves killed.'

'Great,' Jem said sarcastically.

'Or, I could cast it on Lily and let you save yourself, you ungrateful pig,' Alice spat.

'Woah, all right, Alice, settle down.'

'No, I'm sorry,' Jem held up his hands. 'I need to shake this mood off. I'm sorry, Alice. Fire away.'

Alice nodded, looking satisfied. She took both of their hands in hers and closed her eyes. Muttering under her breath, a warm breeze blew around the three of them. Lily felt as if warm, golden honey was running over her bones. It was a pleasant, if unnerving, sensation, but it didn't last long. A few moments later, Alice opened her eyes and the warm breeze faded away. 'There. That should help.'

Lily embraced her friend. 'Thank you.'

'Yeah, thanks, Alice. Look after everyone for me?' he said sheepishly.

'You know we will. Now go, before it's too late in the day.' She gently shoved them both through the doorway and closed the heavy door behind them.

They were plunged into total darkness. The cold, damp walls of the short passageway made Lily feel sick. She had never been a fan of confined spaces, nor of the dark. Breathing deeply, she tried to remain calm. Edging forwards, her hand found the broad, warm shoulder of Jem in front of her. She felt his hand close over hers, and he led her to the end of the passageway. In mere moments, that felt like hours for Lily, a shaft of light broke through the darkness as Jem pushed open the other door. They stepped out into the rain, and Jem pushed the door closed behind them, before sending out a short, sharp whistle.

They heard Alice whistle back, and then watched as the door melted into the wall, covered with ivy and moss once more. To the unknowing eye, it was impossible to see.

'Come on.' Jem threw a casual arm around her shoulders. 'Let's go.'

Chapter Seven

Alice Blackwell wandered back down the snowdrop-lined pathway, focusing on the sound her boots made on the crumbled, decorative ground beneath her feet. She was alone again. The hole in her chest that had opened up when she and Grace had started fighting gaped worse than ever with Lily's absence. It was as if she could feel the life within her fading with every step Lily took away from the manor.

The rain was falling thick and fast; she was already soaked to the skin and shivering, but it didn't matter. The thrum of her magic felt distant. She was trying not to think about how hard conjuring a simple protective spell had felt. Usually, magic came to her as naturally as breathing or blinking, but in that moment, facing the prospect of losing Lily once more, conjuring it had felt like trying to run from a bear with feet made of rocks: exhausting, slow, painful.

The rain at least almost fooled her into thinking her struggles would be fixed by a warm bath and dry clothes. It gave her an excuse, something to blame, but deep down she knew that this had nothing to do with the weather, except for the fact that it was a kind of cruel pathetic fallacy. Her mood felt like the rainstorm that raged in the clouds above.

As she pushed open the door to the manor house, there were children running about, playing, laughing. They were untouched by the pains and traumas of the world, but their time would come. One day, that sweet laughter that burst from their lungs would be replaced by misery, and they too would look upon the innocence of children with envy.

Hecate was deep in discussion with Rowenna and Ailsa, the two girls who had originally been her friends when she had first arrived at Midnight Manor. They hated Alice now, just because Alice had lost her temper once in training against the two of them. She had had no protector, which had given the girls an advantage that they had fully exploited. So Alice had nearly killed Ailsa, a water witch, with the flames of her fire magic. Alice knew she should have been strong enough to resist the bait, but she hadn't been, and she wasn't about to apologise for it. The girl had had it coming, plain and simple.

As Alice dragged her dripping wet self through the entrance hall, Hecate moved away from Ailsa and Rowenna and stormed across the room. Each step seemed to make the very floor of the place shake.

'Alice!' Hecate growled.

Alice ignored her and slumped towards the central staircase that would take her to the north wing and the silence and peace of her own room. She briefly looked up towards the top of the stairs and her heart lurched painfully. Grace, holding an open book in one hand that she was reading intently, was making her way down the stairs, oblivious of Alice. Suddenly, speaking to Hecate looked like the more attractive prospect.

She turned on her heel and tried her best to smile at the priestess. 'Yes?'

'Come with me.' Hecate turned and walked across to the other side of the entrance hall, through a narrow doorway. Alice followed, not daring to look up to see whether Grace had spotted her looking like a drowned rat. She hoped she hadn't.

Hecate led Alice down a wood-panelled corridor lined with glass display cases filled with insect specimens that made her skin crawl. Insects belonged outdoors, in the forest or the meadow, not locked in glass cases, pins piercing their tiny bodies. Dragging her feet, she found herself in a room she'd never been in before. It was a small study, with a little round window that didn't let much light in. Candles filled almost every surface, their wax dripping freely. There was a fireplace on the back wall that was flickering happily, and there were bunches of herbs hanging from the mantel, swinging gently in the heat from the flames. A large grimoire was lying open on the desk that sat beneath the window, and in the centre of the room two weathered chairs sat, plump and comfortable-looking, on a thick, luxurious rug. 'Have a seat,' Hecate said, gesturing to the chairs.

The woman flicked her wrist and the dampness left Alice's clothes. She was still chilled to the bone, but at least she was no longer saturated.

'Thanks,' Alice said, sitting down.

'I just didn't want my chairs getting ruined by the water.' Hecate shrugged. She didn't sit down next to Alice.

'What do you want from me?' Alice asked, exhaling deeply. She was tired to the bone. All she wanted was a bath and her bed. Conversation didn't come easy for her at the best of times, but, right now, she couldn't think of anything worse.

'Your magic is weakening.' Hecate was leaning against the wall by the fire. The light from the flames cast a strange, shadowy glow across her that made her look ethereal, ghostly. After all this time, Alice still found herself in fearful awe of this woman, even though now she knew her motivations and her weaknesses. Hecate was still everything Alice could ever hope to be, so this observation stung.

'Yes,' Alice replied.

'What are you planning on doing about it?' Hecate said sharply.

'I didn't think there was anything I could do. I just thought I'd—'

'Sit it out? Wait for everything to blow over and hope

you didn't need your magic in the meantime?' Hecate snapped.

Alice couldn't believe the unfairness of it all. Did Hecate think she enjoyed feeling weak and feeble? Did she think she was unaware of her own inadequacies? 'I'm hardly powerless.'

'You may as well be!' Hecate's voice was getting louder, and Alice understood now why this conversation was happening in this room, far from prying eyes and ears. Hecate wasn't afraid of people hearing her shout, but she was afraid of people hearing the tell-tale sound of emotion in her voice, the high-pitched intensity that gave away the affection she held for Alice, when the rest of the manor was used to her cold, quiet darkness. Hecate very rarely raised her voice, and she was all the more frightening because of it. 'You may as well be.' She regained her temper, and her control, and her voice became strong and firm once more. 'This needs sorting out, and it needs to be done soon. We cannot afford for you to be weak if the Brotherhood comes at us with a more sustained attack. I need you, as much as it physically pains me to admit it. But I need you at your best. And that means you taking some responsibility for your damn self, girl!'

Alice blinked in silence, overwhelmed by Hecate's admission. 'How do I do that?' She had no power left in her voice and hated how pathetic she sounded. She was no longer the Alice that lived in exile, wishing for magic, wishing to be lifted out of her obscure life. So why did she suddenly feel like her again?

'I have two suggestions, and I hope you'll take me up on both of them. In fact, if you don't, I'll need to seriously reconsider your place alongside me through this war and beyond. I need someone by my side who prioritises their own power, their own wellbeing. If you're unwell, you're useless to me. It's as simple as that.'

Ouch. Alice clenched her fists tightly, trying to focus on keeping her anger in check.

When Alice didn't respond, Hecate continued. 'Number one: the little girls, twins, with the black curly hair. I sense a power in them that I haven't sensed in anyone since I first met you. They are practically fizzing with untapped potential. I need you to take them in, guide them, help them to release their magic and then show them how to control it.'

Alice nodded. 'Brenna and Maeve. I thought I felt something in them too, but I brushed it off as paranoia.'

'I don't care how you release their magic, as long as you get it done.'

Alice swallowed. Her own magic had been released by pain and torture. Lily, Jem, and Grace would have her head if she so much as thought about hurting the twins. She would have to be creative. 'All right. I'll do it. What else?'

Hecate sighed, pushing herself away from the wall. She started to pace backwards and forwards in front of the fire. Her heeled boots clipped violently against the wooden floor and the slit in her dress revealed legs on the dangerous side of slim. Alice looked at Hecate, properly looked at her, and noticed that every part of the priestess was on the dangerous side of slim. Her face had taken on a gaunt look, her cheekbones were too defined, her eyebrows too strong, her lips dry and cracked underneath the thick layer of red. She was disappearing in front of Alice's eyes, and suddenly she didn't care if everyone thought Hecate was the root of all evil, she knew she would do anything to regain her trust and bring this woman back to the mighty power she had been for so long. 'You need to get Grace back – and I don't mean as friends.'

Alice's heart dropped. 'I can't—'

'You must.' Hecate had stopped pacing and stared directly into Alice's soul. With her long hair, slender figure, and dark, piercing eyes, Alice felt like she was looking at a version of herself as an older woman. A version of herself that didn't prioritise her own wellbeing, that didn't look after her heart, that didn't leave space in her life for happiness or peace. Hecate was the product of a lifetime of hatred and revenge. She couldn't allow herself to become what Hecate was.

Alice sighed and stood up, mirroring Hecate's stance. 'What do I need to do?'

'Win her back. I don't care how. You were the strongest you've ever been with her by your side. Your magic flowed like breath from your lungs; nothing was difficult, everything was natural. She made you glow. Without her love, you are a husk of your former self, whether you want to admit it or not. You still love her, and that is slowly killing you. If she won't have you back, then you need to cut off every tie to her and begin a new, different life.'

Alice wanted to spontaneously vomit at the thought.

'I know that sounds impossible, so you need to do everything in your power to make it work between you. And believe me, I'm the last person on earth who should be giving advice on matters of the heart because last time I checked, I didn't have one. So you have to choose your own path to redemption with Grace. But, Alice?'

'Yes?'

'For all of our sakes, do it quickly. You've spent enough of your life moping. It's time you took your power back with your woman at your side.'

Alice nodded. 'All right. I will try.' The feeling of nausea hadn't left her yet, but she knew Hecate was right.

It was time to apologise to Grace.

Chapter Eight

The sound of frantic bag-packing filled a room in the far corner of the north wing. The room, being on the very edge of the manor, benefitted from having two large windows, one on the front wall, and the other on the left wall. A bank of light filled the room, making the lit candles redundant. Morven liked the atmosphere they created though; their flickering warmth made any space feel like home, and after having had so many homes over the years, she was happy to cling to anything that made the transitions easier.

She had her back to Cass, who was stuffing belongings into his bag as if it might explode if he didn't work fast enough. She herself preferred a calm, measured approach, so had decided to pack once Cass had finished steaming about like an angry stag. She stood in front of the mirror, tying her mousy-brown hair back into an intricate braid that snaked down from the nape of her neck and over her shoulder, finishing just beyond her waist. She had found some pretty enough dresses in the clothing room that Alice had pointed them towards and had decided to wear her favourite today to give her the courage she would need to walk away from the predictable safeness of being surrounded by her friends.

The dress was a dark shade of mauve, with delicate embroidery that wound around the neckline, the ends of the V-shaped sleeves, and the hem that sat at the perfect length, just above the floor. She had fastened a leather belt around her waist, from which she hung a dagger she and Lily had bought, amongst other weapons, from the blacksmith in Greywicke. Lily had also left her several bottles of ointment and tinctures in little leather pouches that she was able to fasten to her waistbelt, too. For the first time in her life, she looked at the girl in the mirror and felt proud to be her; she didn't notice the crookedness of her nose, the thickness of her eyebrows, the broadness of her shoulders, or the softness of her tummy. Instead, she saw a girl of strength and character, with a fierceness in her eyes and rosiness in her cheeks that made her look full of life and hope.

She and Cass hadn't been on their own for a while, not on this kind of journey. It was risky, but she was ready. There was a great world out there to be explored, and she tried to think of what Lily would do in this situation. Lily had the courage of an explorer, heading out into the world with unflinching confidence in her own abilities – or at least that was how Morven was sure she must have felt. So Morven was determined to channel Lily on this adventure and seize every opportunity that came their way.

There was a knock at the door, but before either of them had time to respond to it, the door flung open. Farlan was leaning against the doorframe, twirling his stick casually. 'Hello...' he said, when neither of them responded to his dramatic entrance.

'What do you want?' Cass said impatiently. His clothes were still strewn in a chaotic mess across the room and his cheeks were violently pink. Morven wasn't sure if that was from the exertion of his intensive packing or from being interrupted in a state of disarray by this boy who neither of them really trusted.

'Oh well, if you're going to be rude, I won't bother offering my help.' He turned on his heel and went to leave.

'Wait!' Morven shouted, and he turned back around again, smirking at Cass. 'Wait, please,' she said again. 'Why don't you come in?' She gestured with her arm for him to take the crooked wooden chair next to the mirror she was standing by.

He walked forward, and she could see he was trying to conceal his limp. 'I'm Farlan, by the way.'

'We know,' they said in unison.

'You were listening last night then. Well, I know you're Morven and Cassius, too, so I guess we're all even there.' His voice was silky and brazen, like he was used to getting his own way.

'It's Cass.' Her brother sounded short-tempered, which wasn't a great surprise when there was a young man in the room sitting so close to his sister.

'Cass.' Farlan held up his hands. 'I apologise.'

'How can we help you, Farlan?' Morven asked, doing her best to mimic the natural hospitality Jem showed to everyone.

'I have heard, through sources I'm not willing to disclose, that the two of you are planning a midnight flit.'

Morven took a step back, surprised. 'How do you know that?'

'Like I said, I'm not willing to disclose where I gained my information. But I'm not here to warn you against the idea or to discipline you or anything. I'm no Jem Rafferty.' He smirked again, but his joke clearly wasn't received in the way he was expecting, as Morven didn't break a smile, and neither did her stepbrother.

'So why are you here?' Cass snapped.

Morven turned to him with wide eyes, silently saying *stop being so bloody rude*.

'I'm going to ignore your impoliteness and presume it's only because you're feeling anxious about your imminent escape. I'm here, genuinely, to offer you help. I don't know where you're planning on going, but if you're heading anywhere near the border, my home is there. If it hasn't already been taken over by the Brotherhood, you're more than welcome to let yourselves in and stay there for a night or two before you continue. There will be food in the kitchens, money everywhere, comfy beds – you name it, it'll have it. Go wild.'

'You can't be serious?' Morven asked, stunned.

'Deadly, my dear. I have no use of it since I'm unable to return there, so someone may as well enjoy it before the bastards lay waste to it all.'

'Wow…' Morven took a few more steps backwards and sat on the edge of the bed. 'Thank you.'

'Why would you help us?' Cass asked. He had always been the more cautious, suspicious of the two of them, and it rarely annoyed Morven. But right now, it was annoying her greatly.

'Because you're young and from what I've heard, you've been through a lot. I've done a lot of really dreadful things in my life, and I'm starting to wonder if I've been brought to this forsaken place to learn how to actually be a useful, good human being. Before now I've only ever known how to be a spoilt brat, bored and seeking entertainment in all the wrong ways. It's time I redeemed myself.'

'Hmm,' Cass huffed, unconvinced.

Morven, however, was feeling more trusting than her stepbrother. 'That's really kind of you. I'd invite you to join us, but I can't imagine Hecate would be too thrilled at the idea of losing you so soon after she's laid her claim.'

Farlan chuckled. 'I think you might be right there.' He leaned against his stick, cocking his head like a curious puppy as he looked at Morven. 'But I appreciate the offer. Perhaps another time?'

'Another time,' Morven repeated, feeling warmth rise to her cheeks. She cast a glance at Cass, who was seething in the corner. She knew she shouldn't have invited Farlan, but there was a sadness to him, underneath his expensive suits and arrogance – she was sure of it.

'I do have something else to offer the two of you, though, as a parting gift.'

'Oh?' Cass's curiosity had clearly overtaken his impatience with Farlan.

Farlan looked smug. 'If, perchance, you're going to attempt to cross the border, you'll need papers, signed by a baron, explaining who you are and what your purpose is.'

'Oh,' said Cass and Morven synchronously.

'Exactly.' Farlan tapped his stick twice. Sparks shot out of its end as it hit the floor, and then all of a sudden, pinned there by his stick, there were two pieces of weathered-looking parchment. He bent down, picked them up, and passed them to Morven.

'Wait, you have magic?' Cass asked.

'Of a sort.' Farlan shrugged. 'It's only useful for this kind of thing, really. I'd be a great criminal and swindler, if only I had the heart for it.' He smiled. 'But hopefully this goes some way to proving that I am friend, not foe.'

Morven looked down at the parchment. It was a mottled yellow, covered with words in an exquisite scroll. At the top right of the page, there was an artist's impression of her, with her signature braid. Written next to the illustration was the name Elswyth Croft. Beneath that was her age, which had been artificially inflated to list her as nineteen. There was also some information about her being a researcher, and that her purpose in the Shadow Lands had been to investigate the local flora and fauna, and that she was actually a native of the world beyond, a place Farlan had listed here as Hythlund. The other parchment clearly displayed an artist's impression of Cass, even including his freckles which made Morven smile. His name was Alwyn Croft, also nineteen, her twin brother. Morven hoped that wasn't too much of a stretch, considering they looked nothing alike. On the parchment, he was listed as being her chaperone, so that she didn't have to complete her research tasks alone and at risk from rogue Shadow Landers.

Morven shook her head. 'I thought they were supposed to be more progressive in the world beyond. Why on earth would a grown woman need a chaperone?'

Farlan laughed. 'Don't ask me. I think they believe everyone across the border is murderous and threatening. It's easier this way than to list you as husband and wife.'

Morven recoiled. *Husband and wife? Gross.* 'All right, fair enough. Chaperone it is, right, Cass?'

'Absolutely, Sis. I've got to keep these ruffians away from you, after all.' He looked at Farlan with slightly too much of a serious expression.

Morven rolled her eyes and ignored him. 'Thank you, Farlan. Is there anything we can do for you whilst we're away?'

'Nope,' he said, shaking his head as he headed for the

door, 'just make sure you both come back safely, that's all. I barely know any of you, but I do know you've all had enough grief and pain recently to last a lifetime. So stay safe. Good luck!' he said as he flounced out of the door, not looking back.

Cass flopped backwards onto the bed, puffing out his cheeks. 'Well, that was weird.'

Morven looked back into the mirror, mortified at the colour of her cheeks. 'Yeah,' she said, tucking a rogue hair behind her ear, 'really weird.'

Chapter Nine

'Sorry for being a grump,' Jem said, hands in his pockets, staring at the ground as he walked.

He and Lily had been walking all day, barely stopping to catch their breath or to eat the food they had parcelled up into daily portions in their packs. On the map, they had marked a cross-country route that would take them directly to Alder Vale, instead of via the coast. This meant that, should they keep their pace, they would be able to traverse through the mountains and come down above Alder Vale, past Alice's cabin, that very night. Their plan was to rest up there and then head into the village the following morning, where they both hoped a plan for dealing with Alf would come to them as they walked.

They had moved across damp moorland for the first few hours, but as they descended, they became ensconced by thick moss-covered forest that looked as though it hadn't been touched by the recent snow or frosts. As they picked their way through the trees, keeping a gentle bumbling river to their left at all times as their guide, Jem looked around at the landscape he knew Lily loved the most. She had long since abandoned her boots, which were now hanging by their laces around her waist, and her bare feet were bright red from the cold of the air. She didn't seem to mind though.

'You weren't a grump, don't worry. These are stressful times for all of us,' Lily replied, passing him a paper bag filled with nuts that had been covered in honey and then roasted.

He took the bag, smiling with appreciation for both the nuts and her kindness. 'You don't have to be so nice, y'know? I was in a foul mood, and I wasn't very nice to you.'

'I know,' she said, shrugging, 'but like I said, no hard feelings, all right? We've got more important things to worry about than your ego.' She poked her tongue out, which made him laugh.

They fell into a comfortable silence. Every now and again, Lily would pull the map from its home tucked into her waistbelt and examine it carefully. They had travelled further than they thought they would, and were well over halfway there. The Shadow Lands had always felt huge and frightening to Jem, who had convinced himself for a long time that the world was full of dangers. Life in the lighthouse had been happily isolated; he had skulked around stealing food in the dead of night when the only people around were harmless drunks in stupors, and the rest of the time he had been safe on his stormy little island with enough books and plenty of good company to keep him contented.

He thought back to that version of himself, the one who had fought through losing Grace, who had managed somehow to allow Lily beyond his fortress of defences, even amongst all of the fear and hurt and pain. That version of Jem had thought Oakencliff was miles away, too far to bother with. Now, as he walked, he realised their world was miniscule, a compact, compressed universe filled with every single joyful thing in nature: the ocean, thick forests, endless moorland, mountains that tickled the clouds high up in the sky. Even if he remained within these borders, he could find joy and purpose in each one of those vast and changeable landscapes. He was no longer just Jem from the lighthouse, with no family except for Grace and no knowledge of where he had come from.

He was Jem Rafferty, friend to many, explorer of their tiny world, reader of books, and baker of bread only slightly better than Lily's. He was proud of who he had become, and excited for the first time in a long time for what the future would hold. He just had to hope against hope that the war they all knew was coming would leave those he loved untouched.

'We should start climbing uphill soon,' Lily said, deep in thought, squinting at the map which she'd placed in a shaft of light that shone through the canopy of the trees. 'The source of the river is here,' she pointed, forcing Jem to return from his thoughts, 'which is when we need to head west, up and over this hill, and then we'll be heading in a straight line back down the hill to Alice's cabin. Easy.'

'You say *easy* as if you haven't just explained that we need to literally summit a mountain before we get there.' Jem nudged her, but secretly felt a little nervous at the thought. Jem Rafferty had ocean storms running through his veins; he wasn't supposed to be that high up, or this far away from the salty waters of home.

'It'll be fine. I've brought a rope, just in case.' She shrugged, packing the map back into her belt and continuing on, following the river.

Jem gulped. 'Why would we need a rope?'

Lily smiled to herself as she walked. 'In case you slip, of course. I'll have it attached to us both across the ridgeline. That way, if one of us throws ourselves off a precipice, the other can just use their body weight as an anchor to stop them from falling all the way down the mountain.'

'And how exactly do I do that?' He felt his hands getting clammy.

'It's easy really. Everyone in Alder Vale knows how, thanks to the mountains being so close by. I just jump off the opposite side of the ridge that you've fallen down and we balance each other out. Then, once we're stable, we both clamber back onto the ridge and carry on. Honestly, don't worry. It wasn't ever a proper Alder Vale winter if someone hadn't accidentally thrown themselves down a gully and needed to be rescued. But,' she said, placing a hand on his arm, 'it's fine. I've spent many a winter in these hills. They're not as bad as they sound. I promise.'

'Why don't I believe you?' He ran a hand through his hair, catching a knot at the back and wincing.

'Because you don't know what's good for you, Rafferty, that's why.' She grinned.

Soon enough, as Lily had predicted, the path cut sharply upwards, and the forest thinned and thinned until they were surrounded by snow and rocks instead of green moss and trees. The sky was crystal clear and blue without a hint of a cloud in sight, but that did mean the higher they climbed, the colder it got. After a while, Lily threw her backpack on the ground and dug out a rope, and then tossed a pair of thick woollen gloves at him, before pulling on her own.

'Now' – her voice had taken on the tone that she used when explaining to the twins why they shouldn't play too close to the fire – 'according to the map, we continue up a little and then we have to traverse a ridge before we can start the descent. There are ways around it but they're a lot longer and we wouldn't make it by nightfall. This is by far the safest, and swiftest, option.'

He just nodded. His mouth had dried up and he was trying his best not to show his fear to Lily, which clearly wasn't working as she kept looking at him like he might implode any moment.

When they reached the ridge, he wished there were a few more low-lying clouds around. The clarity of the afternoon sun meant that he could see every single inch of the fall to the bottom of the valley on either side. At least if it had been foggy, he wouldn't have been able to imagine so vividly what it would feel like to fall all the way down there or how it would feel to hit the ground.

Jem stopped, dashed a few steps away from Lily and then bent double to vomit.

Note to self: stop imagining imminent death.

He took a few deep breaths, grabbed a handful of snow to wash the taste from his mouth, then wandered back to Lily, trying to look confident and dashing. He feared he looked anything but.

'Everything all right?' she asked, kind enough not to reference the fact that he'd just emptied the contents of his stomach.

'Yep,' he exhaled, 'let's do this.'

'Right.' She tied one end of the rope around her waist, just above her belt and then tied the other end around his waist. Suddenly Jem couldn't breathe. She tied the knot tightly and then tapped him gently on the shoulder. 'As I walk across, I'm going to weave the rope around boulders and outcroppings of rock that we scramble past. If one of us falls, they'll create some really useful friction to stop us from falling too quickly. As you follow, you can undo the parts of the rope that you pass. We'll have a little routine down in no time, me weaving, you undoing, all along the ridge. You'll be so focused on the rope that you won't notice the height.'

'And the bit about... falling?' Jem tried to regulate his breathing, but he was struggling.

'Yeah. The other person, whoever hasn't fallen, would throw themselves down the opposite side of the ridge to balance the fall.'

'So, actually throw myself off the cliff?'

'Exactly. But the opposite side to the side I've fallen down, otherwise you'll just pitch us both off this mountain and we'll be dead.' She smiled her world-brightening smile and for a moment, he was almost convinced things were going to be fine.

'No pressure then,' he said. 'Is this a good time to mention that I don't like heights?'

'As good a time as any, my dearest Jem! But the longer you dilly-dally, the worse it will be. So let's go.'

Lily made her first step onto the ridge, weaving the rope as she promised she would. 'Keep the rope tight if you can!' she called back to Jem, who couldn't find any words to reply with.

When the rope was what he hoped was sufficiently taut, he took his first step out onto the sharp rock. The ridgeline wasn't that long, and it bridged the gap between two hulking grey mountains. It undulated up and down, meaning that he and Lily had to climb down and scramble up multiple times to get across it, and whichever side he looked down, there was an enormous drop.

Don't look down. He had to keep repeating it to himself. *Don't look down. Don't look down.*

Intermittently, Lily would call out words of encouragement, words of kindness and affection designed to keep him strong and moving forward. If they survived this, he was going to confess every single feeling he had ever had for that girl, and he would do it proudly and without fear. Because this was real fear; being high in the sky with only the eagles for company, picking his way across dangerous-looking rocks, hoping that he wouldn't fall.

With his focus on the rope and on Lily, he found that she was right. He was halfway over the ridge, and they were really getting somewhere. Each step was deliberate and slow, but they moved synchronously, silently working together, Lily laying the rope, him picking it back up. Step down here, climb up there. He was getting confident, perhaps even overconfident when—

'ARGH!' Lily screamed and Jem felt his heart drop to the floor.

He looked upwards to where her shout had come from and saw her hanging from a tiny shard of rock, swinging in the mountain breeze.

'Help!' she cried. 'Jem! I'm going to fall!'

He tried to scramble up the rocks to where she was, but in his haste, his hands and feet couldn't find safe holds and he kept slipping, almost careering himself off the cliff as well. He paused, trying to catch his breath. He looked around at where he was standing, stuck on a ledge just below her, and calculated the angle from himself to Lily above him. He was trying to think straight through the panic coursing through him, desperately trying to get a hold of himself so he could find a solution.

'Hold on,' he cried. 'I'm coming to get you!'

Jem gathered what was left of his frayed courage and tried to scramble up towards Lily again, this time breathing slowly and calmly, focusing on where he was placing his hands. Each movement was deliberate and thought through, as he tried to think only of the importance of ignoring his fear and making his way towards Lily.

Hand hold. Move foot up. Pull yourself up. New hand hold. Move other foot up. He turned the climb into a series of singular movements, until he found himself just above Lily, on a small flattened piece of rock on which he was able to lie down on his stomach.

'Give me your hand,' he said, reaching down to Lily, who was white as a sheet.

'I can't—' she sobbed.

'You can and you must, Lily Knight. We are not dying here. Give me your hand.' The firmness in his voice caught him by surprise. It seemed to kick Lily into action as well, as with two big breaths, she swung herself upwards so she could reach his hand. As he grabbed her hand, he used her upwards motion to give him the strength he needed to heave her up a little further. 'Can you find somewhere to put your feet?' he asked.

Lily scrambled around, until—

'Yes! Yes, I've got my feet on a ledge,' Lily choked.

'All right, now catch your breath. I've got you.' He looked about himself and saw another sharp boulder jutting upwards. He threw the excess rope over the boulder, so it would act as a makeshift winch system, and then positioned himself to pull her up. 'After three, Lily, I'm going to start lifting you. But I'm going to need to let go of your hand to make that happen. You're going to have to hold on to the wall. You won't fall; the rope's got you. Keep finding those holds as I pull you up, all right?'

Lily grunted and nodded, finding a solid place for her first hand and then, holding her breath, he watched as she eyeballed a second hold and let go of his hand to take it.

'Nice job, Lily. I'm going to start heaving you up in three, two, one—' He pulled. The rope didn't move for a few breaths and then it finally, finally started to lift Lily from her stranded position. He promised himself he wouldn't stop pulling, not if his hands were shredded and bloody, not if he felt like his arms would explode from the exertion.

An agonising few minutes passed. With each heave from Jem, Lily had to reposition herself on the rockface. But finally, he spied the fingers of her gloves curl over the edge of the cliff, and with one more pull, Lily tumbled over the edge and onto the relative safety of the ledge by Jem's side. She lay there for a few moments on her back, gulping in the fresh freezing air, trying to calm her heavy breathing.

Jem felt like his heart might burst of the panic and the fear. The thought of losing Lily had grasped him like a golden eagle clings to its prey and he couldn't bear the image for one moment longer. He shuffled himself carefully across the ledge and lay down beside her, allowing his own lungs to open up and regain all of the air that had been lost to the breathlessness of the moment. She was alive.

'We're almost there,' Lily said between breaths, breaking the silence. 'We've done the worst of it. We're off the ridge now – it's all downhill from here.'

Jem felt her take his hand and he squeezed it tightly. 'We need to move before we freeze to death,' he said, more for his own benefit than for hers. The cold of the stone they were lying on had started to seep through his thick layers and crawl into his bones. He carefully pulled himself to his feet, and then helped Lily to hers.

A few more steps, this time holding on to each other's hands for dear life, and they were on the summit. Lily untied her own rope, and Jem copied her, packing it away in her bag. In silence, the two of them started the long walk down the other side of the mountain, hand in hand, towards Alice's cabin.

It was almost over.

Chapter Ten

Grace Rafferty stomped from her room in the north wing of Midnight Manor and aimed straight for the front door. She didn't know where she wanted to be or what she wanted to do, but she couldn't bear another moment of pacing in her bedroom in the deafening silence of pure unadulterated loneliness. With Jem gone and Morven and Cass just about ready to disappear, she felt more alone than she ever had before. A huge part of her heart yearned for a reconciliation with Alice, but then she thought about it and stressed about it and talked herself out of it every time she found herself almost tempted to knock on Alice's door.

This was how she'd found herself, yet again, in such a state of disarray that she had to throw herself outside into the fresh air. In the warm darkness of her bedroom, she had decided that she was going to walk calmly over to Alice's room, knock very politely, and then initiate a calm, measured conversation about their situation. Then, two steps away from Alice's room, she had bottled it.

Coward.

As she sprinted towards the front door, it opened unexpectedly. Grace was moving too fast to stop herself, and barged directly into—

'Alice. Shit, sorry.' She and Alice had collided and banged heads rather spectacularly. Grace took a few steps back and allowed Alice to walk through the door. Alice looked much more put together than the last time she'd seen her, when Grace had watched her following Hecate like a sheep follows its shepherd. This Alice, the one standing in front of her, looked far more like *her* Alice. Confident, if a little surprised, headstrong, gentle.

'That's quite all right,' Alice said, brushing herself off.

Grace went to move around her and make a swift exit, but Alice continued.

'Actually, I was coming to look for you.'

'F-for me?' Grace stuttered. The two of them hadn't spoken, not properly, since Alice had left to re-join Hecate. Grace's blood still boiled at the thought, but her immediate hatred had ebbed away now she'd had the chance to think carefully over Alice's motivations, which Jem had explained to her, and which Lily had apparently explained to him. But, after her outburst, which included Grace holding a cutlass to both Alice and Hecate's throats, she hadn't been able to find a way back to how they used to be. She didn't know if it was even possible, after everything that had happened.

'Yes.' Alice looked down, unable to meet Grace's eye. Was it possible she was overthinking this too?

'How can *I* help *you*?' Grace said, and then immediately hated herself for how short and sharp the sentence was that had left her mouth.

If Alice noticed, she didn't react. 'It's Maeve and Brenna you'd be helping, really. I've started to facilitate their training, but they're showing signs of a witch and protector bond like ours. Since I can only provide insight into my side of things, I thought we would all benefit from your input. Plus, they trust you. More than anyone else.'

Grace gulped. She didn't like the idea of Maeve and Brenna being embroiled in all of this, but the longer they left it, the worse it would be. The last thing they all needed was an outburst from them; the whole manor could go up in flames. 'All right. Where do you need me?'

Alice smirked and Grace blushed. *Why am I blushing?* She couldn't believe the state she was in after a miniscule conversation with Alice. Hadn't the power dynamic always been the opposite way around? Wasn't she the one who was supposed to be smirking and causing Alice to stutter and blush? She shook herself off. This would have to stop immediately. She breathed in, stood up tall, placed a hand on her hip, and smirked back.

'We were going to head out into the gardens. That way, if anything does happen, we're less likely to cause any serious damage to the building. Plus, it's a nice day and I think we've all been cooped up far too long.'

'Agreed.' Grace said, holding the door open for Alice to go back the way she had come. 'Are the girls already out here?' she asked, joining Alice as they walked across the gravel, through the rose garden, around past the back of the greenhouse and into a large, open lawned area spotted with a few huge, ancient oak trees.

Alice gestured to one of the trees and Grace saw what she was pointing at. The snow had completely melted away and the twins were practising their handstands in the wet, muddy grass. 'Apparently nothing fazes them; rain, mud, cold, you name it.'

Grace laughed. 'I know. When we took them in, the night I rescued them from some backstreet hellhole where they were hiding from that awful man, the weather was absolutely horrendous. Driving rain, wind strong enough to knock over a full-grown giant, and a strange girl asking them to come with her and get in her boat to sail through stupidly high waves to an island. Through all of that, they just got on with it. Not a word of complaint, barely any tears, just this steadfast determination not just to survive but to thrive. That attitude, *their* attitude, has carried me through some of my darkest days.' She exhaled, blowing out her cheeks. She hadn't meant to talk so much.

'Wow,' Alice replied.

Grace waited for her to say something else, but she didn't. They just walked in an almost-companionable silence until they reached Brenna and Maeve. Grace held out a hand to wave, but as soon as the girls saw her, they careened towards her, wrapping their skinny arms around her waist.

'Hi,' she said, patting them both on their identically curly heads. 'You guys all right?'

'We are now,' said Brenna, as she unravelled her arms from Grace. 'Now you and Alice are in love again.'

'Wait—' said Grace, her heart hammering.

'We're... we're not,' Alice said simultaneously. They were both spluttering like a pair of drowning kittens.

'Oh,' said Maeve. 'All right then.' The girl shrugged.

'We wanted to talk to you guys about some things. Do you know about witches and protectors?' Grace changed the subject swiftly.

Her eyes met Alice's, and Alice widened her eyes as if to say *oh my goodness, thank you*. Grace just smiled.

'I know about witches. Broomsticks, black cats—' Maeve was in danger of listing off every single thing she personally associated with the concept of witches, so Alice interrupted.

'But you know I'm a witch, don't you? And Lily. Hecate too, and lots of other people here at the manor.' Alice rubbed her hands together and then clicked her fingers, causing a spark to shoot from one finger up into the sky. The spark exploded just above their heads, making little balls of glowing light rain down over them like a beautiful silent firework.

'So a protector is what Grace is, then?' Brenna asked, looking surprisingly engaged in the conversation.

'Exactly,' replied Alice. 'Now, don't be fooled into thinking that because witches need protectors, witches are weak. That's not the case.'

Grace watched as Alice started to pace, talking passionately with her hands. This was a side of Alice she'd never really seen, guiding and teaching young people. It suited her. She would have fit right in with her and Jem in the lighthouse.

'Protectors are there to shield the witch from enemy attacks, so the witch can focus on conjuring her own spells.'

The twins nodded in unison. 'So, which is which?' Maeve asked.

'Which is which... what?' Grace responded.

'Which witch is which!' Brenna burst into giggles. 'Which of us is the witch and which of us is the protector?'

'Well...' Grace looked at Alice, hoping she had a bright idea, but Alice said nothing. 'We have to work that out for ourselves. Hecate has always used *archaic*'—she glanced at Alice—'methods to spark the first magic from a witch. I don't think that's always entirely necessary, not when you're both still so young and full of life.'

'Um... all right,' Brenna said, nervously tucking her hair behind her ears.

'What do *you* suggest then?' Alice shot back.

'I think we just teach them as you would teach the youngest groups with Hecate. We'll show them a spell – an easy one – they can both try and channel the power needed, and hopefully the witch will show herself. Then we'll do the same, but for a protector charm; that way they'll both hopefully develop their powers without any nastiness.'

Alice nodded, deep in thought. 'The shield spell is a nice simple one. It comes with an incantation. which will make it easier to muster.' She looked around at the floor, before stopping to gather something from the ground beneath the great hulking oak tree. 'If we throw these at the two of them,' she held up a shiny acorn, 'they won't hurt them, but they will be easy to deflect with a shield.

'What do we need to say?' asked Brenna, fists clenched, a look of fierce determination on her face. Her sister, Maeve, looked much less confident. She was staring at the ground, arms folded gently over her body like she was embracing herself.

Alice knelt down in front of the twins to speak to them, seeming not to mind about the wet ground soaking into her heavy black velvet dress. 'The word is *savailech*, but when you say it, you need to visualise a great big shield right in front of you, stopping anything from coming towards you. Can you do that?'

Both girls nodded.

'After three,' Grace said, picking up some acorns from the ground too. 'One, two, three.'

'*Savailech*!' the girls shouted, again and again. '*Savailech, savailech, savailech*!'

Brenna's face was screwed up with the intensity of her

effort and she didn't flinch every time an acorn thrown by Alice or Grace bounced off her. She gritted her teeth, closed her eyes, and kept growling the words.

Maeve, on the other hand, was more peaceful and gentler in her approach. She closed her eyes from the outset and held one trembling hand out in front of her. The incantation came out of her mouth as barely a whisper.

All of a sudden, the ground shook violently. Branches snapped and fell from the tree above them, Grace felt the tremoring in her bones, but Maeve hadn't noticed. The girl still had her eyes closed and her hand outstretched, except now it looked like she was standing behind a wall of fog.

As if acting on instinct, Brenna turned herself towards her sister, her hand still outstretched. The fog grew larger, denser, and the more acorns Alice and Grace threw, the stronger the fog seemed to become. Wind, stronger than anything Grace had ever experienced, whipped around them all, coursing straight through Grace's thick jumper and shirt to raise goosebumps on her skin.

'What's happening?' Grace shouted to Alice above the storm.

'I don't know!' Alice shouted back, moving closer to Grace so they could communicate better. 'I think it's the twins! But this is unlike anything I've ever seen before!'

Before long, they had attracted a crowd, and still there was no change in Maeve's deep, intense focus and Brenna's determination to support her. They were surrounded by muttering and speculation.

The shield grew taller and taller, thicker and thicker, until most of the lawns were surrounded by it. Brenna didn't flinch, Maeve kept repeating the incantation, and it was almost like they had no limits on their power. No torture needed.

Almost as quickly as it started, the girls stopped. They opened their eyes, and smiles as large as the full moon in the night sky flooded across their faces.

'We did it!' Maeve cried.

'Did it work?' Brenna asked, looking to Grace and Alice for support.

The crowd around them burst into spontaneous applause, and the twins' faces turned red as beetroots.

'Yes, it worked! Brenna, Maeve' – Grace took them both by the hands – 'you are so strong! Stronger even than I am!'

Brenna and Maeve just looked at each other, folded their arms, and grinned.

Chapter Eleven

A pale sun drifted lazily beneath the horizon, leaving behind a sky laced with ribbons of violet and mauve. Overhead, there were the subtle hints of snow clouds building and the temperature had been rapidly dropping since dusk.

Cass found himself standing by his step-sister's side, gazing open-mouthed at a manor house even more grandiose than the one they had left. It had been easy to sneak away from Midnight Manor, easier than either of them had expected, owing to the fact that there had been an earthquake of sorts and a commotion in the gardens. Everyone had been so busy rushing over to the oak tree to discover the source of the disturbance that no one had noticed the two of them, cloaks up and bags on their backs, as they slipped through a secret exit to which Farlan had led them. Neither of them knew why Farlan had taken such pains to help them, but in reality they had no complaints; he had equipped them with everything they needed to go on their own adventure, and that was enough for them.

They had both known that Farlan was rich, but as they stood on the gravel pathway that led all the way up to the front door through manicured lawns that looked like the harsh winter weather hadn't touched them at all, their understanding of the word *rich* had shifted somewhat. Back when they were in and out of the poorhouse, or skulking around deserted towns at night to find food or clothing to stop them from freezing to death, their idea of richness had simply been all of the merchants and their families in their small, comfortable townhouses: food on the table, soft blankets on the bed, warm clothes to work in. And then they'd met Jem and Grace and discovered another type of richness: friendship, familial love, compassion, comfortable isolation. Yes, they all still had to forage for food and things hadn't been easy, but they had always had each other, and Cass would always consider their time in the lighthouse as the richest he had ever been.

But this, this was something else entirely.

'Should we knock?' Morven asked Cass, as they stood on the immaculate doorstep. There didn't seem to be any sign of life about the place.

'Probably,' Cass shrugged. 'There could still be servants

around. But it doesn't look like the place has been ransacked as Farlan feared. Maybe they came to find him but left when they saw that he wasn't here anymore.'

Morven shrugged and knocked on the door.

Knock.

Knock.

Knock.

Silence. No footsteps, no shouting, nothing. They were entirely alone.

Morven pushed the door and it creaked painfully, opening up into a grand hallway. A huge, elegant staircase dominated the space, and after a few cautious moments, the excitement overtook Cass and he was the first to break the silence when an uncontrollable guffaw sprung from his mouth.

'Ha!' he shouted, his voice echoing around the cavernous hall. 'Remind me to thank Farlan when we get home, Morv. I'm not denying he's a strange kind of person, but this really is ridiculous.'

Morven stepped alongside him, grinning. 'Where should we explore first?'

They glanced at each other before simultaneously breaking into a sprint up the stairs, shoving each other as they went, laughing heartily. At the top, they both went in opposite directions. Cass sprinted across the lush, thick scarlet carpet down an endless corridor punctuated by many doors. At random, he charged through a door on his right, and then stopped in his tracks.

Beyond the threshold was the biggest bedroom he'd ever seen in his life. In the centre stood a ginormous four-poster bed, with navy-blue curtains dotted with tiny golden stars and layers of luxurious-looking duvets and blankets. The walls were papered with an exquisite night sky pattern, and the hulking chair underneath the great window was a rich chocolate-brown leather. Also by the window was a telescope, something Cass had read about in the library of the lighthouse, something he'd always been itching to try. There was a small table next to the chair stacked with books, and the nightstands by the bed supported expensive-looking candlesticks. How was it that this room, chosen entirely at random, was perfect for him? He had always loved the stars, the constellations, and had read every book on astronomy he could find throughout his life.

He wandered through the room, gazing wide-eyed at every little detail that seemed to have been put there just for him. It felt immediately like home, which wasn't a feeling Cass was used to experiencing; he had always had to make places feel like home, what with him and Morven moving around so much. But this room, in this strange old manor house, was undoubtedly his.

'Morv?' he shouted over his shoulder, once he'd shaken his head, rubbed his eyes, and made sure he wasn't imagining things.

There was no reply.

He walked to the doorway and shouted again.

'Morven?'

After a few more moments, there was a reply. 'Coming!' Sure enough, her hasty footsteps came rushing down the corridor until she found his room. 'Wow,' she said, as she walked through the doorway. 'How on earth is this your perfect room?'

'That's exactly what I thought...' He hoped she wasn't about to dampen his high spirits.

'Hmm...' She eyed him suspiciously. 'I'll take the room next door, since this one's clearly going to be yours and you'll never be talked out of it.' She winked, and then disappeared back into the corridor.

He heard her open the next door along. Then a curse word broke the silence. 'I can't believe it!' He heard her shout. 'Cass, get in here right now.'

Panic-stricken, he rushed to where her voice was coming from, and then ground to a halt, mouth hanging open. The room Morven was standing in was also completely perfect for her. It had opulent velvet curtains around a very expensive-looking four-poster bed, piles of books in every corner, a fireplace adorned with a beautiful bouquet of dried flowers, and a dressing table with the most exquisite mirror he had ever seen. 'Is this some kind of trickery?' he asked.

They both walked back into the corridor and then, at random, chose another room each.

'Oh my—' Morven gasped.

'What the—' Cass said simultaneously. He was standing in his astronomer's room. Again. Everything was identical.

The bed, the star chart, the chair, the books, everything. 'Are you seeing what I'm seeing, Morv?'

'I imagine so,' she replied. 'The same room?'

'Mmhmm.' He couldn't muster much more of a response through his surprise.

'Well,' Morven clicked her tongue, 'at least we're aware magic exists thanks to everything that's happened recently, or else this would have given me a heart attack.' She chuckled. 'There are worse places to find ourselves, Cass.'

He agreed, and then the two of them wandered back out of their respective rooms in search of something to eat.

'What exactly are we going to do?' Cass asked, as he dropped his spoon into his finished bowl of stew. His cooking wasn't a patch on Lily's, but he was proud that he'd managed to make something edible and not entirely unpalatable.

They were sitting in a grand dining room. It was possibly the most magnificent room Cass had ever been in, and that included his magical bedroom. The dining table itself was long and outfitted with enough cutlery and crockery for a banquet. There were not one but *three* golden chandeliers hanging from the intricately carved vaulted ceiling and the wallpaper was delicately painted trails of ivy and gold strands on a background of the palest blue. Every piece of furniture was polished so heavily that he could see his reflection in every surface – not that he wanted to. When he caught sight of the bedraggled, freckled face that looked up at him from the table where he sat, he moved his bowl to obscure it.

'I was hoping a plan would pop into my mind as we walked, but I don't know. I'm not used to the weight of responsibility.' Morven sighed. 'I didn't realise quite how much effort it took to make decisions. I don't know how Jem does it.'

'Well, we know we want to see the world beyond, and we're almost there. Perhaps, across the border, something will take our fancy and we'll find our plan.'

'Aren't you worried, though?' Morven shifted in her seat across from Cass at the table.

'Worried?'

'Cass, we've left the people we love the most at a time when there is danger around every corner. Have we made a mistake, leaving now?'

He huffed. 'Jem and Lily left too.'

'Yeah, to further our cause, to find out what exactly the Brotherhood is planning. What are we doing?'

'We're doing something useful too.'

'Are we?' She gulped. 'Or are we just bored and irresponsible? Jem said to look for somewhere for us all to live, after, but I don't think we're likely to stumble across somewhere, and it feels like a futile task.'

'What do you suggest then, if you're so clever?' Cass snapped, growing impatient.

She sat for a moment in silence, drumming her fingernails on the polished mahogany dining table. 'The Brotherhood, they want to kill everything and everyone we love. They hate and they terrorise and they ruin. But that's all we really know, isn't it? We don't know anything about who leads them, not really. We don't know their tactics, how they fight, what it even looks like when they attack. But across the border, we're closer to their strongholds. What was it, Farlan called it? The place, the place beyond.'

'Hy-Hythlund?' Cass racked his brains. 'I think that was it.

The people of Hythlund will know far more over there than we do here.' She looked up, mischief in her eyes. 'We should gather intelligence. We could spy...' Her face was glowing with excitement, and it made Cass nervous.

He took a deep breath inward to calm himself before he responded. 'How are we supposed to spy in a place we've never been, in a world different to ours?'

'Ach.' She waved a nonchalant hand at him. 'How different can it be? It's only across a border. I'm clever, well-read; I can fool them.'

Cass pushed his bowl away and stood up from the table. He walked to the large bay window that dominated the dining room they were eating in and looked out at Farlan's lands. 'So we spy. We gather information quietly, and quickly, and then we get out. That's all I'm agreeing to.'

'That's all I'm asking for.' She shrugged. 'It's a purpose at least. It gives us a reason to be away from home. The longer we stay away, the more uncomfortable I am with the idea of this trip being purely gratuitous.'

'When did you swallow a dictionary?' Cass whipped round. 'Don't go getting airs and graces, Morv. You're a waif and a stray, just like me.'

'I'm just trying to get into character. Tomorrow, we are Elswyth and Alwyn Croft. I'm a researcher – I've got to sound distinguished.' She lifted her chin. 'Don't doubt me, Cass. You and me, we've survived far worse that Hythlund can throw at us, I'm sure of it.'

He shook his head, but didn't reply.

Cass felt a heavy weight settle in his chest; this had been his idea, to come away, to get some space, but Morven was right. The longer they stayed away, the worse the timing felt. But they couldn't turn back now. Cass wouldn't let them. They were too committed to skulk back to Midnight Manor without at least something to show for their time away. He wanted Jem to be proud of him. So he'd make sure he was. As much as he hated Morven's plan, he had to admit it would be quite the story when they returned home.

Chapter Twelve

The violet hour cast eerie shadows through the thick, unrelenting forest. The low light and total absence of beautiful birdsong that usually filled the air made Lily feel like a stranger in her own lands. Occasionally, the tell-tale hammer of a woodpecker broke through the otherwise silent landscape, any other sounds muffled by the blanket of snow that had smothered everything. There wasn't even the peaceful, meandering trickle of the river, because that too had frozen over. Lily had spent plenty of time in these woods in the winter, but they had never felt unfamiliar, like they did now. She couldn't work out if it was the world that had changed, or herself.

'We're nearly there now,' she said to Jem through chattering teeth. 'Only a bit further.'

Since their accident on the mountain, Lily had struggled to pull Jem out of his thoughts for longer than a few moments. It had been terrifying, but she wasn't used to losing Jem's steadfast strength after a disaster; usually he was the one pulling up his bootstraps and putting on a brave face. A strange thought entered her head when she considered this.

He doesn't feel like he has to pretend in front of me anymore. He can show his true self, his true feelings. What an honour it is to be allowed to see Jem Rafferty, the vulnerable, not just Jem Rafferty, the brave.

'What are you thinking about?' Jem asked, falling into step alongside her. He was wrapped in a spare blanket from his rucksack and he held it tightly together underneath his chin. He was shivering even as he walked.

'Oh, er...' Lily stumbled, thinking it was hardly appropriate to tell him what she had actually been thinking about. 'Nothing really. Oh!' she cried. 'We're here!'

From out of the woods, a glade had appeared. It was small and roughly circular, but even in the low light Lily couldn't mistake the ramshackle cabin with its log-stacked exterior and crooked chimney sitting right in the middle. Alice's cabin.

'Cosy,' Jem said, as they walked up to it.

Lily couldn't tell if he was being serious or sarcastic, but was too relieved to have reached their goal for the day to care. She banged her boots against the doorframe to knock off the excess snow, and then heaved open the front door and walked into the house that had been Alice's sanctuary for so long. It felt strange to be there without her best friend, but there were pieces of Alice everywhere, even though she'd taken her belongings away when she had left. There was still a small ceramic jug filled with long-dead foliage on top of the mantelpiece, a perfectly neat stack of logs and kindling next to an axe by the fire, and her bed was still covered in a myriad of quilts and blankets that Lily had made for her over the years. Lily had never realised back then, when she had been full of criticisms of how small and pokey the cabin was, how much it felt like a second home to her.

Seeing it now, with a thin layer of dust covering everything and the hearth cold and dark, emotion overcame her, and as Jem wandered in behind her, she found herself weeping.

Without even asking what the matter was, Jem enveloped her in a hug and let her cry into his chest. He muttered words of comfort and stroked her hair gently, letting her process everything that had happened. She realised, as the tears flowed, how little she had allowed herself to actually think about what she had been through, what she had lost, and what she still had to overcome to reach a place of peace and happiness again. It had been a long road, and with a war coming it would be longer still.

She snuffled and stepped slightly back from Jem, wiping her eyes on her jumper sleeve. She looked up at him and he smiled lightly, without an ounce of pity in his face.

'Shall I get that fire started then?' he asked, still not prying.

Lily nodded, cleared her throat, and then got to work clearing the surfaces and sweeping the floor of dust, before rummaging in her bag for whatever food she could find. She hoped, if nothing else, that they could fill up their stores tomorrow in Alder Vale, because stale bread and cheese was starting to get a little depressing.

As the fire started to flicker, she unwrapped the blanket from around herself and laid it in front of the hearth, so they could sit and eat by the warmth of the flames. It had been a cold and stressful day, so the simple act of sitting and staring into the fireplace was exactly the tonic she needed. Jem finished stacking logs over the flames and dropped himself down to sit next to her on the blanket. She offered him a hunk of bread and the round of cheese, and then passed him the canteen of water.

'Do you think things will ever go back to normal, Jem?' she asked, still staring into the flames. The cold was starting to leave her bones, but she still felt the shivering from deep within her body.

'Well…' He shuffled closer, wrapping one half of his blanket around her shoulders so that it enclosed them both. 'That depends on what you think *normal* looks like.'

'Hmm.' She nodded. It hadn't been the answer she was looking for.

'All I mean is, normal for you once was living in a small, gossipy village with your uncle, visiting a miserable, lonely Alice in this cabin. Is that what you want to return to?'

Lily sighed. 'No, I guess not. But I suppose it's easier to

yearn for what once was, even if that reality just wouldn't be possible anymore, than it is to find something new.'

'But you don't have to find something new, Lil. You've found your family in us – or at least I hope you have, otherwise I've sorely misinterpreted your actions.' He chuckled, nudging her gently.

His laugh filled her with a warmth that the fire couldn't compete with. 'No, you're right. I have found family in you all. At least I won't have to search for connections, now. And Alice, I think, is happier than she's ever been. Or she would be, if she and Grace could reconcile.'

Jem nodded, passing her the bread and cheese. 'There's nothing we can do there except wait and hope. They've both done stupid things, but they'll find a way back to one another. People destined for each other always do.'

'Do you really believe that?' Lily asked, heart hammering in her chest. She tried to eat, but the food felt like sand in her mouth.

'I do.'

She gulped. 'I suppose I'm also worried about where we'll live when this is all over. We can't skulk around at night to feed ourselves and the children forever. We need to establish something real and solid, somewhere we can actually help young people to find their way in life. And we need a safe, comfortable home, with enough space to be able to do that.' She looked down at her hands, feeling the urge to tear at the skin around her fingers building.

Jem must have known what she was thinking, because

he took her hands in his and held them tightly, gently, so that she didn't have to rely on her willpower. 'I agree. We're old enough to find a solution that doesn't rely on stealing and skulking. I just don't know what that looks like yet. But we'll figure it out. We always do. At least we've got something to aim for. And hey, hearing you speak of it all as if it's what you actually want to do with your life brings me more joy than you know.'

She leaned her head on his shoulder. 'Of course I do. I could run an apothecary, which would bring us in some coins, at least. I could apprentice some children, too, which would give them a good set of life skills to go forwards with. You could write, Jem, and see if you can make some money from books. We'd figure it out as we went. It will be hard, I know that. But will it be harder than what we've already had to live through? I doubt it. If anyone can do it, it's us.'

'You're a wonder, Lily Knight,' he said, stifling a yawn. 'But I think it's time we considered sleeping. We're going to need our strength and our wits about us tomorrow and starting the day tired won't do us any favours.'

Lily nodded, and then her heart dropped. There was only one bed in Alice's cabin. She knew this – she had always known it – so why did it now seem like a dreadful realisation?

'What's the matter?' Jem asked as he clambered to his feet.

'Er,' Lily said, feeling awkward. She shivered, feeling the loss of Jem's body heat now she sat alone.

'Don't worry, I can sleep on the floor by the fire. Go and get yourself warm.' He pointed to the bed, smiling kindly.

Lily felt guilty, but she wasn't going to complain. She popped the food back into her bag and lifted the bag onto the table, just in case there were hungry mice at this time of year. She threw one of the blankets from the bed over to Jem, and then climbed into Alice's bed. Underneath the quilts and blankets, it was cosy and warm, and she felt all of the day's worries and stresses melt into the fabric. But then she saw Jem trying to make something remotely comfortable and warm on the cold stone floor by the fire and she couldn't bear it.

'Jem,' she said, carefully, 'stop being chivalrous.' She pushed herself up on her elbows. 'You said it yourself, we need to get a good night's rest tonight. Bring the blankets and come over here.' She tried to look non-threatening, and then realised how stupid that was.

'Are you sure?' he asked, looking like a frightened deer.

She couldn't resist the opportunity to tease him. 'I promise I won't compromise your virtue,' she said, laughing.

He rolled his eyes and then grinned.

'Don't be silly. Of course I'm sure. It's bloody freezing. You'll be no use to me in the morning if you've frozen to death overnight.' She pulled the covers back and gestured with her hand. 'There's loads of room,' she lied. 'It'll be fine.'

Tentatively, Jem pulled up the blankets from the floor, shook them off, and then tossed them over the bed. He unfastened his boots slowly, as if he was trying to delay the inevitable, and then finally tucked himself into the bed, surrendering to the warmth and cosiness. 'All right, I'll admit this is a much better situation than over there.' He smiled, turning his head to face her.

'See?' she said. 'Nothing to worry about. Now, let's get some rest.' She turned over, still shivering slightly.

'Night, Lil.' He shuffled closer and wrapped a warm, strong arm around her, pulling her in so they could share each other's warmth. 'Sleep well.'

Lily closed her eyes and entwined her hand in his.

If the whole world burns in this war, she thought, *but Jem remains, I'll be perfectly content.*

Chapter Thirteen

'They're coming.'

Farlan Aelfdene charged into Hecate's study without knocking, sending papers flying.

'You know nothing about my magic, but I felt the energy through the ground. I followed the source, pressed by ear to the dirt, and I heard it. They've crossed the border and they aren't even trying to pretend they're coming in peace. I can hear the violence in their marching. I can hear the threats in their voices. I can hear Fenn Crydlund.'

Farlan looked up to find Hecate staring out of a window, watching something intently.

'Did you hear me? They're coming! We need to prepare.'

'Why do you care?' Hecate asked breezily. She didn't seem to understand the urgency.

'Why do I—? Why do I care that the man who banished me, broke my legs, and ripped out my eye, is on his way to conquer the lands I've called home ever since I was exiled? Why do I care that he's heading right this way? Oh, I wonder!' His words were sardonic and sharp, but the shake in his voice betrayed his deep, unrelenting fear.

'Don't get insolent with me, young man,' she spat, still staring out of the window. 'Now come here and tell me what you see.'

Frowning, Farlan walked over to her, the tapping of his stick echoing around the room every time it struck the floor. She moved aside slightly to allow him to have a good view through the glass. He squinted, allowing his eye to focus in the bright light that contrasted the darkness of the study. Outside, he could see the rose garden, still slumbering, with no early signs that the roses would spring back to life in the summer. Standing in the rose garden were four figures: Alice, Grace, Brenna, and Maeve. It looked like Alice and Grace were teaching something to the younger girls, but their movements didn't flow and the two of them weren't synchronised. 'What am I looking at?'

She tutted. 'You're looking at the future of the Shadow Sect, the two women I wanted to found the School of Shadows with. And they aren't communicating.'

'And...?' He looked at her expectantly.

'And, I need you to help them.'

Farlan was so confused. 'Help them communicate?'

'Alice and Grace are in love, Farlan, they just don't know it yet.'

Oh. *Oh.* 'I thought there must have been something between them. But in love? Is that even allowed?'

'Don't bring your prejudices in here, Aelfdene, or you'll be exiled again before you can say *magic*.'

Farlan felt like the sun had passed over him for the first time, bringing with it clarity of understanding. Stuttering, Farlan continued. 'No, it's not prejudice. It's just that... I didn't know *I* was allowed...' The face of a boy flickered in his memory, his curly hair, his bright, laughing eyes. Farlan's stomach flipped.

'Allowed to do what, you stupid boy?' Hecate snapped, running out of patience with him.

'To... love... someone, who wasn't... a girl...' he spluttered.

Hecate turned to him, the shadow of a smile on her face. 'There are many things you can do in this place that will land you in deep trouble, Farlan, but being true to yourself and who you are isn't one of them. You can love who you like here, so long as you remain sensible and appropriate.'

This was not the direction he had expected this conversation to go in when he had stormed through the study door.

'Now, if you're quite finished having an existential crisis, boy, I need you to use your newfound knowledge for good. Start spending time with them. Gain their trust. And for goodness' sake, remind them that they are stronger together. I have no interest in love or romance, but I need Alice and Grace sharper than ever if we're going to win this, and *soon*, if your predictions are right. They're stumbling at the moment, unable to flourish underneath the stress of not knowing where they stand with one another. It's stupid, and foolish, but I suppose love often is. Help them find their way so we all have a chance of surviving this thing.'

'I never took you for the romantic type, Hecate. I thought you were all about torture and chaos.' He smirked. 'It doesn't suit you at all.'

She turned to him and narrowed her eyes, and he suddenly felt his throat constrict. Struggling to breathe, he clawed at his neck, trying to remove the invisible hands that gripped him with vice-like strength. Then the feeling subsided almost as quickly as it had arrived, and he was left bent double, spluttering.

'I could still strangle you on the spot, boy. Don't push me,' she growled.

Farlan took that as his sign to leave.

With an unenthusiastic wave, he flounced from the room, wondering what he was going to do.

Out in the gardens, Farlan could hear not just Alice and Grace training, but the majority of the residents of Midnight Manor. He hadn't spent much time out of his room because he was, although he didn't like to admit it, a little overwhelmed by all of the new people and new experiences after so long living in exile with just a few members of staff to keep him alive.

It was a remarkably beautiful day, with the kind of crystal-blue sky that only appears in the middle of winter. The air was crisp and cold, but not uncomfortably so. He sighed as he walked, watching the little white wisps of breath dance in front of his face.

He had read about the Shadow Sect back home and had presumed they were all women. He himself had magic, and called himself a witch because, well, what other word could he use? *Wizard* sounded too comedic, and when he read about magic, he could only discover about the four magic user types: earth witches, air witches, fire witches, and water witches. So he hadn't consciously attached gender to the titles, but even still, he was surprised to see a small number of young men training outside with the young women.

Some were training in physical combat, swinging punches and kicks at each other, crying out when they failed to avoid being hit. Others were practising offensive and defensive skills, and more than once Farlan had to duck or flinch away from a rogue spell that hadn't found its intended target.

What he did notice, though, was that everyone seemed contented. The books he'd read about the Shadow Sect had painted them as these awful, cruel, terrible creatures who lived to kill and torture. In the books, Hecate was the queen of terror – even her title, 'the Priestess', had filled him with fear at the very thought of her. She was supposed to be evil. But then, his understanding of evil had always been Fenn Crydlund, and if Hecate was fighting him then how evil could she really be?

He walked around the back of the manor and found Grace, standing by the side of Maeve, and Alice by Brenna.

'Hello, there!' he shouted, feeling strangely awkward. He paused, assumed the invisible mask he always wore, and tried again. 'Hi.' He sauntered forwards, raising his stick in greeting.

Grace turned to him, narrowing her eyes. 'Can we help you, Farlan?'

'Er...' He hadn't actually thought of a realistic reason to hang out with them. 'I was just looking for someone to train with.'

Grace gestured around at everyone else outside. 'And none of these people that you had to walk past to get to us would suffice?'

'Grace,' Alice interrupted, 'leave him be.'

'Don't tell me what to do,' Grace snapped back.

Well, this is going to be harder than I thought. 'I just thought, seeing as you're training Brenna and Maeve in the basics, that I could benefit from those lessons too. You see, I've only learned what I know from books.' *Nailed it.*

'That sounds fair enough, Grace,' said Brenna, looking up at her mentor. 'I don't mind him staying.'

'Me neither,' replied Maeve, smiling sweetly at Farlan.

'Fine,' Grace said. 'Just don't get in the way.'

'Come on,' Alice said. 'It'll be fine.' She gestured for him to join them. 'Which team do you want to join?'

'Er, yours, obviously,' he said, in response to Grace's attitude.

'Tough, idiot. You're on my team,' said Grace, smiling acerbically at him, and he suddenly realised he was more frightened of her than he was of Hecate.

Everyone assumed fighting stances, hands out in front of them, knees bent, each team facing the other.

'But he doesn't have a protector,' Maeve said. 'Who's going to keep him safe?'

Grace sighed and rolled her eyes, 'I will, if I have to. But you focus on landing your spell over there and knocking Alice off her stride. I'll focus on keeping you protected. Brenna will keep Alice safe, and Farlan will just be dead weight anyway so don't think about him.'

'Woah, all right then,' Farlan said, unable to contain himself. 'There's no need to be so rude. Why are you so angry all of the time?'

Grace dropped her hands and huffed. 'I'm only angry when you're around, Farlan, I'm sure you can work it out.'

'That's not true. You're angry, full stop. But that doesn't sound like who you are. I've heard plenty of stories about you from the others, Grace. They say you're kind, and practical, hilarious, spirited, and generous. They tell stories of you saving lives; they say you're a pirate, which is why you dress so funny. All I've seen is, quite frankly, a horrible attitude, impatience, and unkindness. You don't sound anything like the Grace Rafferty I've heard of. I thought Alice was supposed to be the grumpy, prickly one, but all I've seen of her is patience and politeness.' The words had fallen out of his mouth before he had the chance to stop himself. He was supposed to be integrating himself into the group, not calling them out. He'd ruined it before he had chance to begin.

Grace exhaled, blowing out her cheeks. 'Well, shit.'

Brenna and Maeve giggled.

'Look,' Farlan continued, 'I'm sorry. That came out all wrong. In all honesty, I wanted to get to know all of you. I met Alice the day she kidnapped me'– he grinned at Alice, who rolled her eyes – 'and knew that she was someone special. Then I heard the stories and the tales of adventure about all of you, about what you've all been through while I was sitting in a mansion bored out of my brains, waiting for my life to start. I guess, in a way, I'm envious of you.'

'Envious?' Grace snapped. 'Mate, we've just had the most horrific few months of our lives. How can you be envious of people who have suffered?'

'Because in amongst that suffering, you've found companionship. You've found love.' He gulped, his voice breaking unexpectedly. 'I've been alone my whole life, an outsider, unloved, unnoticed. And I see you all, with your family bond, and all I can think is how much I'd be willing to suffer, if only I had the strength of those I loved around me.' He didn't know how much more he wanted to continue, but he couldn't seem to find a way to stop now he'd started. 'Through you two, I myself realised it was all right to love in a way that the world would see as unconventional.'

'What do you mean?' Alice asked, seeming genuinely touched.

'You love each other – or you did… I don't know,' he stuttered, and Alice and Grace exchanged a look. 'In a romantic way. And you're both women. You've shown me that I don't have to follow what I thought was the norm. Because I'm not *just* interested in women, but I didn't know I had a choice to act on those feelings I had for men. I've realised now that it doesn't have to be the case. You both showed me that. So whether you like it or not, you've changed my life.'

'Well, *shit*,' Grace repeated.

'Are you just going to stand here and swear, or can we actually do something useful now then?' Farlan asked. 'Because I've just poured my heart out and, I'll be honest'– he leaned foppishly on his stick – 'I'm feeling a little vulnerable and I'd appreciate it if we could all move on now.' He smiled, feeling shy for the first time in his life.

'All right,' Grace said, looking at Alice who nodded. 'You can stay. And I'll try to be less of an arse.'

'Which will be hard,' Alice piped up, 'because you're such a natural.' She grinned at Grace and to Farlan's relief, Grace grinned back.

Chapter Fourteen

Strange, glowing orbs of light at the top of long metal sticks lined a busy street that was in the throes of a market. People dressed in bright, unnatural colours, their faces plastered in powders and paints, inspected the wares of the market sellers and the setting sun didn't seem to suggest to any of them that they should start their journey home.

Morven, with her bare face, mousy hair and dowdy clothes, felt instantly out of place. She and Cass had passed through the border with the paperwork Farlan had given to them without much of a problem. In fact, she had been more on edge because of how easily they had been allowed to pass through. From what she'd read, she had been expecting a heavy dose of suspicion from the guards, but they had barely flinched after writing down their details and taking their descriptions. The problems had started when they stepped out onto the busy street, in the centre of the busy border town. Hythlund, the name for the world beyond, was stranger than Morven could have possibly imagined.

For years, Morven had dreamed of escaping the Shadow Lands, of being an explorer. All she had read was how backwards and old-fashioned her world was compared to the world beyond, but now, standing amongst all this artificial light and colour, she longed for the natural quietude of home. If adventure looked and felt like this, then Morven suddenly wasn't interested.

No, she thought to herself, it's just new. It doesn't mean I can't grow to appreciate it. I'm sure all the explorers I've read about had trouble adjusting to new places, and I'm no different. But she couldn't shake the feeling of unease, no matter how hard she tried to convince herself that it was normal to feel that way.

She shook her head, trying to make sense of her conflicting thoughts.

'I don't like this,' she whispered to her brother as they edged through the crowd, trying not to stand out. 'I don't like this at all. It's almost night-time – how is it so bright?'

Cass reached out and took her hand as they pushed through the swathes of people. 'I don't know. Look at the lanterns lighting the street. There's no flame in them, and they make my eyes all sore and funny when I look into them, like I'm looking into the sun.'

'You don't think they're… tiny suns, do you?' Morven

looked up and realised her brother was right. There was no flame, and yet the streetlamps were illuminated. How was it possible?'

'If I wasn't looking at them, I'd say you were mad but... I don't know how else to explain them!'

They kept moving, conscious that they didn't want to draw attention to themselves. Above, there was a strange kind of bunting hanging from building to building. 'Cass...' Morven had a sinking feeling in the pit of her stomach. 'Do you remember when Jem and Grace told us about the celebrations in Oakencliff?'

'Yeah, why?' He was only half listening, she could tell. In situations of fear or peril, Cass always puffed out his chest and pretended to be brave, but he had never fooled her.

'This bunting, above our heads.... it's the same – or at least, it looks like how they described it: black, red, and gold.' She exhaled, trying to convince herself she was making something of nothing. 'Jem said they were celebrating the Brotherhood. What if... what if the Brotherhood is here?'

Cass shook his head. 'Why would they be?'

'Well, if the main fear is that the Shadow Lands will come under attack by the Brotherhood then surely crossing the border here is as logical as any other place. These banners could be a celebration of their might, a leaving parade of sorts.' Morven was scaring herself now, and Cass could tell.

'Stop it, Morv,' he said. 'It's fine. We're safe. Why don't we head to an inn, spend the few coins Farlan gave us, have a drink and something to eat, and then if you still feel this nervous, we can leave. We'll just hop back over the border and head home. No harm done.'

Morven nodded. That sounded like a reasonable plan. She couldn't deny she'd be disappointed to head back to the manor without having achieved anything, but she decided that she would rather be safe and comfortable, than in danger far from home.

'Come on,' Cass said, leading her off the busy street and into the relative early-evening peace of a tavern.

As they walked through the heavy double doors, they saw that the tavern, too, was lit by the strange, fire-free lanterns and sconces around the room. It was much smaller than Morven had imagined a tavern would be, with a central bar, a few barrels to sit on and a couple of comfier-looking red leather armchairs by the side of a fireplace. Morven was aware that they were very young to be in a tavern, but hoped since the men on the border believed they were both nineteen, that they could carry that good fortune onwards.

Cass wandered up to the bar to order and Morven took one of the leather fireside armchairs. They were even comfier than they looked and, as she sat, she sank down into the cushioning like it was embracing her. She sighed, feeling the weight of the world that she carried on her shoulders lessen a little. Maybe this world wasn't going to be too bad after all. Just as she was feeling her eyes grow heavy, she had the sudden realisation that it was getting dark and they had nowhere to sleep. Could they make it back to Farlan's mansion? Or would they be stuck on this side of the border until morning?

As the thoughts wheeled around her head, Cass returned holding two glasses of what looked like ale, and a basket of fried potatoes. 'What's the matter now, Morv?' he asked, looking concerned, if a little impatient.

She explained her worries and he listened diligently until she had finished.

'Well, I have to agree with you about us leaving sooner rather than later. I thought it was going to be entertaining to experience the world beyond, I thought there'd be a lot to learn and so much to see, but I've got a bad feeling about this. The woman behind the bar was talking to the other gent – you'll see him if you look behind me, the one in the golden robes.'

Morven tried to look subtly and accidentally made eye contact with the man. Blushing, she looked back at Cass and tried to force her eyes not to look at the man again. 'Yes, go on…' she encouraged, feeling panicky.

'Well, they were talking about the Brotherhood. They were saying that it was only a matter of time now until the Shadow Lands fall. *Fall*, Morven. They're all talking about it as if taking our land is going to be quick and easy. They don't care about the people who live there, or about the lives we have.' He looked as flushed and worried as she felt, and it didn't fill her with confidence.

'What are we going to do?' Morven asked, although she knew the answer already.

'We have to go back and warn the others. We can't risk anything happening whilst we're away. It would be too horrible. I hate to say it, but I think we've made a mistake. I'd rather be there, at our friends' sides, helping them keep our lands safe and free of the Brotherhood than be stranded here in this strange, brightly coloured world. We don't belong here, Morv, and I don't think we could if we tried.'

Morven nodded, taking a big swig of her drink. It tasted of sour honey and rotten apples. She recoiled, pulling her face. 'What is this stuff?'

'Ale, apparently. Although if it is, I've no idea how my father ended up addicted to the stuff. It's awful.' He was also pulling his face. 'But we've paid for it, and it'll give us strength and courage to get back over that border. So down it, and let's go.'

Morven did as he asked and drank the whole glass in one go, choking as the liquid burned the back of her throat. She shivered, and then felt a comforting warmth rise up from her tummy. 'Right,' she said, 'time to go.'

As they stepped back out onto the street, a man – the one Morven had made eye contact with at the bar, the man with the golden robes – stepped out in front of them. He grabbed Morven's shoulder so that she ground to a halt. 'Not so fast,' he said in a gruff, threatening tone.

'Now hold on,' Cass began, standing up taller and swatting the man's hand from Morven's shoulder. 'Don't touch her.'

The man and Cass squared up to one another, nose to nose.

There was a shout, so close it made Morven's ears ring. 'There they are! They're the ones with the dodgy papers!' Morven's blood ran cold. Cass whipped round, looking towards the man who had shouted. In his momentary lapse of concentration, the golden-robed man grabbed Cass's hands and tied them with thick rope behind his back.

'Hey!' Cass shouted. Morven could hear the fear in his voice; could see it in his eyes. 'Run, Morven!' he shouted.

But Morven couldn't run. Her feet were nailed to the ground with shock. This wasn't supposed to happen. None of this was supposed to happen.

The man who shouted was running towards them. Morven recognised him as one of the guards who had let them through the border. He was flanked by two other figures, one man and one woman, both in identical scarlet uniforms and carrying strange weapons. Morven recognised them as the *pistols* Grace and Jem had warned them about.

Morven held her hands up in surrender. What else could she do? She refused to leave her brother behind. She would never have been able to forgive herself. No, it was better they faced whatever was ahead together, than force him to face it alone.

'Shadow Landers,' the golden-robed man hissed. 'You can spot them a mile off.' He was talking to the guards who were pointing their pistols straight at Morven.

'We were just leaving,' Cass said. Before he could say any more, a gag was tied around his mouth and a black bag was forced over his head.

'No, there's only one place for people like you,' the man snarled. 'We can't have you going back to your world and telling them all about us before we're ready. We don't want those backwards people on their guard. No, you'll go where you belong. To the poorhouse.'

'No!' Morven cried.

Cass struggled beneath the bag, and Morven could hear him trying to cry out as he wriggled and writhed in panic. The man kicked him to the ground, where he fell into a muddy puddle.

Morven dropped to her knees to help her brother, but her own hands were grabbed and tied with rope as soon as she hit the cobbled floor. She, too, was gagged, with a bag thrown carelessly over her head, turning the world as black as it felt.

'Surrender to the Brotherhood,' the man said. The people around them joined in, and it made Morven's blood run cold. *'Surrender to the Brotherhood.'*

They were bundled into what Morven eventually realised was a carriage of some sort. Heavy doors slammed behind them, deafening the noise of the jubilant laughter from the streets. Clearly Hythlund residents were happy to see the persecution of Shadow Landers. The chants continued, alongside clapping and cheering.

Beneath her hands she could feel smooth, polished wood, and when they began to move, she could feel the rumble of the wheels that carried them away, away, away.

Chapter Fifteen

Dawn crested the horizon, bathing the shimmering, icy world in a rosy glow. Lily and Jem had already been walking through the snow for a while, after rising early, plagued by thoughts of the day ahead.

Jem had spent the first moments of the night staring into space, not wanting to fall asleep in case he did something embarrassing. Curled up with Lily underneath the blankets, he had listened to her gentle breathing, waiting for her to drift into a deep sleep before he, too, could consider sleeping. She had been warm, and lying there with her had been a great comfort, even if he had ended up with a rogue strawberry-blonde curl up his nose whenever she shifted in her sleep.

The morning had been a calm, simple one. They had heated a little snow on the fire, dropping a few sprigs of pine in to their – or rather, Alice's – mugs, and had eaten another round of bread and cheese. They had both been eager to continue on their way, so things had moved smoothly and efficiently, without any friction.

Jem hadn't told Lily, but there was something in him that was excited to see the place where she had grown up, the place that she had called home for so long. There was something special about the idea to him that he couldn't quite put his finger on. But there was something deeper, more concerning, that weighed heavily upon him. Alf had betrayed Lily once before, and now they were walking straight into his home and trusting that they were going to be able to pull the wool over his eyes. He wished he could see Lily's home without the weight of that distrust.

He hated the plan. They had been through it a hundred times as they walked, and yet he still hated it. But Lily had looked him in his eyes and promised him that she knew Alf better than anyone in the world, and she trusted that he wouldn't betray her again. 'I remember the look in his eyes, Jem,' she had reassured him. 'Hurting me destroyed him. We walk back in there now, hands raised, all forgiven, and he'll do anything for us. I promise you. Can you trust me?' And he had trusted her. But that didn't mean he liked it. It didn't mean he could relax.

They broke through the forest and found themselves on a driftway where the snow had been compacted by a few early risers. As they wandered down, Jem could see the village of Alder Vale sitting in the mists of a cloud inversion. The cottages were made of warm stone, many of them with intricate thatched roofs, and there was a little snow-covered green in the centre. It was such a Lily-like place. Everything about it was cosy and welcoming – or at least, that was how it looked from a distance; like it belonged in a painting. Just like Lily.

'What do you think?' Lily asked, her eyes glowing despite the anxiety he knew she felt about coming back here.

'It's beautiful. I was just thinking how it looks like a very "you" place.' He smiled, tucking his arm through hers. His throat felt constricted as they walked, and he hoped Lily couldn't see the worry in his eyes. For her, he wanted to be unflappable.

They walked together into the village. It was early in the day, but there were already a few people milling about on their morning errands. Jem spotted an old woman with an angry frown tottering towards them, and he felt Lily tense by his side.

'Let me guess,' he whispered. 'Is that Jemima or Orla?'

'Jemima,' Lily whispered back. 'Although, since I'm accompanied by you, it looks like she's having second thoughts.'

Lily was right. The woman who had previously been making a beeline for them had slowed a little and was now just watching suspiciously from a distance.

Jem looked around the square of the village at the different shopfronts. There was a lovely-looking bakery, a butcher's, a blacksmith's and—

'The Apothecary.'

Jem said it out loud without meaning to. If he could have sketched a picture of what Lily's apothecary would look like, he realised he would have drawn exactly what was in front of him: a huge, beautiful window with sea glass hanging from strings to catch the sunlight; a hand-painted sign on the outside, 'Knight's Apothecary'; a front door painted sunshine-yellow, the colour of Lily's soul. It was all so perfect, and yet so bittersweet. This place could never be Lily's home again. Too much had changed; there had been too much sadness and betrayal. In his mind, he captured the apothecary, and promised himself that he would help her recreate all the beautiful bits when she had her own one day.

'Are you happy with our story?' Lily asked, bringing him back from his thoughts.

'Yes, I think so. I guess all we can do now is hope he buys it.' Jem gulped.

'He will.' She squeezed his arm. 'I'm sure of it. Let's go and get this over with.'

Arm in arm, Lily and Jem walked across the green to the door of the apothecary. Lily opened the door and Jem followed closely behind. His heart was beating a tattoo in his chest at the thought of seeing Alf. The inside, much like the outside, was exactly as he had imagined. Endless shelves of brown and green bottles, bunches of herbs hanging from the ceiling, wicker baskets to carry shopping in, and a workbench covered in books and papers that he knew would be organised perfectly, even if to the untrained eye it looked chaotic.

The one thing in the apothecary that he hadn't imagined was standing behind the workbench. A man in golden robes. *Golden robes.* Like he had seen before, in Oakencliff. Golden robes could only mean one thing: danger. *Where was Alf?*

Before Jem had time to say anything, to check in with Lily, his question was answered. Alf, looking pale and drawn, appeared from the back of the shop with his arms full of ingredients. He looked up, saw Jem and Lily, and dropped everything.

The golden-robed man swore. 'What are you playing at, man?' he yelled, and Alf apologised profusely.

'I just lost my footing, that's all. Gave myself quite the scare. But we appear to have customers, Wilfryd. I'll serve them and clean up after myself – I know you have errands to run in the village. Go on, I'll handle this.' Alf shooed the man out of the door. The man, Wilfryd, looked angry but glad to escape the confines of the apothecary. Jem, for reasons he couldn't identify, felt even more nervous now he couldn't see the golden-robed man. Anxiety prickled across the back of his neck. Something wasn't right here.

As soon as the man was out of sight, Alf rushed forwards and pulled Lily into an awkward hug. She didn't return the affection. He stepped back, looking sheepishly between his niece and Jem. 'What are you doing here?' he asked in a hushed voice. 'I thought you said you weren't ever coming home.'

'Things have changed, Uncle,' Lily lied. 'I realised I wanted a normal life, but I couldn't leave Jem behind. I love him, you see, Uncle, and we want to start our life together. A normal life, you've got to understand. We left everyone else behind, but we realise we really need to hunker down somewhere whilst we figure out the details of our new life together. I thought I could work here and Jem could head out and find work somewhere in this village or the next.'

Jem's stomach contracted uncomfortably when Lily said she loved him, even though it was a line in the story they had concocted together on their journey here. He knew it couldn't be true, but that didn't stop his mind from reeling at the thought.

Lily elbowed him in the ribs, and he remembered what he was supposed to do next. Jem held out his hand to Alf. 'Pleasure to meet you, sir. My name's Jem Rafferty, and I want to assure you that your niece is in good hands with me. I'll look after her.'

'But...' Alf stuttered. 'You've still got magic, though? You're still a witch.'

'Well, yes, but...' Lily stumbled. They hadn't rehearsed an answer to such a question. They had worked on the premise of Alf accepting them back, no questions asked. *Stupid*, Jem thought. *Stupid, stupid, stupid*. 'Yes, but I don't have to use it. Like I said, we want a normal life.'

'Witches can't have normal lives,' said an unfamiliar

voice from behind them. The door bounced open as the voice spoke, and Lily and Jem reeled around to see the golden-robed man, red in the face with rage, looking between them and Alf. 'Well done for keeping them talking, Alf. I knew you wouldn't let me down.'

Jem watched Lily look back at Alf with tears in her eyes. They had planned for everything – everything except Alf betraying her again. Even though he'd suspected it, Jem hadn't considered what he'd do if it actually happened. This entire trip had been fuelled on hope and trust. Jem realised they had been fools, but that didn't make the sting of the duplicity any less brutal. Rage lit a fire within him, but before he had time to lash out, the golden-robed man had tackled him to the ground. Jem struggled as he felt a foot settle heavily on his throat.

'I have people coming to take them away now, Alf. You won't have to do this again. Crydlund will remember this and accept you back into the Brotherhood, I'm sure. This is the ultimate act of loyalty to the Brotherhood.'

Jem could hear Lily screaming, beating Alf on the chest with her fists. He wanted to cry out, to help her, to wrap her in his arms, but he couldn't do anything.

It was all over.

Chapter Sixteen

Farlan wandered aimlessly around the manor, looking for something to do. There was a relentless, maddening nature to the feeling of knowing something big was about to happen, and not being able to do anything to stop it or even prepare for it. He spent most of his days just pacing, filled with a mixture of dread and anticipation.

His feet led him to the library, as they often did. He found comfort in stories of heroes and villains, of war and of romance. They stopped him from thinking too much about his own life. As he wandered down past the study tables and tall bookshelves, he caught sight of two little girls sitting cross-legged behind one of the rows of bookcases, hidden away from the rest of the world. Quietly, he wandered over to them and sat himself down, wincing at the pain in his legs.

'Brenna, Maeve, what are you doing back here?' he

asked, hoping he wasn't disturbing them too much. He craved company, and the simple delights found in the company of children was hard to beat.

'Just talking,' Brenna responded. 'We're bored. Alice and Grace are busy today and the weather looks like it's going to get really bad, so we thought we'd hang out in here.'

'What are you doing?' Maeve asked.

'Honestly? The same as you. I didn't really know what to do so I just thought I'd come here and see if there was a book that could distract me. But I found you guys, and you're way more fun than a book.'

Maeve smiled.

'Can I ask you a question, Farlan?' Brenna uncrossed her legs, rearranging her flax trousers at the waistband and pulling her woollen jumper over her hands. 'What happened to your eye? And your legs?'

Farlan always enjoyed the straightforwardness of children. He had met plenty of adults who had just stared, or given him pity, but none of them had ever so directly asked him what had happened, or how he wanted to be treated. He didn't want to be treated like an invalid, that was for sure. 'It's a long story, and it's not a happy one,' he warned.

'We have time,' said Maeve with a kind smile, 'and our story wasn't very happy to begin with either. But it had a happy ending, because we found Jem and Grace, and yours will have a happy ending too, because you found us. Right?'

'All right, if you're sure as well, Brenna?'

'I'm sure.' The twins nodded in unison.

'I am the son of a lowly baron,' Farlan began. 'He ran a tiny fiefdom on the border of the Shadow Lands called Hythlund. I spent the first few years of my life in a luxurious mansion with everything I could have ever wished for. Everything, except the love and care of my parents. My mother ran away, you see, just after I was born. My nursemaid told me she had been an impossibly sad woman, and when I came along, that sadness was too much to bear, so she left. My father didn't notice, because apparently even when my mother had been around, he had had mistresses.'

'What's mistresses?' asked Maeve innocently.

'Oh, er…' He wracked his brains for a child-friendly explanation. 'It means he had lots of women that he loved in his life. He kissed lots of women that weren't my mother, and that's not a very nice thing to do when you're married.'

'Oh,' they said together, pulling their faces.

'So my father had lots of mistresses to keep him busy, and I spent my days reading, playing outside, fencing, that kind of thing. I wasn't unhappy because I didn't know what I was missing, but I was bored and unsatisfied in life. I felt like I wasn't reaching my potential, even when I was really young.

'One day, my father made a terrible mistake in court. Court is where all the barons gather and socialise, with their wives and their mistresses. It's a place where lots of wine and rich food is consumed and people say things they don't mean. Well, my father had had too much to drink and said some very rude things to a much more senior baron from a neighbouring fiefdom – I forget which one. But these courts are strange places, and instead of punishing my father directly, it was decided that it was I who would be punished. One day, a man in golden robes arrived at the mansion and dragged me away from my nursemaid and took me to the very centre of Hythlund. I now know that the man in the golden robes is the leader of the Brotherhood, Fenn Crydlund, and this was one of the first things he did to gain favour with the barons.

'In the middle of the town square, with hundreds of people watching, Fenn broke my legs and took my eye. I was twelve years old.'

The girls were holding each other, their faces etched with horror.

'I'm sorry, is this too much?' Farlan asked, realising he'd lost himself in the storytelling.

'No, no,' Brenna insisted. 'Please continue.'

'Well, I expected after that horrible day that my father would want to spend more time with me, to apologise. He paid for a very expensive surgeon to fix my legs and sew up my eye, but that was all. Instead, my father felt humiliated by what had happened to me, and how my infirmities reflected on him. From that day onwards, the very sight of me filled him with embarrassment and shame. So he sent me away, to the mansion in the Shadow Lands. I was well cared for; my nursemaid came with me, along with a couple of other servants, but I was renounced as his heir. He trusted that one of his mistresses would give him another son, and that he could forget that I ever existed.

'So I lived in the mansion from then on, without friends or relatives or anyone really to talk to except the servants. But even they resented me, because they had had to leave their families to care for me across the border. Father kept me well stocked up with food and with money, but always on the proviso that I kept quiet, stayed away, and never tried to reclaim my title as the heir to his baronage.

'To protect myself from the harmful words of others, I assumed an invisible mask to wear in social situations, a mask that allows me to walk with a swagger instead of a limp, a mask that helps me to make jokes about myself so that other people don't have to. All of the bravado, the cheek, the power you see me wield, it's all a defence mechanism, designed to keep people from getting too close to me.

'And that, my friends, is my sad little story about my legs and my eye. I'm sorry that it's not a happy one, but you're right – just because my start in life wasn't very happy, doesn't mean I'm destined for a miserable life. From now on, life is exactly what I decide I want it to be. And that's the same for you two as well. If you're not interested in any of this magic stuff, just tell Grace and Alice. They'll understand.'

Maeve got up from where she was sitting and wrapped

her arms around Farlan. 'I think you're the bravest person I've ever met.'

Brenna laughed. 'Maeve, you think everyone is the bravest person you've ever met.'

Maeve huffed, letting go of Farlan. 'Well it's not my fault everyone we know is really brave, is it?'

Farlan laughed. *The bravest person Maeve had ever met.* That was a title he would wear with pride from now on.

Chapter Seventeen

It was as bad as Cass remembered. Worse, even, without the distance of memory to soften the edges of the brutality. The sound of crying children, begging for their mothers, the smell of tired, sweaty bodies that didn't fade no matter how many times they were forced to dunk themselves in ice-cold barrels of water to clean themselves, the mottled, hazy light that shone pathetically through the tiny windows high up on the walls so all they could see out of them was the cold sky. Poorhouses were all the same, it turned out, in the Shadow Lands and in the world beyond: miserable, wretched places filled with miserable, wretched people.

At least he had Morven with him; that was one saving grace of all of this. Had they been as old as their forged papers had suggested, they'd have been sent to different poorhouses all together, torn apart without knowing how they could ever reunite. The thought made his skin crawl. Separating Cass from Morven would be like separating a person from their limbs; agonising and unthinkable.

Every night since they'd arrived, Cass had woken up in a panicked sweat from a dream where Morven had been shipped off somewhere else. It terrified him more than he was willing to admit to his sister, although he knew she felt the same. They had been each other's strength through so much pain.

They had arrived at the poorhouse quickly after being bundled away from the town. Which meant, Cass was pretty sure, they were close enough to the border to be able to escape back into the Shadow Lands if they were lucky enough to find a way out of this squalid cesspit of a place. The thought of escaping was the only thing that had forced him out of the dirty, itchy bed that morning to go and work.

Work, in these places, was always incredibly difficult. That morning, Cass had left the dormitory he shared with twenty other boys and been marched down to the stone-breaking area. He tried to get there as early as possible because if all the slots were filled, he'd be forced to tease out old rope instead. He'd only done that once in the last poorhouse and had walked away with torn and bloody hands from the relentless work. He still had the scars. So stone-breaking had always been his preference, beating large lumps of stone with a hammer until they were small enough to use to cover highway surfaces.

After the working day was done, long after the sun had

disappeared from the sky, they were fed a measly meal. *The best part of the day*, he thought, as he wandered to the dining room, his hands still cramping from being wrapped around a hammer all day. He scanned the large room, lined with three long straight tables, for his sister. The air smelled faintly of burning, with an undertone of something disgustingly sour, but he didn't mind; after a long, horrible day, food was fuel.

A small hand at the far end of the left table drew his attention and he saw that the hand belonged to Morven. She had saved him a seat. He dropped himself next to her and gave her a quick hug. 'Are you all right?' he asked, looking at his sister in the candlelight.

She nodded, not meeting his eye.

'Morv?' he pressed. 'Morv, show me your face.' He felt like he knew what he was going to see before he saw it.

On the far side of Morven's face was a darkening bruise, a cacophony of blues, purples, and yellows across her cheekbone and up to her browbone. Her right eye was barely able to open properly because of the swelling. 'It's nothing,' she said, trying to smile.

'What happened?' he asked, trying to keep his voice, and his temper, measured and controlled. They had only been here for a few days, he wasn't sure how badly punished he'd be for causing a scene, and they'd both agreed to keep their heads down whilst they worked out an escape plan. Anonymity would be their only chance at slipping out unnoticed.

'I was in the washroom today, for work. I forgot to change the water between washing the red uniform of one of the guards, and the barrel is so dark it's impossible to see the water colour. I washed the table linens in the same water, and they came out mottled pink. A guard saw, called me some horrible names and then when that didn't upset me, he hit me.' She exhaled.

Cass swore. Loudly.

'Shhh!' Morven hushed him. 'Don't draw attention to it. We're staying anonymous, remember? I've already drawn enough attention to us today. The best thing we can do is keep our heads down. I know it's not all right that he hit me, Cass, but, before you ask, I'm not going to point out which one it was. I don't want to give you that kind of temptation. We have to move through this.'

'How can I move through it?' Cass hissed under his breath. 'I can't have someone going about hitting people, least of all you. How many other kids has he hit?' It was a rhetorical question, but Morven's face made him repeat it. 'Morv, how many other kids has he hit?'

She swallowed, sighing. 'All of us now, I think. I was the last one left in our group, but that was only because I'm new here. It seems like a common occurrence, although I want to believe that isn't true for my own sanity, and for yours.'

'I can't just sit on this, Morven—'

Morven grasped hold of his hands tightly. 'You must,

Cass! You must if we are to stand any chance of getting out of here.'

He squeezed her hands, trying to breathe through the pulsating anger he felt. This was a place built on abuse, a place he had hoped never to end up in again. How had it come to this? 'We should never have left Midnight Manor, Morv.'

She nodded. 'I know, but hindsight is wonderful.' She unfastened her mousy plait and let her long straight hair fall in a curtain over her bruised eye. 'We'll make it out of here, I promise.'

'How? How can we possibly get away?' Cass's voice cracked, much to his shame.

His sister sighed. 'We'll find a way. I know us. We're never stuck for long.'

They fell into silence, turning to their miserable bowls of potato stew. Stew was rather a generous term for the food, Cass realised with his first mouthful. Stews at home, made by Jem or Lily, had been filled with meat and root vegetables in a thick, flavoursome broth. This watery, measly amalgamation of ingredients in front of him barely warranted the name.

Time passed, and soon enough they had finished their paltry supper. Cass was about to stand up to leave when a commotion drew his attention elsewhere. A few seats along on their table, a young boy, no older than Brenna or Maeve, was crying. In front of him stood a guard in the scarlet uniform Morven had been washing earlier. They weren't close enough to hear what the guard was saying, but the boy's wailing was ear-splitting. He looked heartbroken.

'STOP CRYING!' The guards voice rang out across the dining hall and brought every other conversation to a standstill. Now they could hear the guard perfectly well. 'You insolent child! First you neglect your latrine-cleaning duties—'

'I just forgot where I was supposed to be today!' the young boy cried. Cass felt an unbearable rage on behalf of the boy, and for every child in this place. It wasn't a fate he would wish on his worst enemy.

'Forgot? Forg—' The guard lost his temper. Without a second thought, the grown man swiped the back of his hand hard against the child's face, sending him flying to the floor where he landed in a crumpled heap, eyes closed, unmoving.

Cass could hear blood pumping in his ears. His face flushed red and angry, and before he could stop himself, he seemed to lose control of his body. All he could think about was Glenn, and how Cass had watched as he had been struck to the floor, how he'd done nothing about it, how Glenn had never forgiven him. Cass wouldn't let that happen again. He couldn't. He pushed himself away from the table, vaguely aware of Morven hot on his heels, and charged straight for the guard before anyone could get in his way.

The room was deathly silent. Every other child was watching with bated breath and Cass could hear the chattering of their teeth, the trembling of their tiny bodies wracked with fear. No other child would be treated like this; he wouldn't stand for it. 'Hey!' he shouted, and the guard turned on his heel to face him.

As he did, the guard seemed to recognise Morven. 'Oh, hey, stupid girl. How's the eye?' he spat.

That was it. Any inclination Cass had had to go easy on the man disappeared with those seven words. The guard seemed to realise what was about to happen, but even with his instinct, he didn't respond quickly enough. Cass's punch landed squarely across his jaw, sending several teeth flying across the room.

Chapter Eighteen

Lily's ears were ringing, and she couldn't shake the nausea that had her in its vice-like grip. All she could hear was the sickening rumble of wheels beneath her, and all she could feel was the bone-rattling of those same wheels on rough ground. The world was black, although she knew that wasn't true. The bag over her head blocked out any light and muffled most of the noise.

She couldn't believe Alf had betrayed her. Ever since finding out about his involvement in the Brotherhood of Light, she had wanted to give him the benefit of the doubt; perhaps he'd made mistakes in his past. That would have been acceptable to her – forgivable even. What he had done was dreadful and had caused Hecate Winter to be born from the grief of losing her mother in such horrendous circumstances. But still, she could have worked on forgiving him, because he was the only family she had.

After this, though, she knew forgiveness was impossible. He had betrayed her to the very people who had exiled him, and all for what? Reverence? A ticket back into their dark world? And because of Lily's blind trust, she had dragged Jem into all of this too. *His* only crime had been to trust her.

She could feel her hands heating up with the kind of magic that only appeared when she felt emotion this strong coursing through her body. It was a dangerous magic, uncontrollable and unpredictable. She couldn't let it take over, because then she'd be putting Jem in danger. The pain of hurting him would be enough to kill her; she knew that in her bones.

'Jem…' she whispered, hoping he would be able to help her find some peace. 'Jem, my hands are glowing. I'm scared. What if I can't control it? What if I hurt you?' The tears were rolling down her face uncontrollably and her voice cracked uncomfortably as she spoke.

She heard shuffling near her, and felt his head come to rest on her shoulder. She could feel his strength, his fortitude, even though she couldn't see him or reach for his hand. 'It's going to be all right, Lil. Don't lose control, not now. You need to save this strength, store it up somehow—'

'I'm not sure I can,' Lily spluttered, not letting him finish.

'You're not a defeatist Lily – it's not in your nature. So don't let it crawl in now when you need your strength of mind the most. You've got this – you know it as much as I do.'

She nodded, trying to let his words wash over her.

'Look,' he continued with a new power in his voice, 'this is all perfect. We couldn't have planned this better.'

'We didn't plan it...' Lily muttered.

She heard him sigh. 'I know we didn't, but even if we could have concocted a plan, it wouldn't have worked half as well as this is going to.'

'Go on...'

'We're infiltrating the Brotherhood of Light, Lily. We'll be going straight to their heart, straight into the very core of who they are. There's no chance they'd take captives that had just been with your uncle, the exiled hero, and *not* take them right to their stronghold. We're getting past the front gates without even having to sneak or lie. This is better than any plan I could have thought of.' His voice sounded certain, without an ounce of doubt or fear.

Lily couldn't tell if all of this was just for her benefit, but she was glad of his stalwart nature. She had always known that Jem was someone to have by your side in a crisis, she had just never imagined a crisis quite like this. 'But... we're going in as captives. That gives them a major upper hand. We have no cards to play, no power here. How will we make it work?'

The carriage they were in went over an alarmingly large bump and Lily found herself flying sideways, landing straight in a heap on top of Jem. She banged her head on something hard and sharp, and instantly felt the bruise rising on her forehead.

'Ouch,' Jem muttered. 'Are you all right?'

'I'm… fine…' Lily winced, wishing her arms were free so she could feel the lump on her head and check it for any blood. Instead, she was stuck, unable to properly move her limbs, on top of Jem. 'Are you?'

He laughed breathlessly. 'I would be if I could breathe. Something's fallen on me.'

'Jem, it's me. I'm the something,' Lily said, barely able to stop herself from laughing at the surreal ridiculousness of it all. Barely any time had passed since they had saved each other from falling from a dangerous winter mountain, and now look where they were.

Jem chuckled knowingly. 'That was a joke, Lil.' She could hear the smile in his voice. 'Can you manage to get up, or are we stuck like this for ever?' And then, as if the anonymity of the bag over his head gave him extra confidence, he said, 'And I wouldn't mind that one bit, if I'm being totally honest. I'd just rather it not be in the back of an enemy carriage on the way to our inevitable doom while we're—'

Before he had a chance to finish the sentence that had made Lily so lightheaded that she forgot about the raging heat of her magic in her hands, the sound of a door being wrenched open stole her attention.

'Right, you two,' she heard a booming voice say, 'we've arrived.'

Chapter Nineteen

Snow fell in thick flurries, banishing any sense of sunrise or sunset from the days as they passed. Soon, the pathways around Midnight Manor were so heavily shrouded that it became Ailsa Merryck's full time job to keep everything clear. Every time Alice walked outside, she couldn't help but find a strange, bitter joy in watching the water witch casting spells to clear the paths, only for them to be covered in snow again by the time she reached the end of the day. It was futile, relentless, thankless work and Alice found a dark satisfaction in her struggle.

Alice herself was battling to make any sense of her emotions, and had been from the moment Lily had left. When she and Grace had been in the lair, she'd had Grace to help her find her way through the darkness. And then, when she had first come to the manor, she had had Ailsa,

Rowenna, and Hecate to keep her on the right path. Now, in a world that was looking more and more hostile by the moment, Alice realised she craved the wisdom and kindness only Lily could provide. And that realisation made her feel horribly guilty for taking Lily for granted for so long. If she wasn't careful, Lily would carve her own way through life and Alice wouldn't get to be a part of it, and that thought filled Alice with the most intense sense of loss.

She walked the snow-cleared path towards the great oak in the grounds of the manor. The oak tree had always reminded her of Lily, who, back home, had spent many a day underneath her own oak tree, watching the world as it passed by. Alice felt sure that she would be able to connect to Lily in some way, even if just in her imagination, if she went to the oak and spent some quiet time mulling over her thoughts for the afternoon, before darkness forced her back inside for another endlessly long evening alone.

As she approached, squinting through the heavy flakes of snow that were still falling relentlessly, turning her raven hair silvery with their magic, she saw that someone else had had the very same idea. She swore inwardly. Her trajectory was too obvious; she couldn't turn around now, else the person at tree would know she had turned around at the sight of them. Usually, Alice wouldn't have minded making a bad impression on an unknown person, but there was something pulling her towards them, something she wasn't able to put her finger on. It wasn't, couldn't be, Lily underneath the tree, but she had a sense in her mind that Lily would want her to keep walking, to make peace with the stranger, to break through this fear of being seen. And, Alice reminded herself, if she was going to be a great witch, a leader of people, with her own powerful coven, she could hardly shy away from human interaction.

Alice exhaled, puffing out her cheeks as she waded through the thickening snow, rubbing her hands together to create sparks of heat. This was going to be fine.

But as she got closer, she could see more clearly through the falling snow. The outline of a distant figure became the very clear shape of a woman in a heavy structured woollen coat; a woman with sharp jaw-length hair underneath a wide-brimmed hat; a woman with brown skin and a brutal, jagged scar across her face. A woman she still longed for in every single moment of the day.

Grace.

Alice felt her heart quicken. She and Grace had only spent time together in the presence of the twins, and had focused their energy on training Brenna and Maeve, supporting them through this wild and unpredictable time where their magic was at its most ferocious. The thought of being alone out here in this weather, of making conversation, of looking Grace squarely in the eye was enough to break Alice even at her strongest. And she definitely wasn't at her strongest.

She felt her heart quicken as she slowed her pace. Maybe Grace hadn't noticed her. Maybe she could just turn around really slowly and walk back to the manor and everything would be fine because Grace wouldn't have noticed.

'Alice.'

Alice swore under her breath. No chance of a quiet escape, then. She was going to have to do this.

'Grace!' she said, trying to keep her voice light and friendly, when inwardly she wanted to scream. 'I didn't see you there,' she lied.

'Hm,' Grace responded.

'How are you?' Alice felt painfully awkward as she came to a stop by the tree. Instead of standing directly ahead of Grace, she decided to lean backwards on the tree. That way, she could look out at the snow and Grace wouldn't be able to see just how red in the face she was.

'Fine,' Grace responded.

Alice looked up into the bare branches of the oak tree. This conversation was going nowhere. Much, it seemed, like their relationship.

And then Grace spoke again. 'Alice, I've been thinking.'

'I know,' Alice said, sighing. 'I'm not who you thought I was, and what I did to you was unforgivable. I know all of this. I've been a complete arse and I'm ready now to hold my hands up and say I messed everything up. You don't have to say anything.'

Silence fell.

Alice tried to steady her racing heart by counting each snowflake that she felt fall on her nose.

'I was actually going to say that I've been thinking about the way I've behaved,' Grace muttered.

Risking a sideways glance, Alice saw that Grace was uncharacteristically ringing her hands, staring at the floor. Snow had gathered around the brim of her hat and her cheeks were flushed in a way that made her look so beautiful Alice thought her heart might fall out. Then she realised that Grace seemed to be waiting for a reply. 'Oh, er,' she stuttered, 'the way you behaved...' she repeated, wanting to slap herself on the forehead for being so dim.

'Yeah...'

'All right.' Alice tried to regain her sense of composure. 'But I was the one who behaved dreadfully.' She hated herself every day and she hoped that came across in her voice.

'No, I could have handled things better.' Grace sighed so hard it came out as a growl. 'This is really awkward, isn't it?' She smirked one of her famous smirks, and Alice couldn't help but smile back. 'Bloody hell, why is this so awkward?' Grace burst into laughter that seemed to dissipate all of the horrible, heavy emotions that had settled over them both.

Alice, too, laughed heartily for the first time in what felt like for ever. 'It is very awkward!' she said between breaths. 'What happened to us?' she asked, still laughing, and then fell silent. *She* had happened to them. She had mistreated Grace, and then left her. 'Grace, you have every right to never want to see me again.'

Grace's laughter had fallen into silence too, but when Alice looked up from the floor, she noticed that Grace had moved closer. She was now standing directly in front of Alice, who had her back still pressed against the tree. 'But, what if that sounds like the worst possible outcome of all this?' Grace asked, taking another step closer so that every time she exhaled, Alice was bathed in the dancing ice crystals of her breath.

'What... what do you mean?' Alice stuttered.

'I mean,' she said, her deep voice almost dropping to a whisper, 'that never seeing you again is my worst nightmare. When you left, I fell apart. But while I was gone, I forgave you because I finally understood what it was that you needed.' Grace lifted Alice's chin so she was looking directly into her eyes. 'And then you came back to the castle, and *she* was with you, and it was like a burning rage was lit inside of me and I couldn't see or think straight because I'd forgiven you and there you were, standing by the side of a woman who had destroyed everything we hold dear.'

'I know,' Alice choked, tears rolling down her cheeks. 'I know how it looked, but—'

'I'm still speaking, Alice,' Grace said firmly, cutting her off. 'You were standing with her and all I could feel was hatred all over again. It drowned every other feeling I had. But then we came here. You saved us all. And you've asked nothing of me. You haven't pleaded with me, or given me bullshit excuses. You've just gone about life in your quiet, Alice-like ways, doing what you can for those you love.'

Alice didn't know what to say. She had barely allowed herself to hope through all of this. Ever since Grace had held that blade to her throat, she'd known she would never be able to get back what they had lost. But suddenly she wasn't so sure. 'Would it have been better if I had pleaded?' Alice asked, her heart beating violently in her chest.

'No, I don't think so,' Grace said, a small smile tugging at the edge of her lips. 'Because the space has allowed me time to process and to think. But it has also allowed doubt to creep in.'

'Doubt that I was never right for you in the first place?'

'Doubt that I've left it too long to get you back.' Grace looked Alice straight in the eye, and all Alice could see was sincerity.

Grace still wanted her. After everything she'd put her through, after all of the pain and the torment, the silence, the betrayal. 'But...' Alice stuttered, not wanting to say the wrong thing. 'But I hurt you. So, so badly. I didn't mean to, nor did I want to, but the fact is that I did. We'll never be able to forget that, for as long as we live. How are you supposed to love me after all of that? It should have been me begging and pleading on my knees for you, Grace. I would have deserved rejection even after all of that—'

'Alice,' Grace interrupted, her brow furrowed and heavy. 'Are you trying to talk me out of this?'

'No, I—' *Shit*. 'No, I'm not, I just... I want to... I don't want to hurt—'

Alice didn't have the chance to finish that sentence, as Grace cut her off by kissing her deeply. It was like every moment of pain and stress of the recent weeks had melted away into that kiss and it felt like a first kiss all over again. She felt renewed. Grace was kissing her, and she was kissing Grace, and they were underneath the great oak like a pair of lovers in an oil painting.

Chapter Twenty

The guard, blood streaming from his mouth, looked incensed instead of in pain and vulnerable. His whole body shook with rage and he growled like an agitated wolf at Cass, whose fist was still throbbing from its impact with the man's jaw.

Before the guard could respond, Morven had climbed the bench beside them and launched herself at his back, knocking him to the floor. The little boy from earlier had shuffled himself upright and was now watching with unblinking eyes as Morven and Cass fought his oppressor.

Guards started filing into the room, but Cass didn't care. All he wanted to do was punish this man, and all thoughts of anonymity had disappeared like the guard's teeth. But for some reason, as he was throwing punch after punch at the man, no one had carried him away yet. He risked a glance behind himself and saw the most unbelievable scene.

The children were rioting.

Shouting echoed across the dining hall of the poorhouse. Pewter jugs and plates were being thrown, as well as fists. The children had broken into a ruthless attack the moment Morven and Cass had defended the poor young boy who had been assaulted so cruelly by the guard. Every other guard in the place had filed into the room, but they were massively outnumbered. It looked to Morven like they deliberately didn't station many guards in these children's houses because children were submissive and harmless. *Ha*, she thought, *that'll show them.*

Morven had never been one for violence, and on more than one occasion she had declared herself a pacifist. But there was something special about standing up for someone else in need that made her forget all of her morals. She felt more alive than she had in a long while, even if she didn't particularly enjoy throwing punches.

For a moment she took a step back. One advantage of the chaos was that no one else was paying attention, which allowed her the space and brief snippet of time to actually think about what they were going to do next. There would be no going back from this, which in a way was a very good thing; she had wanted to get as far away from this place as possible the moment they had arrived. But it was no longer just about her and Cass. There were thirty or so children in this place who were going to be punished for their actions, and punished badly. Could she live with herself if she just left them to suffer? She knew the answer without having to think about it. *No.*

But what would she do with thirty vicious, angry, half-starved and overworked children once she broke them out of this cesspit? She looked around at them throwing themselves around the small dining room, pushing aside the long tables, throwing chairs, roaring with the relief of a captive animal that has just had its first taste of liberation.

And then she realised, and suddenly the idea was so obvious she was annoyed that she hadn't thought of it sooner.

With a deep breath, she threw herself back into the fray in search of her brother. Most of the guards had been subdued, knocked unconscious, or driven away, but there were a few still clinging on. She spotted Cass tying one guard's hands behind him to render him useless, and Morven was glad she didn't have to see him punching anyone else. It still made her nauseous after all of his fights with Glenn, and being in a poorhouse again didn't make those feelings any better.

'Cass!' she cried above the noise, dodging several children who were chasing after a lone guard who was running like a frightened rabbit away from them. 'Cass, I have an idea!'

It took barely a few moments for her to explain her plan to her brother and for him to agree.

'It'll be dangerous, Morv,' he warned, once she'd stopped speaking.

'I know.'

'And they might not all make it.'

'I know.'

'But we can't leave them here. How will we find our way?'

'There are those stupid illustrated maps in every room, some strange attempt at making us proud of the land we're in, but Hythlund is no different to the Shadow Lands with how they treat their poor and unfortunate. And we didn't travel far from the border, so it won't be too bad, and then once we're in the Shadow Lands again, everything will be easier.'

But Cass wasn't listening anymore. He'd run across the room to peel a huge guard from the small girl he was beating relentlessly. This time, Morven didn't look away when Cass's fists found their mark. It took all of her strength not to charge on over there and join him, but she had other matters to handle.

Like how she was going to help thirty children to escape from a poorhouse so that she could get them all to the safety of Midnight Manor.

Chapter Twenty-One

The silence was unnerving. No birdsong, no breeze, just heavy, aching silence. Lily felt the sting of gravel against her knees as she tried to clamber up from where she had been thrown after she and Jem had been flung from the carriage, and the ringing in her head was making it hard for her to focus on her surroundings. Where was Jem? Where had they brought them?

'Are you all right?' She heard a whisper, and glanced to her left, her eyes finally adjusting to the light after so long spent with that horrible bag over her head. Jem was also on his knees, barely three strides away. He had a horrible bruise that covered most of his right eye and cheekbone, and his hair was limp and matted.

Lily couldn't find the words to respond, so she nodded firmly in the hope that Jem would believe her. She didn't have a plan, but Jem might, if he avoided getting distracted by worry for her wellbeing.

She looked upwards towards the sky from her hunched position on the ground and tried to decipher where they could be. Directly ahead was a wide grey staircase that led to a grey door that sat in a grey building. Grey, grey, grey. No trees, no life. Everything was made from the same dull stone.

'Get on your feet, the lot of you.' The deep voice that had come from the man who dragged them from the carriage returned.

The lot of us? Lily thought. What a strange way to talk about two people.

But that was when she heard it. Now the ringing in her ears had subsided and the strange silence no longer distracted her, she could hear the wheezing. A glance to her left confirmed what she desperately hoped wasn't true.

Alf was here. He had sacrificed them, and had been dragged here all the same.

Lily couldn't bring herself to feel anything but sadness.

She knew most people would be quietly glad to see their betrayer brought to justice of any kind. Familial love would be dead; pity would be impossible; sadness, an alien, distant concept they were unable to apply to their situation.

But for Lily, it was love that she felt. Love, heartbreak, grief, pain, yes, so much pain. But not for the reasons she knew Jem would presume. She couldn't bear the idea that her once blissful, sun-soaked, spring-filled life was over.

From this point onwards, she wouldn't have an Uncle Alf, even if he escaped. His betrayal had brought a sword down on the throat of her childhood, and she had no choice but to rise from the executioner's stone a woman. So it would be with love in her heart, not hatred, that she would face whatever was about to befall her and Jem and Alf.

They were dragged to their feet but allowed to walk unaided. Lily seized Jem's arm and held him tightly against her side. He kept his eyes ahead, but his hand found hers and squeezed it tightly. This was not what they had planned, and his optimism at their being able to infiltrate the Brotherhood from the inside seemed to have dissipated.

They walked up the stairs and through the great doorway into the dull grey building. The inside, somehow, was even more grim and depressing than the exterior. Everything was angular, with clean straight lines and smooth polished stonework. Shining silver candelabras hung from the impossibly high ceiling. Lily had never seen a tree reach as high into the sky as this building stretched, and the candles that shimmered in their holders cast strange, eerie shadows that made the ceiling look both a thousand leagues above them and as oppressive as a cave.

They walked down a long, slender aisle flanked on either side by empty seats. It didn't look like their capture was significant enough to warrant a roomful of people, which Lily hoped would play to their advantage if they tried to escape. At the end of the aisle stood a man. He was staring, unblinking, at them as they approached, with a wry smile on his face.

'Alfryd!' the man called, and Lily looked behind her to see Alf being dragged, instead of walking of his own volition, behind them.

She and Jem stepped aside to allow his captors to pull Alf past them, and as they did, her uncle found Lily's eyes with his own. A pained whisper broke from his lips. 'Don't listen to them, Lily.' That was all he could manage, before he was dragged too far away to crane his neck any further.

Jem leaned into her and whispered gently into her ear. She was expecting him to tell her everything was going to be all right, or to ignore her uncle, or to be brave. Instead, he asked a simple question that came straight from his heart. 'Are you all right?'

All Lily could do was nod. It was a lie, of course. She was about as far away from all right as it was possible to be, but this was no place to show weakness; it was no place to surrender to her tears. She had to be strong if she was going to figure out how the two of them would survive this.

'Alfryd!' the man ahead repeated. Alf had reached him and had been flung onto the cold stone floor beneath his feet. 'Alfryd, you must introduce me to our lovely guests.'

Now the man was looking directly at Lily and Jem, and Lily was certain she saw Alf gulp. His mouth opened and closed in silence.

Something about this man was familiar. He had the same kind of authority as Hecate, and reminded Lily of when Hecate had stood at her own altar in the cave when she and Jem had broken in to rescue Grace and Alice. He, too, stood with an aloof confidence. He, too, was impeccably dressed and sleek. But that wasn't why he was familiar.

Lily looked into his intelligent eyes. They were the colour of violets. His golden hair was smooth and pin-straight, brushed over to the side and slicked into place. His skin was alabaster, although the passing of time had left deep crow's feet by his eyes and mouth, and his pale forehead was etched with lines. But he carried himself like a man who hadn't aged a day over twenty-one, and he was tall and slender. The longer she looked, the clearer he became. When he spoke, his voice had that quiet confidence of the soul alongside which she had spent so many years. He looked, sounded, dressed, and moved exactly like Farlan.

Lily stumbled as she walked, and the only thing that stopped her from hitting the ground was Jem's arm that she was still clinging to with all of her might.

'Ah,' the man continued, 'I suppose I will do my introductions myself then. Esteemed guests, my name is Fenn Crydlund, and I am the leader of the Brotherhood of Light. You are all here on my orders. Alfryd Knight betrayed you long ago. We have been lying in wait to capture you and at last,' he paused, inhaling the scent of his victory, 'here you are. And with a bonus addition. Who is this dashingly handsome gentleman I see before me?'

He was looking at Jem. Alf still wasn't speaking. Jem himself stuttered; she knew he was hardly expecting to be noticed directly. He had spent a lifetime skulking around out of eyesight, and even now he was standing in the shadow of Alf and Lily. Lily knew the task fell upon her shoulders to speak, but she could hardly form the words now that she looked upon Crydlund's face. How was it he looked so much like Farlan?

She shook herself, but as she went to speak, Jem also opened his mouth. 'My name is Jameson Rafferty, and I believe you've made a mistake. Lily and I have no place in this mess. It was created, orchestrated, by her uncle, but she had nothing to do with it. She doesn't belong here.'

'Ah, my fellow, that's where you're wrong.' Fenn cleared his throat. 'Your Lily over there has magic, does she not?'

Jem stuttered again, but no words came out this time.

'Your silence tells me all I need to know.' Alf was still on his knees with bound hands beneath Fenn. He was shaking. 'Alfryd, for once in his pathetic little life, wasn't lying.' Fenn patted Alf on the head like he was a disdainful lapdog. 'That doesn't mean he's forgiven though.'

'No…' Alf choked.

'Oh yes.' Fenn appeared to be enjoying himself. 'You see, Lily, I was a young man when Alfryd Knight tried and failed to kill Catherine Winter, the woman you all know as Hecate. I watched him fail and I promised myself that I would never stoop to the levels he did when he failed. We chose to banish him for his failure, and he begged and begged with all of his strength to be forgiven, to be given another chance. He promised that he would do absolutely anything to regain our favour. And so we made him promise that he would do exactly that; when the time came, he would drop everything and prove to us that he was still loyal, that he still lived and breathed our cause.'

Lily looked at Alf, and then tore her eyes away. She couldn't bear the pleading, tearful look in his eyes.

'When Hecate began to rise again, we stamped them out. The Bloodletting of Oakencliff? That was only possible because of the knowledge given to us by your uncle. He whispered, he stole secrets, he planted information, he spied, all in pursuit of his lost honour. But after that, he decided rather foolishly that our cause wasn't one he wanted to follow anymore. Ha! As if he had a choice.'

'Lily, don't listen to him,' Alf pleaded.

Fenn paused, seeming to await Lily's next instruction. 'Go on,' she muttered.

'We investigated the root of this disturbance in his loyalty, and discovered *you*.'

'Me?'

'He chose to wander off the path because he wanted to protect you. We knew you were the one thing preventing him from continuing to do our bidding. We never had any intention of allowing him back within our ranks, but as a simpering coward who would do almost anything to win back our favour, he was valuable. That is, until he stopped being valuable. Our sources tell us his sudden reluctance to continue was sparked by his return from a journey. A journey, it would seem, to visit his delightful, innocent niece, living in a distant castle, far away from prying eyes. Why, I wondered, did this trip push him over the edge? What changed, after all those years of sneaking around when you were asleep above the apothecary, of lying to your face when you asked why he was heading out on another trip to collect ingredients you knew there was plenty of in your stores? Then we realised. There was only one thing in the world that could have made Alfryd Knight suddenly so reluctant to drive out magic from our lands. You had to be a witch. You had to have become his very worst nightmare. And so, he attempted to betray us. He told us where to find you, but gave us the wrong place. After that, we placed one of our guards with him at all times, confident that you would eventually find your way back to the comfort and familiarity of your home after so much trauma. And here you are.'

'So he's been trying to protect me, and that's why you're so angry?'

'Protect *you*?' he sneered. 'But you are what the world needs protecting *from*, my dear. You and your little band of witches think you can rule the roost. You think you have a *right* to live amongst us, all because you were born *freaks*; because you are abnormal.'

'But the Brotherhood has magic!' Lily exclaimed. 'How can you profess a hatred for something you yourself take advantage of?'

'I'd be stupid to waste an opportunity, and my morals aren't nearly as strong as yours, child. Once this is over, between you and me, there will be no witches allowed to exist, no matter whose side they fight on.'

Lily couldn't find the words. And then they came to her in a torrent. 'All of this because you're afraid of something different? All of this pain and torture, all of this murder and heartbreak because a bunch of miserable, pathetic, talentless men can't bear the thought of others wielding a power you could only wish for. Now it all makes sense. You are frightened of us, and of anyone who looks or speaks differently to you.'

It was Fenn's turn to stutter.

Lily took advantage of his silence and continued. 'Why kidnap us? Why not just kill us there in the apothecary and use us as an example?' And then the realisation dawned upon her. 'Ah, because that wouldn't play into your idealised vision of yourselves, would it? If you were to be seen murdering someone well-known amongst the villagers, you wouldn't be seen as a benevolent leader with their best intentions at heart. You would, instead, be viewed as what you are. Intolerant. Cruel. *Pathetic*.'

'Enough of this nonsense!' Fenn had regained his ability to speak. 'You are just like the stories of my dreadful nephew. He, too, has joined with Hecate, I have heard. My brother would be turning in his grave. But that's what he gets for falling in love with a cunning woman; a long line of disgusting creatures born from one man's pathetic mistake.'

'Your... nephew?' Jem asked, confusion etched across his features.

'Farlan Aelfdene. Farlan Crydlund, if he had been given her true name. Aelfdene was the disgusting name of his greatest conquest.'

'No...' Lily had realised that he looked like Farlan, but had hoped against hope that it was a coincidence. This was too much to bear. Her own uncle being part of the Brotherhood was hard enough to bear, but Farlan's uncle leading it? There was too much at stake in all of this. Hecate had brought Farlan within her walls. Alice, her dearest Alice, trusted him implicitly.

'Yes. He, and Hecate of course, have been key to my motivations as leader of this group of brave soldiers who just want to see their homelands united and free of such poisons as yours. I rid the world of you, and this ends.'

'Does Farlan know you exist?' Jem asked, his voice sounding clear and confident all of a sudden.

'Yes, in a roundabout way. He knows me as the man who caused his many afflictions, but the weight of the knowledge of my bloodline is too powerful and I intend to wield it when the time is right.' Fenn smirked. 'But enough talking. You've heard my explanations, though you don't deserve them. Now we can get on with why we're here.' He puffed out his chest, his eyes darkening. 'Alfryd Knight, you have betrayed the Brotherhood one too many times. You will not have the opportunity to do so again.'

In a movement as fast as a nuthatch flits from branch to

branch, Fenn Crydlund unsheathed a dagger from his waist and swiped it violently in a straight line across Alf's throat.

Alf fell to the floor, blood streaming from the wound in a constant flow of scarlet. Lily fell to her knees before him. The screams that tore from her throat felt otherworldly, somehow. She felt simultaneously immediate in the agony of the moment, and also a million leagues away, watching herself howl like a wolf mother.

Alf was dead, and one look at Fenn's eyes through her tears confirmed what she already knew in her heart.

She and Jem would be next.

Chapter Twenty-Two

Bright sunlight, the colour of shimmering gold, streamed through the open window. Even though it was still winter and the warmth of spring was yet to appear on the horizon, the fresh air that floated into the room was refreshing instead of bone-chilling. On the breeze, the scent of snowdrops and damp earth was intoxicating, and the only sound that broke the silence was the sweet music of birdsong.

Alice felt sure she had died. She knew in her heart that real life could never feel this full of joy, and she was content to know that death had taken her gently, and led her to the land beyond life, where she could live in perfect peace for eternity.

But then she felt movement beside her; heard the deep, calming breaths. How could this be real? Alice rubbed her eyes and allowed herself to take the scene in, slowly, gently.

For if it was real, she wanted to remember every single detail.

She was in a bed not her own, but one that was cosy and comfortable. The duvet was soft and heavy, like a warm embrace. On top of the duvet was a thick knitted blanket in alternate squares of mustard and cream wool and another of plain soft brown. The room had a large window, much like her own, and had the same tired wooden floorboards and delicate wallpaper on the walls. Aside from the gently floral and earth scent of the outside world, she could now also smell other things – must, leather, seawater – the combination of which she hadn't smelled in so long that the heady scent brought tears to her eyes. Because if she could smell that, it would mean—

Grace was by her side.

Slowly, she turned herself and allowed her eyes to fall on the sleeping soul next to her. She looked peaceful, content, like all the troubles she carried with her every day had finally lessened a little. Her straight chocolate-brown hair was ruffled and untidy, just how Alice liked it. Her skin was flushed slightly and looked dewy in the early morning light, and Alice couldn't quite believe it was possible for one person to be so beautiful.

Alice snuggled down into the duvet and thought through every event that had happened yesterday, from the moment beneath the oak tree on, analysing it all to ensure she hadn't said or done the wrong thing. She had only had Grace back for a few delicious hours and already couldn't bear the thought of ever losing her again. But then she did think through everything that had happened – how they had managed to hold it together as they walked through the manor with straight faces so as not to betray their feelings, how all barriers had fallen away the moment they had found themselves alone together in Grace's room, how they had melted into one another in new and thrilling ways after an agonising period of distance and grief.

Alice felt her cheeks grow warm at the thought of their night together, and the thought of more nights like the one they had just had. Butterflies had exploded in her tummy yesterday afternoon and they remained there still. She closed her eyes and analysed her own self, too. Her magic, the magic that had felt forced and difficult within her for so long, felt like golden light once more. She could feel the strength in her bones, the determination, the power. It had all returned, thanks to Grace.

Grace's eyelids fluttered and a yawn contorted her features before she opened her eyes. She smiled, which turned into a smirk, before she grabbed Alice tightly and pulled her in closer. 'I see you're still here, Blackwell?' Grace asked with faux coyness.

Alice cleared her throat, trying to keep a straight face. 'Well, I can leave if you—'

A hand shot from under the covers and plastered itself across Alice's mouth, preventing her from speaking. 'Shush now. You're never leaving me again.'

Alice grinned for the first time in forever. 'I know.'

After they had finally torn themselves from the bed, Alice and Grace got swiftly dressed and headed out in search of breakfast and a plan. Their training with the twins had been going swimmingly, but Alice knew they needed something more solid to aim for; Jem and Lily were on such an important mission that they needed to be properly prepared for them when they returned, and fully prepared for war if this whole ordeal got that far.

Even with the horrendous thought of war on the horizon, Alice had a spring in her step that she just couldn't dampen, made even better by Grace's insistence on holding her hand. 'We have nothing to hide, anymore,' she had said as they got dressed. 'Most people knew back at the lair, and they tried to weaponise it. Now we are strong and we are happy and we are together. That's all there is to it, and I won't hide it any longer. I love you, Alice, and I don't care who knows it.' So, side by side with Grace who swaggered in her usual confident style, Alice found herself walking with her head high and her boots practically skipping across the floor.

Breakfast was always an event in the manor, and even more so since they had arrived back from the trauma in the castle. It was almost like everyone felt like the end of days was closer than it had ever been before, so mealtimes were special. Hecate sent different scouts out every week to local markets, and Alice half suspected that they pickpocketed the majority of the gold they used to buy the food, but she never asked. Who was she to question their contentment?

In the breakfast room as they walked in hand in hand, Alice spied Hecate in her usual corner, away from the hustle and bustle but watching with keen eyes as her wards stuffed their faces with pastries, bread, cakes, sausages, and eggs. Considering Alice had been so cruelly treated in the beginning, as had the majority of them, Hecate had softened into someone she could almost understand. A life of resentment, rejection, and loneliness had created a monster. But with the legacy she had built, Hecate had been able to find purpose amongst the chaos, and the cruelty was more for keeping up her fearsome reputation outside of these walls than it was *her*. With every new person who joined, she had to ensure they knew how terrible she was, for if they ran away she needed their reputation as the Shadow Sect to be one of greatness and power. Alice felt something stirring in her heart, as she watched Hecate watching everyone else, that was somewhere close to tenderness. Hecate was a mother-figure, in her own way, and Alice hoped there would be a place for this strange, complex woman in her future with Grace, Lily, and the others. She had for so long missed having an older woman in her life to show her the right path, and it was Hecate who had begun to fulfil that role.

She and Grace walked over to the breakfast spread and loaded up their plates before taking their seats by Hecate, who was alone at her table in the shadows. Up until their reunion last night, Grace hadn't trusted Hecate at all. There was too much pain, too much torment attached to Hecate and everything she stood for. But after a few hours of spilling their feelings between the bedsheets, Grace had come round to Alice's way of viewing her. It would take a while for Grace to trust her, but that was something Alice was willing to work on, providing she had Grace *and* Hecate in her life. Grace would see through the bravado soon enough, and they would all find their peace together, in their shared understanding.

'Ladies,' Hecate said, gesturing an unenthusiastic greeting without taking her eyes off the rest of the room.

Grace went to respond with some sardonic comment – Alice could see it in her eyes – but Alice squeezed her hand and Grace resisted.

'Good morning, Priestess.' Grace said through gritted teeth. 'We think we should be doing more to prepare for the oncoming war.'

Alice inwardly cringed, but externally she smiled. 'What Grace means is—'

'I said what I meant, Alice.'

'Oh dear. I thought you two had only just patched things up?' Hecate said with a smirk.

Alice felt prickly all of a sudden. 'We have – we're just tired.' Hecate winked at them and Alice blushed furiously. 'Anyway, actually Grace is right. We need to be prepared for Jem and Lily's return; we need to be ready for whatever news they bring. If a war is coming, as we believe it is, we need to ensure that we are ready.'

'You never take the bait anymore, Alice. I remember when you were full of fire and venom. Where have you gone?' Hecate pretended to be sad, but in reality she looked concerned.

'Don't make the mistake of underestimating me again, Hecate,' Alice snapped back. 'I'm still here, conserving that energy for when it needs to be the strongest.'

'Good. You'd better be. I didn't bestow on you the title as my companion and my successor for you to throw it all away, child.'

'So what's the plan?' Grace was getting impatient. Alice could tell by the tapping of Grace's foot beneath the table, and the fact that she had pushed her plate away with food unfinished.

'Believe me' – Hecate took a sip of her black tea – 'you'll know my plan when I'm ready to share it. For now, find Farlan and win his trust. I have a feeling he's not telling me everything I need to know, and I didn't rescue the boy for him to just be a drain on our resources.'

Alice nodded. 'As you wish.'

Chapter Twenty-Three

Morven sprinted from the room to seek the maps that Cass had mentioned and found them almost immediately. She had spent so long staring at them in the mundane hours of the night that she couldn't believe she hadn't had the same thought. She ripped them from the walls and gathered as many as she could stuff in the pockets of the tattered work pinafore she wore over her woollen dress.

She made a beeline back towards the fighting, her mind racing with possibilities and fears: how would they escape? What would happen to them if they didn't get out? What would happen to them if they *did*?

Her heart was racing in her ribcage, threatening to break free. She gritted her teeth and shook the pessimistic thoughts from her head. This, right here, was her moment of reckoning; her opportunity to do something real and worthwhile for the first time in her life. She had been surrounded by helpless children, desperate for another chance, and she was determined to give them that chance.

Whatever it took.

Her thoughts turned darker as she half ran down the dingy stone corridor of the poorhouse, past tired wooden bedroom door after tired wooden bedroom door. The corridor, having no windows, was lit by intermittent lamps of the same flameless too-bright light that seemed to permeate this entire world. She wanted no other child to be locked up in this place. It was barely fit for the worst of criminals, and yet it housed innocents. It was a disgrace, a shambles, and she couldn't bear the thought of leaving it standing here to entrap more poor young people caught in the crossfire of this clearly broken society. But what could she do about it? She was just Morven, still a teenager, with no real experience of the world. She wished she could burn it all to the ground.

Morven stopped in her tracks.

She *could* burn it all to the ground.

Resolve settled in her heart. She knew what she had to do.

The fighting had reached a natural pause, with all of the guards unconscious, or having been overrun by a few very determined, very angry, very frightened young people who had seen their opportunity to wreak revenge on their oppressors.

Morven appeared in the doorway and scanned the room for Cass. Her eyes found him quickly, his tall, lanky form standing head and shoulders above even the tallest of the children around him. He was wrapping them in the coats of the guards, who had been outfitted in warm, stiff woollen jackets. The uniform also included scarlet knitted neckerchiefs which were purely ornamental on the grown men, but invaluable against the cold for the children. Morven counted the heads.

There were twenty-two, a mixture of ages and genders, but all of them looked rabid and ready to fight again if they had to. She dearly hoped they wouldn't. But whatever happened, they needed to get out. Immediately.

'Cass!' Morven shouted, her voice echoing around the cavernous dining hall. 'Cass, we need to act now. We need to get them out.'

'I will, Morven. I'm just getting everyone togged up.' He waved her away nonchalantly.

Her rage burst into flames, mirroring what she had just seen upstairs in the bedrooms. 'Cass, you don't understand.' She ran at him. 'Cass, I've just set fire to the whole of upstairs. It's all alight. We need to get these children out, and then we need to set the rest of the place ablaze.'

'Shit, Morv!' Cass hissed. 'Right.' He changed his voice to the one Morven always thought made him sound like a schoolteacher from one of her books. He puffed out his chest, too, as he usually did when he was in a position of authority. 'Everyone, grab what you can. Food from the tables, bags and jackets from the guards, anything you can reach right now, and then follow Morven.'

'I'll follow behind,' Cass told her. 'You get them out, I'll make sure no one is left behind, and I'll set the fires in here. I don't want a single brick of this place to still be standing once we're gone. You used the candles, right?'

'Right,' Morven nodded. She passed him a map. 'Let's meet by this bridge, it should provide us shelter and a hiding spot so we aren't in the open while we wait the few moments for you to join us.'

'Good plan. I'll be right behind you, Morv.' He ushered her away.

She pushed to the front of the children. 'You always are, brother!' she shouted over her shoulder. 'Follow me, everyone!'

Morven grabbed a heavy guard's jacket for herself, pulled a satchel off one of their bodies, and filled it with food before wrapping the red scarf around her neck. And then she ran. Every few moments she checked back over her shoulder, and she was pleased to see a sea of determined faces following her, all wrapped up in coats that were far too big, but which would provide ample warmth for their small, underfed bodies.

After a few moments, moments that felt like hours, Morven pushed out of the entrance hall doors and was treated to lungfuls of icy air. There was a thick blanket of dry, fluffy snow on the ground, and she was pleased to see that the maps were correct; the poorhouse was an eyesore, and therefore was quite a distance from the nearest dwelling. No one would see them escaping, and the flames would have engulfed the whole, miserable building before anyone came running to its aid.

She counted the heads as they burst out of the door, and when she was content with their number, she continued running across the flat snow-covered fens until she reached a crooked stone bridge. The river running underneath it was still, frozen solid. The bridge was disproportionately wide and hulking for such a pathetic excuse for a river, but Morven couldn't complain considering the space underneath its arch was more than large enough for their party. Bundling the children underneath, she counted them again.

When she was content that they were all there and safe, she begged them to sit tight, and ran back towards the poorhouse. The flames were visible now, licking the roof tiles, and smoke billowed high into the sky in a dull grey plume. Even ablaze, the building was depressingly grim.

Despite the victory of saving the children, watching a building burn brought back memories of their lighthouse that forced a heavy, dry lump into her throat. She willed Cass to hurry up so they could move from this place, so she could tear her eyes away from the flames and get the horrid, acrid smell out of her nostrils.

'C'mon, Cass,' she muttered, staring at the door.

The flames were getting worse. In the intensity of the blaze, the windows, of which there were only a few on the lower floors, exploded, sending missiles of glass shards out into the snow. Morven flinched, shielding her eyes. The blaze had clearly been set successfully by her brother, as she could see the eerie orange fingers flickering through the glassless windows. So where was Cass?

Her heart was hammering. She willed him to appear. Her hands were clasped together at her breast, as if she could reach into her chest cavity and hold her heart gently, as if she could tell it to calm itself.

A great rumbling noise drew her eyes upwards. The roof was caving in. If Cass didn't get out now, she couldn't bear to think about what that would mean.

'Morv!' She heard a familiar voice shout, and her heart leapt. Cass was standing in the doorway, grinning with pride at all they had achieved. He too was wrapped in a guard's jacket, but it fit him almost too well. He was a man now, or just about, a man she was proud to call her brother.

'C'mon,' she shouted back, but her voice was lost amongst the deafening sound of the poorhouse crumbling.

As Cass took his first steps towards her, the whole building collapsed. He couldn't move, couldn't outrun it. The stone walls fell with great abandon, their brutal weight cascading them to the ground at impossible speeds. But it wasn't the ground they fell upon first.

It was Cass.

Chapter Twenty-Four

A great rumbling, mixed with a cacophony of shouts and screams filled the air, reverberating through the room from outside the great grey doors but Lily didn't care. She couldn't take her eyes away from it, from *him*. Her throat had closed, and tears streamed silently down her face. She neither knew nor cared what was happening outside, or what Fenn Crydlund's next move would be. She didn't care about anything except the fact that Alfryd Knight's blood still ran in a near constant stream across the polished stone floor.

When he had fallen to the ground, she had rushed over to him and held his head in her lap. For a few short moments, he had known she was there, he had known he was forgiven and that she loved him. That was what Lily hoped, anyway, and that was the only thing giving her the strength to avoid an explosion. She knew it was coming; she knew her magic was desperate to be released, but for the first time, she seemed to have some control over it. She wanted to surprise Fenn, and her magic would only buy them a few moments, so she had to be wise. It would do no good to allow it to explode whilst the heavy weight of Alf's head still rested on her lap. She would have to leave him. But that thought alone was painful enough to make the strength of her magic almost unbearable to contain.

She glanced over to Jem, who had taken the noise outside as an excuse to stand up. Fenn had sent two men to investigate, but the rhythmic banging on the heavy door was growing louder and louder still, and his men had not returned.

'You there,' he gestured to another two men dressed in the signature golden robes. 'Go and investigate, and make sure you return promptly. I will have your heads if you take too long.'

The men looked at each other and paused. Neither looked confident nor filled with the courage of purpose. Through her watery eyes, Lily could have sworn they looked fearful.

'I will have your heads now if you don't hurry up!' Fenn yelled, stamping his foot like a petulant child. This seemed to have the desired effect, as the men flinched and then hurried away towards the noise. 'Get up!' Fenn continued.

Lily strained her neck to look round at him, and noticed he was staring straight at her.

'Get up, now,' he demanded.

Lily was hardly in the mood to argue, but the thought of wrenching herself from Alf made her want to sob, bang her fists on the floor, and claw at his face with her nails until it fell away from his skull. But she didn't do any of that. Instead, she took a deep breath, closed her eyes, gently lifted Alf's head, placed it on the cold floor, and stood. Her strong legs shook beneath her dress, which was damp and sticky, the brown material dyed scarlet from her uncle's blood. She pulled her cloak around herself, in a feigned attempt at comforting her grief-stricken body and walked towards Jem.

He held out his arms and beckoned her into them. He didn't wipe away her tears or whisper condolences in her ear. He simply held her tightly against his body and said, just loud enough for her to hear, 'Be ready.'

The incessant banging continued, until—

CRASH.

The doors gave way and a horde of people poured into the great chamber of the Brotherhood's headquarters. Lily froze. Then a laugh, hearty and filled with hope, burst from her lips.

'Jem!' she cried. 'Jem, we're saved!'

She watched as *the whole of Alder Vale* poured into the building. Perhaps it wasn't the whole village, but it was every single soul strong enough to make the journey and brave enough to try. And at the front, hand in hand, were Orla McHail and Jemima Darroch, the two incessant, rude, gossip-mongering troublemakers who, back home in Alder Vale, had loved nothing more than to berate and chide Lily throughout her childhood.

Now they were here to save her.

Lily had always thought them old women, but looking at them as they stood, cleavers in hand, eyes hellbent on revenge, Lily realised they were just without purpose, and their malicious thoughts had aged them beyond their years. Here, in this building, faced with danger and excitement, they looked younger even than Alf, with so much life still ahead of them.

'Orla!' Lily cried, breaking free from Jem and giving him a hopeful nod. 'Jemima!'

'No time for chatter, Lily,' Orla responded in her usual no-nonsense manner. 'We've come to take you home.'

'NO!' Fenn's voice echoed across the room. 'She stays here. She dies here. This ends HERE.'

Lily knew it was time. Jem gave her a subtle nod, ran towards the crowd of villagers, and gave Lily space to do the very thing she'd been holding in since Alf fell to the floor.

She released her magic.

Jem Rafferty's ears rang painfully and his eyes were trying desperately to focus through the flashing stars of intense bright light that had emanated from Lily's body. He knew she had been holding it in, he had known she was ready, but he had expected such an explosion to come from such a small woman. The magic she had released in Hecate's lair was a puff of smoke in comparison to the mighty golden explosion that shattered the windows. Jem was just far enough away that the blast only threw him to the ground, along with the villagers that surrounded him, but Fenn Crydlund had been running *towards* Lily when she let go. The force of the blast sent him flying like a ragdoll against the stone wall, and he now lay crumpled in a heap on the ground. Unconscious or dead, Jem didn't stop to find out.

His focus was Lily. She was lying lifeless on the ground, her skin even paler than normal, her flaming hair haloed around her peaceful face. Her fingers were charred black and she had angry burns up her arms, where her sleeves had once been. The gentle rise and fall of her chest was the only thing that kept him afloat. He had to get her back to Alice and Grace and, though he hated to admit it, Hecate. They would know what to do. They would be able to bring her back to him.

'We need to go,' the old woman Lily had called Jemima said. She was standing above him.

'I can't leave her,' Jem croaked.

'Don't be stupid, boy! Of course we won't leave her. Do you think we came all this way... do you think we followed your damn carriage and broke down this door to give up on her now? No, you need to get her on a horse and take her back to safety.'

'What will you do?' Jem managed, the lump in his throat growing larger by the second.

'We've done what we needed to do here. We will see that you can leave this forsaken place safely, and then we will return home. We will decry this Brotherhood, and ensure everyone in the Shadow Lands knows that it is they who are the evil ones. We will tell them that those with magic are simply defending themselves, and defending us.'

Jem couldn't believe his ears.

'They will come back from this, though, and they'll come back heavy. It doesn't end here.'

'I know,' Jem replied. 'But we'll stop them.'

'We trust that you will. What's your name?' Jemima asked.

'Jameson Rafferty,' Jem choked out. 'Jem.'

'Well, Jem,' Orla said, joining Jemima. 'You bring her back to us when it's all over. She deserves our apologies, and she will always find a home and a hearth in Alder Vale.'

Jem brushed a tear from his cheek, and tried to thank them, but they shook their heads.

'Come on. They've already secured a horse outside.'

Jem stood and then carefully manoeuvred Lily up into his arms. The arm that wasn't pressed against his body lolled lifelessly, but he looked only ahead. He didn't want this Lily to be the one he remembered. He wanted to hold on to the memory of her strength of purpose just before she released her magic. She had looked fierce and beautiful and unstoppable – everything he always knew she was. It was like, in that moment, she had finally seen it in herself. Whatever it took, he would bring her back from this.

Lily Knight would be revered; he would make sure of it.

Chapter Twenty-Five

Alice marched towards the front gates of Midnight Manor, incensed. The gates were still guarded by two witches, on a constant shift pattern through the day and night, but as night had fallen and the watch had changed, the story of the Brotherhood's disgusting attempts to distract and disarm the witches had reached Alice's ears.

'I'm going to kill them,' Alice said aloud, because she knew Grace was hot on her heels.

'I'll kill them first,' Grace growled. 'I'll do it with my bare hands if I have to.'

'How dare they threaten anyone like that. Not even Rowenna and Ailsa deserve such treatment.' Alice, too, thought she would be capable of killing a man with her bare hands after this.

'It's horrifying. Those things, those words they used. I want to vomit. I want to strike them from my brain so I can never hear them again.' Grace had fallen into step beside Alice and was maintaining an almost constant growl. 'That's what those men are like though. I don't know why I'm surprised. If they slither through life without someone teaching them a lesson, they think it's acceptable to threaten and belittle women with threats on their honour.'

'Threaten us with magic, or a fair fight, and I'll respect it. But to threaten *that*, to threaten the forceful removal of a woman's honour, to threaten to *violate* them,' Alice spat, 'is beyond anything I've ever known. I will kill them.'

As they continued marching towards the gate, they saw that someone else had beaten them to it.

Hecate.

She was beyond the boundary of the manor, but the gates were closed again. Alice could see the tell-tale shimmer of the protective spells around the metal. They were on one side, and Hecate was on the other.

She was as incensed as they were. By the time they reached the gate, they could hear her shouts and threats clearly. One man was held up by an invisible hand at his throat; another was already lying dead on the floor.

'Hecate!' Alice banged on the gate. 'Hecate, let us through.'

'I'll be done in just a moment,' she snarled, 'I'm just teaching these men – although they barely deserve the title – a lesson.'

'Hecate, don't be stupid.' Grace banged on the gate. 'You're a sitting duck out there alone.'

'A sitting duck?!' Hecate laughed and then paused. When she saw the expression on Alice's face, she sighed, and flicked her hand. The gates creaked open. 'Only Alice,' she said. The man she held by an invisible hand at his throat continued to struggle, suspended in the air.

'What are you doing?' Alice asked.

'Like I said, I'm t—'

Alice interrupted her. 'No, I mean what are you doing out here, on your own? We need you. If anything happened to you—' Her voice faltered.

'Alice, I've been the leader of the Shadow Sect for more years that you have been alive. I have fought worse fiends than the ones in front of us now. And Fenn, when he gets here, will be just another pathetic man desperately searching for meaning and purpose in his life. He's nothing. And you, my dear' – she looked over her shoulder into Alice's eyes – 'you are everything I could never be. Where I have malice, you have patience. Where I have sharpness, you have understanding. You are me, if I'd been stronger, if I'd been able to shut out the world and its rejection of me.'

'No, that's not true. You are the strongest person I know,' Alice snapped back. 'You are better than all of us, combined. Yes, you've done some terrible things, but who in your situation would have acted differently? I know I wouldn't.'

Hecate tutted. 'You do nothing for my evil reputation, girl.' A smirk tugged at the edges of her scarlet lips. She still looked painfully thin, but there was a flush to her cheeks that Alice liked to see.

The struggling man tried to cry out, but his voice was compressed beneath the weight of Hecate's magic.

'Oh, do shut up,' Hecate said to him, before clenching her fist. An audible crack shattered the night, his neck snapped, and he fell to the floor. Lifeless.

'You really are just like your mother, Alice. Good to the core, even when you try not to be.'

'You hated her,' Alice muttered. Without the distraction of Hecate holding the man by his throat, the conversation had become very real – too real. Alice could feel Grace's eyes on them from the other side of the gate.

Hecate sighed, rubbing her eyes. Her make-up spread itself across her cheeks, but she didn't seem to mind. When she looked up, Alice could see Hecate's eyes were sparkling with tears. 'Hate is the exact opposite of what I felt for your mother, Alice.'

'What… what do you mean?'

'I was in love with her. I had been in love with her from the moment I recruited her into the sect. She was different, like you. Always on the periphery, never quite noticed. And then we met and it was like a spark had been lit in both of us. Except, she could never love me like I loved her. I believe that she wanted to, that she would have loved me if she could have, but she couldn't. So we lived side by side harmoniously. For years, we were together. Just her and me, leading this band of misfit witches without a home. She helped me find the castle, and the lighthouse, and eventually this manor. She was by my side as we grew from a few, to a legion.' Hecate's voice was as measured as Alice had ever heard it. It was like she was finally allowing herself to be seen, to be vulnerable, with all that came with it.

Alice couldn't shift the lump in her throat. She didn't know what to say.

'And then she left me, as you know. She met your father, the bastard. She was so ashamed of her love for him, our greatest enemy, that she ran. She didn't even give me the chance to say goodbye. She didn't tell me where she was going. It was like she crafted her own fate; by not telling me, she broke me. And broken, all I could do was fight. I didn't know how to grieve; I only knew how to kill. So kill, I did. And I'd do it again. But I am glad of one thing,'

Alice felt sick. How could this woman, the woman who had murdered Alice's own mother, have become someone so treasured? It was too confusing. 'What? What are you glad of?' she managed.

'I'm glad I didn't manage to kill you. You, Alice Blackwell, are my greatest achievement.' She smiled, and reached for Alice's hand.

And then her smile faltered. Another man, cloaked in gold, emerged from a thicket of overgrown brambles. She whipped round and held her hands out towards the man, firing every ounce of her strength towards him in the form of huge, terrifying flames.

But the man was one of those fearsome golden-robed witches. He was a product of Hecate *and* Fenn. And he was ruthless.

He, too, flung out his arms, catching Hecate's flames in mid-air.

Alice called up her magic to support Hecate, but Grace's cries at the gate behind her forced her to falter. Should she help, or risk a few moments to allow Grace through the gates, where she would be infinitely stronger.

She had a Protector for a reason. Alice shot towards the gates and wrenched them open, letting Grace scramble through. Together, they called up Alice's magic, ready to defeat this awful man and everything he stood for.

But Alice wasn't fast enough.

With her back turned, another man had crept out from the shadows. Hecate's focus was solely on the witch who was hammering her own flames back towards her. Her teeth were gritted with the unexpected effort. He was stronger than any of them had thought possible. Alice spotted the new man, but before she could react, he had taken advantage of Hecate's distraction and made his move.

Alice stood, helplessly, as the man charged forward with all of his brutish strength, and plunged a dagger into Hecate's throat.

Her flames faltered, and then dissipated. She fell to her knees, a look of total surprise etched across her face.

Alice couldn't make sense of what she was seeing. It was all too quick, too real.

She could feel the heat rising from her toes up though her body. The rage was so strong. She took the two men in her sights and with Grace by her side, she allowed her magic to flow freely, without inhibition. She roared, her magic lifting her off the ground, her black hair flailing around her head. She could feel the support of Grace's protection, and that was all she needed to unleash her wrath on the murderers. They were consumed by flames in moments, their screams echoing through the freezing air. Eventually, their screams stopped, and all that was left of them was two neat piles of ash and dust.

Alice dropped to the floor and dragged herself to where Hecate was lying. Blood seeped in a gentle stream from the wound in her neck, where the dagger still protruded. Hecate's breathing was laboured and her face was deathly white.

'I'm here,' Alice said, trying to fight back tears. 'I'm here. You're going to be all right.'

'No, Alice,' Hecate choked. '*You're* going… to be… all right. You're… going to… finish what I… started.' Her breathing became shallower and shallower.

Until it stopped.

Alice screamed, turning her face to the cruel, cruel sky. Grace was by her side, but none of it mattered.

It was a mortal's death. A violent, brutal mortal's death. It was her mother's death.

And now it was Hecate's death.

She was no longer immortal.

Alice felt the shroud of darkness cloud her vision. Her ears rung painfully. Her screams shot into the night like lightning bolts, and she could barely feel Grace's arms wrapped around her.

She wanted to kill. Death was the only thing that could right this wrong. Death to everyone who had ever wronged her.

'Alice…' She could hear Grace pleading with her, but her voice was far away, at the other end of a long pitch-black tunnel. 'Alice, we need to get back inside the boundaries.'

But Alice didn't care. She flung herself over Hecate's body and let the sobs shudder painfully through her. How could she be anything if Hecate wasn't there to guide her? How could she continue walking along this path without Hecate?

For Alice Blackwell, the world had ended.

'Alice!' Grace was yelling now, pulling at her arm with panicked violence. 'Alice there's more of them coming. We need to get inside.'

More of them? Alice's thoughts were scattered and hazy, but she knew she was in no fit state to handle a full-blown attack. She looked up and realised Grace was right. There was something coming, something on horseback. Hecate wouldn't have wanted her to kill herself, even for vengeance. No, she would have wanted Alice strong, filled with darkness, ready to kill hundreds in her name.

Grace dragged Alice to her feet, but the oncoming rider

was closer than either of them had realised. Within moments, a great black horse was upon them, ridden by a heavily cloaked man with a body flung over the saddle in front of him.

'STAY BACK!' Grace yelled, her voice cracking with the strain and the fear.

'Grace!' the voice came from the horseback rider. 'Shit, Grace, it's me! What's happened?'

It was Jem, which meant the body was...

'Lily!' Alice couldn't bear any more tragedy. 'Is she alive?'

Please, please let her be alive, Alice thought.

She dragged herself to her feet, but her whole body felt like it was made of lead.

'Yes, but she needs to be seen by a healer. She is very unwell,' Jem said, his voice cracking.

Alice wiped her nose and tried to muster any strength she could find. 'Grace, take them inside. Find Farlan. I will set the spells back on the gate and follow.' The power of Alice's voice surprised even herself.

Lily had to live.

'Are you sure?' Grace asked, taking Alice's face in her hands.

Alice gave her one firm nod, hoping her beloved wouldn't see how close she was to total devastation. 'I'm sure. Get her inside, now.' She kissed Grace briefly, forcefully, on the lips to seal her trust, and then watched as Grace artfully jumped up into the saddle behind Jem and the three people Alice had left in the world rode away from her towards the manor.

She ran back towards Hecate's body and dragged it within the boundaries of the gate, and then pulled them closed. The spells to seal the gate fell from her lips without thought or meaning, but they worked all the same. Within moments the gates were locked and sealed, but they didn't hide the bloody desolation just beyond the threshold.

Alice vomited on the ground. She knew, in her heart, that this was just the beginning. But without Hecate, how could she go on?

Chapter Twenty-Six

Jem watched helplessly from the corner of Lily's bedroom. She was no longer still and peaceful, as she had been in the Brotherhood's headquarters and on the journey. It was as though her magic had stayed dormant and controlled whilst he got her to safety, and now it was fighting to be released once more.

She was fitting, jerking uncontrollably, her eyes wide and burning red, her bedsheets singed with the heat of her magic. There was no doctor to send for, no Hecate to stroll in, bold as brass, to tell him what to do or how to save her. He had hated Hecate – he still did – but he couldn't pretend that her knowledge would have been useful at a time like this. And her death had sent Alice down a path he knew they all needed Lily to bring her back from.

'They've poisoned her mind.' Farlan charged in, a heavy tome in his hand. 'I read about it back home, when I first started to become worried that they'd come for me. They deal in a more subtle form of magic, something engineered and not quite natural. Did she touch blood before she collapsed?'

Jem wracked his brains, and then remembered Alf, how she had held him in his last moments. 'Yes, her uncle's. It's what's all over her dress.' He gestured at the dark-brown stains. 'Why?'

'It's blood magic. They must have poisoned him with it, knowing she would touch him in death.'

'That sounds…' Grace frowned.

'Clever? Far-fetched? I know, but either way, it's all I've got.' Farlan flicked through the book feverishly until he found the page he was seeking. 'They have to plant it using the blood of someone who represents home, safety, comfort.' He showed the passage to Jem, his finger tracing the line of text he read from. 'It will cause her magic to eat away at her from the inside, until she is barely a shell of herself. If we let it ravage her, she will be hollow before the day is out. It wouldn't be worth waking her; she wouldn't be Lily anymore.'

'So what do we do?' Jem felt himself cry out. He felt helpless. A hollow Lily? How would he live with himself, knowing he had all but killed her, knowing he would never get to look into her eyes again?

'We make her realise that home is *here*. If her magic recognises itself as being somewhere safer than safe, the poison's hold on her will break. At least, that's what the book suggests.'

'We'll take it,' Alice snapped. 'We'll do whatever we need to do. We can't lose her.'

'No,' Jem agreed, 'we can't.'

'The example in the book suggests that smell is the strongest sense. If a room is filled with scents of home, it can create an atmosphere strong enough to break this.'

'Alice.' Jem looked Lily's best friend in the eye and saw a terror there he knew was reflected in his own. 'I will stay with her, watch over her. You know her better than anyone else. Save her, please.'

Alice didn't, or couldn't, respond to him, but she did nod, before charging from the room, his sister close at her heels.

The sun was sitting low in the sky by the time Alice and Grace returned. The room was bathed in golden light that was so similar to the colour of Lily's own magic that it made Jem's heart contract painfully in his chest. He'd spent so long without her in his life that he wondered now how he had ever managed to live, day by day, without her wisdom, without her company. Even those few short weeks ago, when he had been away from her with Grace, he had felt a strange pull back to her side. It was a feeling that only briefly subsided when he had arrived home in the castle for those few short moments before chaos broke out, and it returned almost immediately whenever he stepped more than a room away from her. Without her, he felt like a saltless ocean, a storm without lightning, a lantern without a flame.

Farlan had taken a seat long ago, before the sun dipped, to pore over his book, but Jem couldn't settle. This boy in the room with him was related to the awful, evil man who wanted to destroy everything he held dear. He paced and paced until he felt the soles of his boots might wear away to nothing; he stacked and restacked the measly pile of books in the corner of the room; he used his shirt sleeve to scrub the haze off the grubby windows to let in more of that intoxicating light. Anything to distract him from looking at Lily, pale, clammy, unresponsive, lying far too peacefully on the bed. She didn't look like she was sleeping – that was the worst part. She looked like she was locked in some kind of nightmare somewhere inside her head; her brow was furrowed, there were bruise-like shadows under her eyes, and her hair was a matted mess of fiery clumps that could no longer be considered curls.

'All right,' said Grace, as she stormed into the room. Alice skulked in behind her, her face ashen and her eyes watery. Both of them were laden down with a variety of items; it didn't look like they were going to take any chances. 'Farlan, what do we do with all of this?'

Farlan looked up from his seat and smiled slightly. 'Arrange them as close to her as possible. It needs to create a strong scent in the air for it to impact her, so the closer the better.'

To assuage his feelings of utter helplessness, Jem took some of the items from Grace and began the process of placing them on the bedside table, the headboard and the bed: old books, cinnamon sticks, brown sugar in a paper bag, sprigs of pine and spruce, winter berries, dried fruit. He lit candles and placed them on the nightstand and wished he could capture the scent of earth after a summer rainstorm, or the ocean as it crashed on the rocks, or the musty, vivid scent of her apothecary that he knew she would always miss.

When they were done, and Lily's unconscious form was surrounded by the range of items that were so gloriously Lily, they took a few steps back. Would it work?

Moments passed, and Jem realised he was holding his breath. He exhaled heavily and turned to Farlan, who was looking sheepishly at the ground. 'How long will this take, Farlan?'

The young man looked up, his lips pursed. 'I don't know. The book made it seem like it would be instantaneous.'

Jem rubbed his eyes until he could see tiny stars beneath his eyelids. He didn't want to open his eyes again to see a world without Lily's energy in it.

Alice cleared her throat. She still looked ghastly, and he knew she would be feeling Lily's loss as keenly as he was. 'I have an idea.'

Thank goodness, Jem thought. *At least one of us isn't incapacitated by helplessness.*

'Jem, we still don't know each other that well...'

He looked up, surprised to be the subject of her speech.

'And I know that your experience of me has been anything but positive... but what I do know, I've heard from the two people who love you the most. Your sister, and Lily.' She looked up from underneath her black curtain of hair and looked him straight in the eye for what Jem thought might have been the first time ever.

Love?

'I don't think I can do this alone, but I think, if you don't mind, I might be able to do it with your help.' She gulped, and Jem was suddenly terrified of whatever Alice was about to ask of him. She held out a hand which, after a nod from his sister, he took and allowed himself to be guided to the bed on which Lily was lying. 'This is going to sound strange, but lie with her. I'll lie on this side, so that we are on either side of her, protecting her.'

Jem suddenly felt like everyone in the room was holding their breath, waiting for his response. He wouldn't allow them to see how flustered and strange he felt on the inside; instead, he did exactly what Alice told him to.

There was plenty of room by Lily's side, so he was able to lie facing her, without actually needing to touch her. Alice did the same on her opposite side, and then placed a gentle hand on her best friend's chest. She gestured for Jem to give her his hand, and placed it atop hers, so that Lily's heart was covered by their hands.

Alice closed her eyes, as if she were in deep concentration, but all Jem could do was wish and hope that this would work. He looked upon Lily's clammy, pale face and damp hair and willed her to wake up, to open her eyes, to breathe deep lungfuls of air instead of short, shallow gasps.

To calm himself, he focused on counting each of her delicate, pale freckles that adorned her nose and cheeks. He'd never really noticed them before, but up close he could see each one, gilding her face like constellations in the night sky that he had gazed at for night upon night back in the lantern room of the lighthouse. Over the years, he had learned the position in the sky of every single star, learned their names, their movements. He realised, lying there by Lily, that one day he wanted to memorise each and every one of her freckles, like he had the stars.

'Jem,' Alice whispered, which brought him swiftly back to earth. He looked past Lily into the emerald eyes of her best friend, and noticed that though there was a darkness, a pain, etched into her features, there was also hopefulness – barely a glint, but it was there. 'Jem, I think it's working.'

He shuffled himself backwards slightly, so that Lily once again came into focus. It was true. Her face had regained a little of its rosiness, and her brow was less saturated. Her breathing deepened with each inhale and her eyelids began to flutter.

Then, almost as quickly as she had fallen unconscious at the Brotherhood's headquarters, the life shot back into her with a forceful vengeance. Lily burst awake, sitting upright, stiff as an old oak tree.

'They're coming,' she croaked, her voice lacking its usual sing-song intonations. 'The Brotherhood. They're coming.'

Chapter Twenty-Seven

Crunch. Crunch. Crunch.
The relentless, trudging monotony of leather boots on frozen snow was all Morven was able to focus on. One step, then another, then another. Sometimes, she could focus on the twenty-two pairs of little feet also making the same trudging sound on the snow behind her, but only sometimes. The rest of the time, it was too painful. There should have been twenty-three pairs of feet. One was, and always would be, missing.

Cass had disappeared under an enormous pile of burning rubble, and that was that. A lifetime by his side, and now a future alone. But Morven couldn't afford to crumble, not when there were still living souls who needed her. It was time for her to channel Jem, and Grace; time to put herself at the bottom of the list and focus on what really mattered: giving these children a second chance at life. That would be Cass's legacy, and she would be the one to make it so. But the pain cut her deeper than she had ever been experienced before.

'Morven…' a young girl with a bruise covering most of her left eye socket and cheekbone fell into step alongside Morven. She realised the girl couldn't have been more than a year or two younger than herself, although she was much shorter than Morven. Her hair, which she wore in two dishevelled braids, was the colour of milky tea. The sleeve of the right arm of her jacket hung strangely. 'Can you help?' the girl asked.

Morven paused and turned to look at the girl, giving her her full attention. 'What is it…?'

She realised she didn't know the girl's name, nor any of their names, and felt awful. They had been walking for hours, diligently, not complaining although she knew they would be exhausted, freezing and hungry.

'My name is Efwyn, or Efi, and this jacket is making things really difficult.' She had a strong, confident voice for such a small-statured girl.

'What's the matter with it?' Morven couldn't understand why the girl wouldn't appreciate a warm jacket in these conditions, even if it was poorly fitted to her slight frame.

'My arm…' Efi shrugged her shoulder slightly and the jacket fell from her. Underneath, her arm ended, smooth and rounded, roughly where her elbow would have been. It didn't look like an injury, and Morven understood immediately how restricting the heavy jacket sleeve would be.

Morven crouched down to where the end of the jacket sleeve hung, and pulled it back over Efi's shoulder. She then rolled the sleeve up, up, up until it was the perfect length to be able to keep her arm warm, whilst giving Efi the freedom of movement she needed. 'There. Is that any good?'

Efi smiled. 'Thanks. And... thanks for everything. Most of us thought we'd die in there. No one was coming for us.' She paused, then continued. 'I'm sorry about your brother.'

Morven gulped, her throat suddenly feeling like she had swallowed an icy rock straight from the riverbed. 'That's all right,' she managed, before starting up walking again. It wasn't all right. Nothing was all right.

'Just because we're children, it doesn't mean we don't understand your pain,' Efi said, and then dropped back into the group, leaving Morven with her thoughts.

She was acutely aware that a crowd of their size would draw attention, so she picked her way across the land, avoiding any main tracks, keeping to the shadows of the snow-covered treelines on the lesser-used trails. She consulted her map every few hours, ensuring they were still heading in a fairly straight line to the border. She was thankful that this time of year was quiet, and the weather had seemed to scare away any travellers. The rambling driftways that weren't suitable for coaches were usually much more solid underfoot, and meant the children were less likely to roll their ankles or scuff their knees than if she had led them directly across country avoiding tracks entirely.

When the trees fell away to moorland, she felt exposed, but she knew moorland meant the border was close. The thought was both a comfort and a terror. How would she get this band of misfits through back into the Shadow Lands?

In what looked to be the final thicket of woodland before they lost the trees altogether, Morven ushered the children beneath the branches. 'We'll sleep here for the night,' she bellowed above their chattering teeth. 'You need your rest and we need a fire. We can make some warm pine tea to drink and we can set off again tomorrow.'

She gazed at the crowd of faces staring back at her, unblinking, as if they'd forgotten how to be children. Their bodies were in survival mode; their faces couldn't remember how to conjure a laugh or even a smile. And yet, they were strong. They didn't complain, even if some of them cried for much of the day. Some were younger even than Brenna and Maeve, and others were close to her in age, as Efi was. She tried to remember what Efi had said, about them understanding, and realised she didn't have to pretend to be brave.

'All right,' she started up again, her voice cracking. *Cass would have been so much better at this*, she thought. She brushed down her overcoat and wrapped it tightly around her chest. 'I need those of you who are feeling strong and brave to collect the firewood and the pine sprigs. Efi' – she gestured to her mousy-haired friend who looked at her with the kind of understanding Morven had only seen before in Jem – 'you know everyone far better than I do. Can you help them see to their tasks? I'll start making the fires for the younger ones.'

She knelt on the snowy ground and wished she had paid more attention. Much of her life in the lighthouse and in the castle had been spent bettering herself: she had read books on famous explorers, learned to curl her hair perfectly with handkerchiefs, identified her strengths so that she might land a good, capable husband who would be able to support her and Cass, and the twins too. She hoped a rich husband would allow her to see more of the world beyond the Shadow Lands, but now she knew that was futile.

The only place she wanted to be was in her bedroom in the lighthouse, surrounded by books and homemade beautifying products, listening to a ranging storm outside the window. It was too late now to realise that she had had everything she could ever want, back then. She recognised it, now that every single thing that she loved in her life had been taken away.

Goodbye lighthouse, goodbye Cass. Goodbye the Morven of old, the Morven who had hopes and dreams of bettering herself. Because *that* Morven didn't pay enough attention to the here and now, and she certainly hadn't paid enough attention to how to light fires and cook food. How much better for everyone it would have been, for her to be lying dead beneath a pile of rubble, and for Cass to be leading them to safety.

Morven gathered dead twigs from the low-lying branches of the trees that surrounded them. She made a small pile on a flat grey rock, and then realised she had nothing to light it with.

She swore, pushing herself up to her feet and stumbling behind a tree away from tiny prying eyes, before the tears consumed her. She collapsed against the tree trunk, her legs giving way beneath her, until she was curled up like a badger in a sett, sobbing until her face ached as much as her heart.

She had been a fool, thinking she could save them all. She had been drunk on the hope of possibility, enamoured by the idea of preventing any child from experiencing what she and Cass had, but now Cass was gone, and she was alone.

A fool, indeed, she thought.

Chapter Twenty-Eight

Rain hammered on the window, the greyish light casting strange, eerie shadows on the wall of Lily's bedroom in Midnight Manor. She rubbed her eyes, trying to recall where she was, and how she'd come to find herself here.

The images came back in flashes, but she couldn't pick out the real from the imagined; they were all as horrible as each other. Blood dripping on a polished floor. Flames engulfing whole buildings. A crush of bodies. A knife to the heart. An army. A pyre. Death. Then there was Alf. Her uncle, Alf, with his rosy cheeks and bushy grey eyebrows, his contagious belly-laugh and his all-encompassing hugs. He came to her, a beacon of glowing light amidst so much darkness and pain. Had any of it been real?

'Lily?' A voice broke through her stupor. She blinked open her eyes once more, this time allowing them to focus.

They fell upon Alice, sitting patiently on the edge of her bed. She was holding her hand so tightly that Lily could barely feel the ends of her fingers.

Reality seeped into her dreams, and she remembered the Brotherhood. Fenn. Alf. Blood. And then so, so many people. Were they there to help them? Lily couldn't recall. She could, however, recall the immense pain of her magic flying out of her control once again. She could feel remnants of it still, as if she were lying on glowing embers.

'Lily,' Alice repeated, and this time Lily really tried to focus. 'Lily, are you all right?'

'I... I think so,' Lily managed, although her throat felt sore, as if she had just consumed a mug of tea straight from the kettle, before it'd had time to cool. 'Where's Jem? Is he all right?' She sat upright, frowning. 'What happened? Where is he?' The realisation that she couldn't trust her own recollections made her want to cry.

Alice squeezed her hand and encouraged Lily to lie back down onto her pillow. 'It's going to be all right. Just relax.'

Relax? Had Alice gone completely mad? 'Where is he, Alice?'

'He's in his room getting some much-needed rest. He's been here, by your side, from the moment you came back. He hasn't left you for longer than a few moments, so I've sent him away now he knows you're going to live. He's not slept this whole time.'

'Why?' Lily couldn't get her thoughts straight. She pulled her hand back from Alice's. She needed to feel like she had control over something, and sure enough, her hands automatically started the familiar motion of picking at the skin on her fingers. The sharp, shooting pain helped her to feel like herself. It helped her to sink into herself, to be present, to try to understand Alice. She knew Jem wouldn't approve, but she wanted him to be here to tell her to stop; the idea of him wasn't enough.

'Why?' Alice asked. 'Lily, isn't it obvious?'

'And everyone else?' Lily asked, evading the question.

'Grace took Jem to his room to make sure he actually got there. The twins are with Farlan…' She trailed off, as if she had been about to say something, and then changed her mind.

'Morven and Cass?' Lily felt panicked again. She rued the day she and Jem had decided to leave; everything felt far too tentative, too fragile. She hated not knowing exactly what was going on.

'They left, shortly after you did.'

'They left?'

'Not permanently. I think they just wanted space and time to figure out who they are, away from other influences. After so much transience and change and pain, they needed a bit of distance, especially when Jem left. They didn't know who to be, so they went out looking for themselves.'

'I feel awful.' Lily sighed. 'I could have guided them better, shown them how valued they both are.'

'You did everything you could, but they're at that stage

in life where they need to make their own choices, their own mistakes. You and I know that feeling very well.'

'Hm...' Lily nodded, her throat feeling strangely constricted. 'And Hecate? Are you still training with her? Is she still on our side?'

Alice gulped and her face turned oyster-shell white. That was when Lily looked at her best friend – really, properly looked at her – and noticed what she should have seen immediately: the black rings around her eyes, the puffy, mottled skin underneath, the drawn, pale complexion, the hunched way she held herself.

'Alice...' She pushed, feeling the same reservations she had felt all those times in Alice's cabin, when her friend had been teetering far too close to an edge for comfort. One push too hard and Alice would be lost to her, but if she didn't push hard enough, Alice wouldn't find the strength to be vulnerable.

'She's gone, Lil.' Her voice cracked. 'I know you hated her – everyone hated her – but she was the only person in the world who believed in my strength. A world without her guidance is a very bleak world. She's left me to fight this threat alone; her legacy rests solely on my shoulders. She didn't finish my training, I don't know what her plans were, I don't know anything... I wasted so much time.' The tears had started to flow now, which seemed to make Alice more angry than sad. Her face had grown red and her teeth were clenched together.

'You aren't alone, Ali. You've never been alone. We will

figure it out together, side by side. If you want to take up her mantle, I'll be there to hold your hand. We're sisters, you and I, aren't we?'

'Sisters of Shadow.' Alice nodded.

'Sisters of Midnight, my friend. We will protect this place, and our people, from the Brotherhood. It's all we can do. Midnight Manor represents everything we have left.'

Alice nodded again. The tears had stopped; her face was set with the determination of a grieving soul bent on revenge. 'You're right. I have you. I have Grace, and everyone else. We can do this.'

'You've never been stronger, Ali.' Lily reached out and squeezed her hand. '*We*'ve never been stronger.'

Chapter Twenty-Nine

Morven shook herself off, wiped the tears from her cheeks, and walked as proudly as she could back to the camp. To her surprise, there were several fires lit. One was more of a small bonfire, surrounded by the majority of the children who were warming their hands a little too close to the flames. Another was heating water in a small tin pot that Lily recognised as one of the serving bowls from the poorhouse. They had very little, but what they had stolen away with them was providing just enough to keep them going. It wasn't much, but it would keep everyone alive for another day. Morven wished she'd asked Lily more about foraging; how magical it would feel to be able to scour these woods to find extra food.

She took a seat next to the fire that was heating the water and tried to smile at the three faces looking at her with intense interest. One of them was Efi. The other was a boy of a similar age, with a crooked nose, hooded eyes, and raven hair, and the other was another girl, who was much younger and had cropped hair, elven ears, and a permanent frown.

'Welcome back, Morven.' Efi gestured to her. 'This is Cuth' – she gestured to the boy who raised an eyebrow but not a smile –'and Mildryd.'

'It's just Mil,' the girl snapped. She was shivering underneath the great guard's coat. The clothes they had been given in the poorhouse were thin and poorly made. She was thankful though that the boots, at least, were made of sturdy leather.

'Hello,' Morven managed. It was all so awkward. She was supposed to be leading these children, she was supposed to be brave and likeable like Jem and Grace, and instead all she could do was wish this responsibility had fallen on someone else. She felt a bitterness rise in her throat that she wasn't proud of, but before she could stop herself, she muttered, 'If you didn't want to come this way, you didn't have to. I was only trying to help.'

'And a fat lot of good that did us,' responded Cuth without looking up.

'I'm serious.' Morven found herself growing angrier by the moment. 'You can leave. You don't have to go where I'm going. I got you out, which means I feel some strange responsibility for your wellbeing. But don't stay here if you don't want to. Go, for all I care. It's one less person to worry about.' Morven was surprised by the venom in her own voice. All of the pain was threatening to bubble over again, and she couldn't bear the thought of having forced these children against their will.

'They're all just tired, Morven. So are you.' This time it was young Mil who spoke, the snappiness completely gone from her voice. In its place was a touch of empathy, amidst the exhaustion.

Morven nodded. She had never felt so out of her depth. She was so angry at Cass for leaving her, and those feelings of anger triggered even heavier feelings of guilt and shame for blaming her brother for something he didn't choose.

Sleep came quickly for the children after the chill had shifted from their hands and feet. They curled up with each other, close to the flames, in little groups. She hadn't been able to give them as much food as she would have liked, as their bags could only carry so much, but Morven was satisfied that at least they'd had snow to drink, and a little food was better than no food at all. She finally succumbed to the tiredness in her bones as she pored over the map one more time. Tomorrow, she was sure, would return them to the manor. Tomorrow, it would all be over.

The sun shone as high as it could this late in the winter and its almost-warmth was a tonic. Morven couldn't believe their luck; Cass, she knew, had to be watching over them, ensuring their safety. There was no other way to believe she had managed to keep twenty-two children alive, and see them through the border safely.

But here they were, trudging through the same thick snow but now in her beloved Shadow Lands. People here didn't walk around with weapons slung over the shoulders, didn't look at her with furtive glances and suspicion. All that had stopped the moment they had been granted passage.

She supposed, now she thought on it, that the border guards were less inclined to let people out of the Shadow Lands; their concern wasn't preventing people going back in. Even so, Morven felt incredibly lucky that her story had landed, and she had been believed.

As they'd approached the border earlier than morning, Morven had rehearsed everything with the children. They were to cough, sniffle, and walk even slower than they already were. She wanted them to look too ghastly to bother inspecting them closely. She'd had Efi join her at the front, and she and Morven had cleaned each other up using snow to scrub away the dirt on their faces and in their hair. It had taken a bit of time and a little persistence, but Morven had been happy with the result; she and Efi had looked respectable, which was what she'd wanted.

They had approached the border, making a fuss, so that people noticed them and noticed the children they escorted.

Naturally, people backed away and covered their faces, so as not to catch whatever affliction the children suffered from. She and Efi bundled the children into the ramshackle border building and marched straight for the first guard they saw. They had stayed calm and firm, but made it clear that their swift passage would be advantageous for everyone. The sooner the children were in the Shadow Lands, heading for their new poorhouse that had been established in the old Aelfdene Manor, the better. They would keep their illness inside the Shadow Lands and no longer endanger the good people of Hythlund, and she and Efi would ensure their safe passage, to make sure no stragglers escaped.

The guard, who had looked young and nervous, took one look at Mil, who was doing her very best impression of a dying girl, and waved them all through without so much as asking for papers.

That had been much earlier in the day, when the sun was barely peeping over the horizon, and even now with the sun high in the sky, Morven couldn't believe they'd actually done it. She felt Cass by her side, giving her strength and confidence, and with each step through the border, she had tried to emulate the calm, selfless trustworthiness of Lily and the strong steadfastness of Jem. She had been so strongly shaped by those she loved in her life, that she felt almost renewed.

A few more miles and they'd be home. Morven had

decided with Efi and Cuth's input that another stop would only hamper the children's strength, so they would bypass Aelfdene Manor and head straight for Midnight Manor. As awful as Hecate was, Morven would be glad to have her protection after so much trauma.

Chapter Thirty

A lone blackbird whistled its cheery tune, breaking the still quiet of the dawn. A gentle fog drifted over the moors, enveloping Midnight Manor in a mist so fine, it was like a delicate piece of lace had been draped over the dark stone building, softening its edges. The contrast of the deep, rich greens of the plants in the greenhouse and the hazy grey of the outside world made Lily's tired heart heave a sigh of contented relief.

She had awoken after another fitful night to a silent empty room. Her companions must have been comfortable with her recovery, for they had all left to sleep in their own rooms. All Lily could remember was snippets of visions that frightened her, so she couldn't bear the thought of going back to sleep. No, the world here, in the fluttering dawn light, was far safer and more secure than the world in her dreams. She had wrapped a woollen blanket over her white nightgown, slipped her feet into her unfastened boots, picked up her flickering candlestick, and headed down to the gardens, being careful to avoid going anywhere near the entrance gates. More Brotherhood spies were positioned there and the witches on watch duty would be growing tired at the end of their shift; she didn't want to cause any unnecessary chaos.

The mist on her skin had felt magical at first, but after a while it had clung to her scraggly red curls and seeped into her blanket until the goosebumps on her arms were so sharp, she couldn't stay outside any longer. The greenhouse, with its trailing vines, orchids, ferns and fig trees, pulled her inside with a promise of warmer air and the companionship of plants. She sat on a humble wooden chair, the same chair she had sat on with Alice when they'd first arrived at Midnight Manor. Time had a habit of passing strangely, and Lily couldn't believe how much had changed. *Again.* As she sat, gazing at nothing in particular, she imagined a future where things didn't change much; the comforting presence of those she loved and trusted around her; purposeful work; a safe home. That was all she wanted. But even with her optimism and imagination, she struggled to truly believe that it could be in her future.

After a few moments of companionable silence amongst the plants, the gable door at the other end of the greenhouse swung quietly and slowly open. Lily shifted to cover more of herself with the still-damp blanket, but held her tongue. Maybe whoever it was would change their mind and go back to sleep. The sun was barely awake; there was no reason to be up yet.

She heard heavy footsteps approaching. They dragged slightly along the floor, as if the person was dillydallying, seeking refuge too, perhaps. From behind a particularly large fern, a familiar face appeared: long, thick russet hair, kind eyes, brown skin, and a look of surprise, turning to relief, turning to embarrassment.

Jem.

'Hi,' she managed, whilst wishing she had pulled on an actual dress before leaving her bedroom. She went to stand up, but he gestured for her to stay where she was.

'Can't sleep?' he asked, as he ran a hand through his hair.

She shook her head, gesturing to the seat across from hers, which he took. 'I keep having strange dreams – visions, maybe. I don't know. But they aren't very pleasant. And when I fall asleep, I have a few painful moments as I wake where I forget everything that's happened. In those moments, Alf is still alive, I'm still normal, and we still live in Alder Vale. And then I realise how much has changed, and the pain is so much worse than just staying awake.'

Jem exhaled, puffing out his cheeks. 'That's a lot to bear alone, Lil.' He was staring, unblinking, at the toes of his boots.

'What about you?' Lily pried. 'Are you all right? You had to bring me here. You had to see all of that alone. If you aren't all right, it would hardly be a surprise.'

He rubbed his eyes and took a sharp inhale of breath. 'I thought I'd lost you.'

Lily thought she heard a crack in his voice, as if he was trying not to cry. She remembered, in that moment, the time they had shared on the rocks in front of Kelseth Lighthouse, on the night of Glenn and Cass's huge fight. Jem had cried his heart out on her shoulder, and that had been the first time he had opened up to her. Since then, they had had many small moments of trust and affection, but she hadn't been able to delve any deeper into the young man he was; there was still always something hidden behind a curtain.

'But I'm here now,' she reassured him. 'I'm not going anywhere, not anymore.'

'But once this is all over,' he said, wrapping his arms around himself, 'you'll go back home. You've got a life there. All the villagers saved us, Lily. They helped me escape from the Brotherhood when you were unconscious and they saved us. You've got a home and family there.'

'You're a silly goose, Jem Rafferty,' Lily responded, feeling more confident all of a sudden. The warmth of the air mixed with the coldness of her skin made her feel giddy in the low light. 'I *am* home. Right here, anywhere in the vicinity of you. *You* are home. So wherever you go, there I'll be alongside you. Alice will follow Grace to the ends of the earth, so I'm sure between the four of us, we'll find somewhere to call home, somewhere we can all be happy. You needn't be far from your sister, Alice and I can be together, and you and I…' She trailed off, her confidence wavering with his silence. 'If that's Alder Vale, then great. If it's right here, in this big old house, then that's fine too.' She stood up, unable to contain the jitters she felt. For some reason, the words kept coming no matter how hard she tried to stop them. 'I've been so afraid to say it, so afraid to be honest with myself, with you.' She sighed and stopped pacing. She turned to face him, and looked him straight in the eye. He looked as though he'd stopped breathing. 'But I'm not afraid to say it anymore, Jem. I'm not even afraid of what you'll say if you don't feel it too, because I can barely contain it.'

'What?' he managed. 'What is it?' He stood too, and took a step closer to her.

She looked up at him. She could hear how shallow his breathing was; it matched hers. Lily felt as though a hummingbird had been placed in her chest as she took in the man standing in front of her, his hair loose around his shoulders, his dark eyes glittering in the candlelight. Suddenly, everything made sense.

'I love you, Jem. There, you have it.' She shrugged, trying not to show how much she was reeling inside. 'That's the truth of it, and now it's out there and I can't take it back, so if you—'

He placed a finger to her lips. 'Shh,' he whispered. 'Thank you for being brave enough to say the thing I've felt in my heart since the moment you washed up on my forsaken island.' He pressed his forehead gently against hers, and Lily entwined her hands with his.

The silence that filled the greenhouse was thick with expectation, with hope.

After a few moments, Lily continued. 'So... just to confirm... you feel the same?'

Jem burst into laughter, his contagious guffaw almost rattling the glass panels. 'Oh, Lily. As if you even have to ask.' He took her face in his hands and gently, carefully, placed his lips against hers. 'I have loved you all this time, and I will love you until the last breath leaves my body. That's a promise.'

Lily wrapped her arms around him and held him close, so that her ear was pressed against his chest. She could hear the hammering of his heart in his chest, mirroring hers, and knew that whatever happened in the next few days and weeks, with Alice and Jem by her side, she could face anything at all. Even if she didn't find her way to a quiet life again, she already had the comforting presence of those she loved and trusted around her. The rest, she realised, was simply daydreams.

Chapter Thirty-One

The dark, ivy-strewn shadow of Midnight Manor rose from the thick mist in the distance, on its little hill in the centre of an otherwise flat moorland landscape. Morven had never been so relieved to see a building in her entire life. She wanted to run to Jem and Grace, to tell them about Cass and then spend the next week crying on their laps about it, as though she was a child again. The world was so full of shadows without her brother in it, and they were the only people that would understand her pain.

There was less comfort to be found in the thought of telling the twins, though. Brenna and Maeve had been terribly fond of Cass, and Morven had always felt like they were older siblings to the girls. How were they going to take this loss, after Glenn? Her eyes prickled with tears and her throat closed up uncomfortably, and no matter how many times she cleared her throat, the obstruction wouldn't budge.

She trudged through the snow-covered heather, trying to muster up the strength and courage needed to guide this band of little misfits through the last few moments of their journey.

'There it is!' she cried out, trying to inspire hope, or at least an ounce of patience, in the children. They were dragging behind, which was unsurprising; they had all been through so much over the last couple of days, but Morven was confident that after warm baths and good food, their strength would return to their bones and they'd find light in their souls again. Plus, Lily always had tonics and tinctures for every possible ailment, so Morven had no real concerns for their wellbeing. She had miraculously kept them all fed and alive, and that in itself was something she couldn't help but be proud of.

As they approached, Morven was so lost in her thoughts that the figures standing on this side of the gate gave her hope. They had walked through the night, and now the dawn light combined with the mist made everything seem otherworldly and ethereal. But as they drew closer and closer to the gate, the figures turned to face them. There were four of them, all wrapped in golden cloaks, hoods up, weapons in hand.

Morven swore. She had forgotten about the secret gate and she had forgotten about the Brotherhood in all of the chaos, and now she was walking the children she had so carefully rescued straight into their deadly hands. She wracked her brains, trying to think how on earth she could get them all out of this situation.

'Stop!' she cried out, and the children halted behind her. The men were moving closer, away from the gate. If they were going to get through this, they needed to draw attention to themselves; the manor residents needed to know something was afoot. The men coming closer to them meant they were all further away from earshot, and that wouldn't do at all. Morven realised she was going to have to do the exact opposite of what her instincts wanted if they were to get through this.

Efi pushed through the snowy heather to join Morven. 'What's going on?'

'Those men, Efi, they're the enemy. We shouldn't have come this way, and I'm so sorry.'

'The enemy?' Cuth asked.

Morven hadn't realised that he had been listening. 'Yes, Cuth. They're very dangerous, and we need to get everyone in the manor to realise we need help.'

'We need to run at them,' Efi said with confidence.

'Exactly my plan, Ef.' Morven nodded. 'We can overwhelm them – for a few moments, anyway. But we need to act fast.'

Cuth nodded once, rearranged his guard's jacket and the pack on his back, pulled the knife from his pocket, and ran.

Straight at the men.

Morven glanced at Efi with horror, and then realised there was only one thing for it.

'Come on!' she shouted, hitching up her skirts as she ran. Behind her, she could hear Efi encouraging the children to use what was left of their strength to run too. They shouted, screamed, swore, as loudly as they could, and Morven was strangely satisfied in that moment with how large and intimidating she felt sure they were. A band of misfit children, like a smaller version of what she had always been a part of since finding Kelseth Lighthouse. Cass would have been so proud.

In mere moments, Morven and her friends had the men surrounded, and they were successfully pushing them back towards the gates. With the sheer volume of bodies, the men struggled to overpower them enough to fight back, and as Morven pushed forwards, she could see the cast-iron gates slowly creeping open. She dearly hoped there was some serious help on the other side.

A searing pain shot across her face, like a red-hot flame. In the struggle, Morven managed to reach a hand up to her cheek and was horrified to find it wet and sticky. She pulled her hand away and saw the tell-tale scarlet of blood dripping from her fingers. The pain was growing in intensity; her whole cheekbone was throbbing, as though she could feel every pump of blood as it leaked from her freckled face. Ahead of her, the eyes of a malicious, golden-cloaked man gazed upon her with satisfied malice, the blade, still dripping blood, held tightly in his fist.

All Morven could focus on was the damage one man could do with such a small weapon. He was surrounded by children, but all of them could be felled by one small swipe of such a knife. It wasn't worth the risk. Morven didn't stop to think; there was nothing to dissuade her. She ploughed forwards, a battle cry flying from her mouth, and tackled the man to the floor.

The children parted as Morven and the man fell, but all Morven could feel was his throat beneath her slight hands. The strength within her flowed, although she wasn't sure where it came from or what she was supposed to do with it. It was as though the rage and the grief of losing her brother, of losing Glenn, of losing their home and everything they had worked so hard to preserve, gave her the strength she needed in that moment and the golden-cloaked man didn't stand a chance.

She looked down at his face as he struggled, and saw that underneath the bravado of the cloak, underneath the power of the name, he was just a man – pathetic, frightened, terrified of anything that looked different to himself. As the life ebbed, ebbed, ebbed from him, Morven felt her own spirit grow stronger. She had never killed a man before. The man beneath her became at once in her mind her awful step-father, Brenna and Maeve's father, Lily's uncle Alf, every soul who had ever hurt another – and then she caught herself. If she killed this man, would she be any different? She looked down into his eyes and saw desperation, pleading her to let him live. He was so, so close to death. Only a few moments more and he would be gone.

'Morven!' A cry filled the air. It was the voice of the man who had taught her that not every one of them was cruel. Jem.

She flicked her head up and took in the scene. People were flooding from the manor, led by Jem, Grace, Alice, and Lily. Grace and Lily were ushering her children through the gates. She could see now how tired and scared they all were, and the feeling of abject failure flowed through her; she had been so hellbent on revenge that in those final crucial moments, she had forgotten what it was she was there to do – to see the children to safety.

Jem was pelting towards her, his thick cloak billowing behind him as he hurled himself through the snow. She pushed herself off the man beneath her and stumbled backwards. As she looked down again, she realised the true horror of what she had done. He was dead.

'I didn't mean to—' she croaked, her hands shaking. 'I didn't—'

All she could feel on her skin was his final moments; all she could see with her eyes was his fear. She was a murderer. She would always be a murderer.

Jem careened into her and swept her into his arms. That was when the tears started to flow. The tears she had pent up and held in this whole time. Once they had begun, nothing could assuage them. She buried her face in Jem's shoulder as he lifted her up and carried her across the heather back to the gates. The woollen jumper he wore felt rough and coarse against her red-raw cheek, but she didn't mind. 'It's going to be all right,' she heard him say, over and over again.

Morven didn't know if it was her he was trying to convince, or himself.

Chapter Thirty-Two

The flickering candle cast strange, dancing shadows across the dark wooden panelling that covered the walls of Hecate's study. It was like a black cloud had shrouded an awakening sun; just as the world had been getting brighter, everything had been plunged back into darkness, as though it was midnight once more. Alice could hardly believe it was still daylight outside. The clouds that had promised snow hung heavily, as if they could barely hold themselves up with the weight of the impending storm.

She had been sitting at Hecate's desk for what felt like a hundred moon cycles. She couldn't move, couldn't breathe for the weight of it, much like the clouds outside. But it wasn't snow that held her down in the scarlet leather of the seat, but the burden of her grief. Momentarily, through the surprise and subsequent chaos of Morven's arrival, with countless other souls that needed care and attention, she had lost herself. She had tried to move with the flow of bodies, finding, treating, and caring for each one, but no matter how hard she tried, she couldn't emulate the easy kindness that flowed from her companions. After a while, she had skulked away to a dark corner to watch Grace and Lily working together to sort through the children and ensure each one knew where they were, where to go, who to ask for help. If Alice hadn't felt so nauseous and hollow, she would have found the sight of the two souls she loved the most working alongside each other heartening. She had been so close to losing Lily, and every moment had felt like a knife through the heart. But now, with Hecate gone, all she felt was loss. It felt like Hecate's death was mourned by no one except herself.

Was that going to be her legacy too? Destined to strive, destined to fail, destined to fall back into obscurity? She couldn't bear it. She had spent her entire life as an outcast; powerless and alone. For a few sweet moments, someone had recognised her potential and lifted her up to new heights of possibility. How could she bear to go back to being a nobody again?

Alice looked around the room. Hecate hadn't left much behind; she had never cared much for accumulating objects beyond those which adorned her person. But in this old manor house, all the rooms were filled with maps and books by default, as if the custodians of the place throughout history had cared only for paper and ink.

Alice tried to force herself to take some deep, measured breaths. Her ears were ringing; her heart felt like it was trying to beat in a vat of boiling tar; her hands were dry and cracked. She could only guess at the state of her face and hair – she hadn't managed to bathe since Hecate left her. It felt as though, if she washed the dirt away, she would wash the memories away too. If the Brotherhood attacked now – which she reminded herself was very likely – what would she do? How could she fight, when the fight had been stripped from her?

She stared at the candle in front of her and clicked her fingers. Nothing. She clicked her fingers again, frowning at the flame as it flickered, taunting her. Nothing.

Something in her snapped. Filled with pain and frustration, loss and fear, she burst from Hecate's seat and swiped her arm across the book-laden desk. Papers flew into the air, an old paperweight fell to the floor and smashed with an ear-splitting crash, and the candles extinguished themselves on their way to the ground in response to the force with which they'd been flung. Alice wedged her hands beneath the impossibly heavy oak desk and heaved with every ounce of strength in her until it was upended and crooked, lying pathetically on its side. She dragged the curtains from their rails and flung them across the room; she kicked piles of books until they were strewn across every inch of the floor. She roared and howled like a wolf had been trapped inside her all this time, just waiting for an opportunity to be let out.

She wanted death. She wanted to kill, or be killed – she didn't mind. Anything to end this feeling of utter despair.

'Alice?' A voice broke through her cries and found its way directly to the centre of her heart. 'Alice? Where are you?'

That was when the tears started. From the anger grew the fear, and from the fear grew the sadness. It was the sadness she had been so desperate *not* to feel, but as Lily burst into the room and found her there on her knees, surrounded by devastation, all she could do was cry.

The arms of her best friend enveloped her, and the heavy snow clouds lifted a little.

'It's all right,' Lily said, rocking her back and forth like she had done so many times throughout the years. 'It's all right. It's all going to be fine. I've got you. I'm here.'

In her heart she felt gratitude, but she couldn't make her voice reflect that. 'I'm fine,' she said. 'I don't need your help, I'm fine.'

'I've known you far too long to believe that,' Lily whispered, stroking the knots from Alice's hair. 'I'm so sorry about Hecate.'

The wave came over Alice again, just when she thought she'd got a handle on it. The relentless crying made her feel so angry. How would this solve anything? She was supposed to be the next leader of the Shadow Sect, a priestess feared and revered by all. But she was just a pathetic child, useless and alone.

'Whatever it is you're telling yourself up there, in your

mind, it isn't true. Just because life is unkind sometimes, doesn't give you an excuse to be unkind to yourself.'

Alice sniffled and pulled back from Lily's embrace, rubbing her red eyes until they were raw. 'What am I going to do?'

Lily took Alice's face in her hands. 'You're going to brush yourself off, magic this room clean, and get back down there to start drawing up a plan. Hecate trusted you, Alice, which means you are the person every single witch, protector, and child will be looking to for guidance.'

Alice started to protest, but with one look from Lily her mouth was closed again.

'I don't care if you don't think you can do it, or if you think they don't like you, or if you think they might laugh at you. Someone has to take the lead before the Brotherhood arrives, and I know the best thing for you to do is to find a purpose; no good can be found in this solitary confinement, Alice. You need to get out there. I'll be right by your side. We are Sisters of Shadow, one light, one dark. You have Grace to protect you, we have Jem to watch our backs, and you have a manor filled with people looking for a purpose, looking for a reason to get up and fight.'

'But why would they follow me? I am nothing without Hecate,' Alice snapped, refusing to display the fact that she had been moved by Lily's speech

'Hecate gave you tools, yes. She's also given you an army. A Protector. A power you never even knew you had. Hecate has done her job, and now it's time to do yours.

Alice, it would be a slight to her memory if you gave up now.' Alice felt her hands gripped tightly by her best friend's, and Lily pulled her up off her knees. 'But now you need to do exactly what you keep promising me that you will do.'

Alice frowned. 'What's that?'

'You need to train me.'

Chapter Thirty-Three

Jem couldn't believe it was true.

Morven had sprinted straight upstairs to her bedroom after he had carried her inside, slammed the door in his face, and refused to answer his questions. He had decided to help with the children for a while to allow her some space, but when he had returned, she had wrenched open the door, fallen back into his chest, and cried three words he had never, ever wanted to hear.

'Cass is dead!'

He stood in her doorway, dazed, his ears ringing. Morven peeled herself from his jumper and stumbled back to her bed, where she sat curled up with her knees touching her chin. Jem took a few tentative steps forward but then he heard footsteps in the corridor.

'What's going on?' It was Farlan. Fenn's nephew. Jem

realised the boy would always be that now. Where had he been? 'Can I help at all?'

Jem cleared his throat and stood up as tall as he was able. He felt like the world had fallen away beneath his feet, and now he was barely floating, held up by an invisible noose at his neck.

Cass is dead. How can he be dead?

First, he had lost Grace, and thank goodness he had found her again. Then Glenn was taken from him. Lily had almost died, and those days of despair without her had been agony. And now this. He was supposed to protect those around him, and yet.... *And yet.*

'Jem...?' Farlan had wandered into the room uninvited, and Morven had turned her back to them both. Jem could see the trembling of her shoulders that indicated she was crying silently.

'It's fine, Farlan. There's nothing to see here. I'd appreciate some privacy though, if that's all right. There are plenty of children downstairs in need of food and a little company. Can you go to them please?' Jem tried to keep his tone light, but the order came out with a venom he hadn't expected. What business did Farlan have here? It seemed like he turned up everywhere, just to annoy him.

Farlan didn't argue. He skulked back into the shadowy corridor and disappeared. Jem heaved a sigh of relief. He didn't feel much like confrontation at the best of times, but this was something else entirely. How could he face Grace, or Lily, or Brenna and Maeve with this?

He sighed, trying to fight back the tears that were threatening to burst out of him at any moment. Not Cass, the bravest, strongest boy he had ever known. Not Cass, who puffed up his chest when given any responsibility, the hero of Brenna and Maeve, the secretly gentle soul with the tough exterior. Cass couldn't be dead. He couldn't.

Jem shook himself and rubbed his eyes. Right now, it was Morven who mattered. He was Jem Rafferty, and he didn't let suffering go untreated. He walked over to her bedside and sat by her, wrapping an arm around her shoulder. 'You've been so brave, Morv. You've come all this way with the weight of his loss on your shoulders. You did all of this, kept all of those children alive, without him. He would be so proud of you, Morven. So proud. I know I am.' He squeezed her shoulder, trying to stop his voice from cracking. 'I was speaking to a young girl downstairs earlier – I think her name was Ef… Ef…'

'Efi?' She sniffled.

'Efi, yes. Efi and Cuth were singing your praises. You led them selflessly; you showed them care and leadership even when you felt your worst. Even when battling such a loss. That's something to be proud of.'

'I never wanted any of this without him, Jem.'

'I know. Me neither. A world without Cass is—' He broke off, trying not to let her hear how much he was suffering. His eyes burned and his throat felt tight and uncomfortable. He wanted to scream, to tear the wallpaper from the walls, to put his fist through a window, to collapse onto the floor in a fit of sobs. But he didn't do any of that. He lifted his chin, swallowed his own pain, and looked at Morven. 'A world without Cass is going to be a hard world to survive in. But survive we will. Together. I promise you, Morven, he would have wanted you to find happiness.'

Morven covered her face with her hands. 'What will I do without him?'

'You will carry on, hour by hour, day by day, living the life he would have loved. That's all we can do, my dear girl.' He scraped his hair out of his face and tied it in a knot out of the way; his tears that were flowing freely now trailed down his cheeks.

She sighed and lifted her head, nodding slightly. 'He wouldn't want me to give up.'

'No, he absolutely wouldn't. Cass had this fight in him, didn't he?' Jem smiled through the agony, recalling Cass's hot temper and fierce loyalty.

Morven chuckled, despite herself. 'Always the first to pick a fight, always the first to apologise. That was Cass.'

He sat with her in silence for a while, her head rested on his shoulder. They watched as the light refracted through the window and danced its delicate waltzes across the walls. The sadness cloaked Jem; he felt it fasten around his throat and weigh down his shoulders. There was only one person in the world he wanted to talk to about this.

'How is Lily?' Morven asked, seemingly out of the blue.

'What?' Jem was disorientated. They had just been

talking about Cass; his own thoughts had strayed, but how would Morven know that?

'You were in a far-off world of your own for a moment. I saw that face enough times at the lighthouse to know it was Lily on your mind.' She nudged him gently. 'Have you told her yet?'

'Told her what?' Honestly, how was she so perceptive?

'You *are* silly, Jem Rafferty.' She pulled her plait over her shoulder, fiddling with the end of her hair and sniffling. 'If you don't know yourself, it'll do no good me telling you.'

Jem shook his head, wiping away a rogue tear. 'I haven't the foggiest what you're talking about, Morv.'

At that moment, in a flurry of curls and gangly limbs, Maeve and Brenna burst into the room at full speed. Brenna grabbed Morven and Maeve grabbed Jem, and they both pulled and pulled, shouting. 'Come on! Come on!'

'Where? What's going on?' Jem found himself smiling, in spite of himself. The twins' energy was contagious.

'It's the best surprise ever! Come on!' Maeve said, pulling and pulling on Jem's jumper until he relinquished control and allowed himself to be led from the room at a pace far faster than a walk.

He glanced behind to check Morven was following, and caught a glimpse of her face; concern and confusion were etched all over it, and she definitely wasn't smiling. 'Morven has had a tough time, girls,' Jem began. 'You need to be gentle with her.'

'We will!' Brenna panted as she skipped, 'but this will make everything better!'

'Everything!' Maeve agreed.

They were dragged down the corridor, down the grand central staircase, and into the dimly lit hall. Jem would remember what happened next for the rest of his life.

Standing in the hall, by the great oak doors, looking broken, bruised, and very tired, was Cass.

Very much alive.

Chapter Thirty-Four

The smell of delicious, home-cooked stew filled the air. Lily had made sure that she and Jem had cooked enough for everyone who called Midnight Manor home, and even though that number was growing by the day, she was content to see that their pantry was barely depleted. Hecate had established a strong routine of sending witches out weekly to keep their stores stocked up, and since her death, they had been continuing the routine in her memory. Lily noticed that without Hecate's guidance, every single person, witch or not, who called this place home had fallen into step, bolstered by the determination to continue doing what Hecate would have wanted.

They had fed everyone else first, and sent them off to bed, leaving the vast kitchen much quieter. On the end of the long table closest to them, Brenna and Maeve sat on Cass's lap, taking one leg each. Morven was sitting as close as she could to her brother without also being on his lap, and Grace and Alice were across from them, listening to his story. Morven was still crying gently. She had started crying the moment she had been reunited with her brother, and hadn't stopped since. Lily could only imagine the depths of Morven's feelings; to have lost someone so dear was unthinkably painful, but to have them return, safe and sound... that was something else entirely. Lily looked across the room at Alice, and felt enormous gratitude that she, too, had found something – or rather some*one* – that she had lost, and ignored the terrible weight in her chest that reminded her she would never have this moment with her uncle.

From what Lily could tell, Cass had survived a horrible accident at the poorhouse he and Morven had been trapped in. He had been wearing a guard's uniform, so when help had arrived they had pulled him out, treated his wounds, and allowed him to go on his way 'in pursuit of the scoundrels who set the fire'. No one had argued with him, of course, and that story had held up through the border, too. He had been relatively unscathed, except for some minor burns, a few cuts and bruises, and a very, very broken nose.

'I just don't understand how you could've survived,' Farlan said.

Lily noticed the boy had distanced himself from the group lately, and most of the things he said were probing questions. Gone was the sweet boy, full of confidence but never arrogance. In his place, this Farlan had grown brooding and suspicious. Lily wondered if Fenn had anything to do with it. Could his influence be felt this far away?

Cass shrugged. 'Me neither. The entire thing fell on top of me. But I was right on the edge of it, and for whatever reason, I was lucky.'

'Well, I for one don't care why or how you survived, my boy.' Jem grinned as he served up the bowls of food. 'I'm just glad you're here. We had quite the scare when we thought you'd...' He paused, unable to finish the sentence. He passed Lily some of the bowls, and the pair of them got to work serving up food onto the long table around which the friends were sitting.

In amongst the chaos of the past couple of hours, with Morven's dramatic arrival, and then with Cass's, Lily had almost forgotten what had passed between her and Jem in the greenhouse. Everything felt the same, except the world felt more vivid now, and every time she caught his eye she wanted to explode. *All right*, she thought to herself, *maybe things don't feel* exactly *the same*.

She took her seat next to Alice, and Jem joined her across the table. There was a momentary lapse of chatter as they all tucked in to their stew; it was a simple concoction of vegetable stock, onions, potatoes, and carrots, but between her and Jem, they had managed to make something rather delicious. Lily had also finally perfected the spell for multiplying things, so the one perfect white loaf she had baked turned into enough bread to feed every single manor resident with some left over.

Whilst everyone was busy eating, Lily stole a glance at Jem, but he must have had the same idea. Their eyes locked across the table and Lily felt her cheeks warm at the exact moment she watched pinkness rise to his. He grinned, and she couldn't help but smile back.

Grace let out an overdramatic moan. 'You guys, we're eating here!' Lily looked down at the table, mortified. 'Can you keep the grossness until after dinner has finished?'

Everyone around the table laughed.

'Don't tell me you've finally found the courage to put each other out of the misery you've both been in all this time?' Grace banged her fist on the table. 'Thank goodness for that! Now maybe we can all think straight, without the constant noise of pining and yearning to distract us.'

'I'll remind you of this attitude next time you and Alice are having a moment,' Jem huffed, although he was still smiling. If Lily didn't know better, she would have said Jem looked proud, almost smug.

'Us? Having a moment?' Grace was smirking now.

Lily had forgotten how nice it felt to have everyone she loved in one room. They made the pain of losing Alf so much softer than if she had had to face his betrayal and death alone. At least surrounded by their comforting presences, she was distracted from her sorrows. And her fears. She still hadn't learned nearly enough to feel confident in her magic, and the Brotherhood could appear any day.

'I think we all need to calm down, focus, and actually think of a plan.' Alice spoke softly, but every person at the table heard her. There was something in her voice – a power, of sorts – and everyone turned to listen.

'Alice is right,' Lily chimed in. 'We don't know how far behind the Brotherhood will be, and they'll be angry. They know we're practising magic here, and we pretty much have every witch left in the Shadow Lands with us. If they wipe us out, they wipe out every last trace of our people, and we lose not only ourselves, but everything Hecate did will be for nothing. That means Glenn will have died for nothing. Everything we lost, for nothing. We can't grow complacent.'

'How do you know they'll come?' Farlan returned with his probing questions.

'Are you going to do anything except sit in that corner and probe us for information, boy?' Grace asked, her features darkening. 'Why are you here, anyway?'

'He lives here, Grace.' Alice said.

'But why? Why here? We can't offer you anything. You have magic but you never use it. Oh, and apparently you're the offspring of the Brotherhood. Why is everyone so keen to trust you?' Grace had grown red in the face. She was clearly holding on to anger that she hadn't dealt with, and Farlan was the easiest target.

'Hecate had a plan for me, that's all I know. I imagine I

was to be a spy or something – I don't know.' Farlan stood up. 'Look, I know I don't fit in, but I have nowhere else to go. I lost my home too.'

Cass swore. 'I forgot!' He swore again, louder this time. 'The Brotherhood has taken your home, Farlan. I'm so sorry. With everything else that's happened, I forgot to tell you all.'

'It's finally fallen?' Farlan's voice crackled. 'I never cared for the place, but the thought is a miserable one.'

'They're using it as some sort of base. On my way here, I was planning on stopping in to freshen up so I didn't arrive looking like I'd just been buried under a ton of bricks…'

'You *had* just been buried under a ton of bricks, Cassie.' Brenna grinned.

Maeve chimed in too. 'Yeah, you stank but we figured that was fine since you could have died but didn't.'

'Almost dying is a very good excuse for getting away with almost anything.' Cass grinned, squeezing the pair of them tightly on his lap.

'What did you see, Cass?' Jem encouraged.

'Flags lining the driveway and the front of the house; the strange symbol they use, of the tree circled in light. Outside, there were dozens of men and women, all in the golden robes. I didn't hang around to find out what they were doing.'

'Them being based so close by doesn't bode well in terms of how much time we have. If they're gathering an army, we need to move fast. We need a plan for those of us who will fight, and those of us who won't.' Lily looked at the twins, who were frowning. 'Don't even bother, either of you.'

They pouted but didn't argue. Lily knew Jem was poised to back her up, if need be, but she was quietly proud that he hadn't needed to.

'I agree with Lily.' Jem stood up and walked around the table to place a reassuring hand on her shoulder. She felt the strength of his affection, and allowed it to comfort the parts of her that were so deeply buried in the trauma of the past few weeks and months that sometimes she thought she might suffocate.

'Of course you do,' Grace muttered slyly, winking.

Alice placed a hand on Grace's shoulder too, mirroring Jem. But Alice's hand was there for a different reason. 'Grace, leave them be, please,' she whispered, just loudly enough for everyone to hear.

'Everyone who can needs to train.' Lily couldn't see Jem, as he spoke from his place behind her, but she felt the authority in his voice. This was the Jem she'd first met; fierce, solid, unwavering. 'Someone needs to stay back and protect those staying at the manor. I suggest me, Cass, Morven, Brenna and Maeve stay behind. We will only hinder you at the front of the battle, and we are all far better suited to defending the manor, treating the injured, etcetera. Farlan, you can choose where you think you'll be the most useful.'

'How come he gets to choose?' Morven complained. It

was the first thing she'd contributed properly since Cass had returned.

'Because I'm not really part of this group, this family,' Farlan muttered, before skulking out of the room with his head hanging low.

'Well, now you've done it,' Grace said, not unkindly.

Lily heard Jem sigh and reached up to her shoulder to hold his hand. He squeezed it gently.

'Come on then,' Lily said, after mopping up the last of her stew. 'We should all go to bed. We've got a full day tomorrow if we're going to be ready.'

The clattering of plates and bowls filled the air almost immediately, as everyone allowed the weight of what was ahead to sink in. Lily hated the idea of not having Jem by her side as the Brotherhood attacked, but she knew being with Alice and Grace was the best place for her to be, and there was no one in the world she trusted more than Jem to ensure everyone else was safe and well looked after.

Chapter Thirty-Five

A spiralling gust of ice-cold air whipped across the manor grounds, leaving a trail of devastation in its wake. It tore up grass and threw stones, and Lily was sure it was the most violent she had ever deliberately been. She held her arms out, as demonstrated by Alice beside her, and sent the tiny tornado across on its path of destruction. It was tiring, but exhilarating. She could do real damage with this spell, without actually seriously hurting anyone. Lily didn't like to think about hurting people, no matter how much they deserved it.

Alice, on the other hand, had shown her stronger forms of fire magic, which set everything, *everything*, in its path alight. Rock, tree, person. There was a fire in Alice's eyes, too, when she cast that spell. A fire that worried Lily, although she didn't admit it to her best friend. She was mostly glad to be here with her, by her side, actually training.

Magic, *deliberate* magic, didn't come easily to Lily. That is, the power itself often came very easily, but the weight of what she was doing was heavy, and she didn't enjoy it. It was a gift she'd never sought, a sense of purpose she'd never needed. Sure, she could see the benefits of being able to imbue her salves and tinctures with little pockets of healing magic so that they would work even in the most difficult of cases, but offensive magic was terrifying. Lily was realising more and more than she wasn't cut out to be a fighter, a warrior. She was a healer.

And yet, sometimes, when her power flowed freely, there was a darkness lurking in the depths of her soul. She felt weightless with it, giddy almost, with the strength of her own power. She hated the feeling, especially after the spell had passed. The guilt was almost overwhelming; if she unleashed the darkness she knew resided somewhere within her, she didn't know what would happen.

But, she remembered, Alice needed her. And if Alice needed her, she would do anything to support her friend.

'You're doing great!' Lily said, watching Alice and letting her own spell fall flat, until the gust of wind entirely disappeared.

'Hm,' Alice said, concentrating.

They were surrounded by every other witch at Midnight Manor. They had all been received the call late last night that they would need to garner their strength and perfect their spells. Lily could see the witches Alice had introduced coldly as Ailsa and Rowenna, the two who had been with her when she had rescued Farlan. There were also a few of Morven's young friends, practising their fighting skills without magic. Lily wasn't sure she was happy at the thought of them marching towards danger without magic, but Morven knew them better than she did. She wasn't even an adult herself, so how could she judge others based on their age?

Nearby, Grace was training with Brenna and Maeve. Their skills as witch and protector had developed so dramatically that Lily was half convinced they would annihilate her and Alice in a duel without much effort.

'Ali?' Lily asked.

Alice dropped her fire spell and turned to her friend. 'Yes, Lil?' Her eyes were still dark with the height of her grief, and the fear of taking on Hecate's mantle.

'I missed you.' She reached out and took her friend's hands. They were impossibly warm, something that still caught Lily by surprise. Growing up, Alice had always been bone-cold, but now that she had her magic it was like fire flowed through her veins in place of blood.

Alice squeezed her hands and managed a smile. 'I missed you too.'

'What are we going to do when this is all over?' Lily asked. She hated how constantly full of fear she felt. She knew it was a waste of energy to yearn for quieter, simpler times, but she couldn't help it.

'We'll sleep for about a week.' Alice managed a smile. 'And then we'll build something magical. Together.'

'You and me?'

'You and me. And Grace. And Jem. Morv and Cass, too, if they like, and of course the twins.' She looked over to where Grace was standing. Her Protector didn't notice that she was being watched, but Lily saw the affection in Alice's eyes.

Lily sighed. 'But that isn't the life you wanted, Al. You wanted adventure, power…'

Alice let out a short, sharp laugh. 'I'm not planning on giving it up, either. In my experience, there's nothing better after an adventure than coming home to a cosy, warm place filled with your favourite people. I know I'm done living alone, Lil. I don't want to go back to how things were for me.'

Lily nodded. That made sense. 'I think I've had enough adventure for a lifetime.' She smiled. 'You and Grace can go on great, epic adventures, have daring fights, and see wonderful things I could only dream of, and then you can come home and tell me all about it. I'll write it down in a little chronicle, and then all the children who pass through our home can know where you are, and what you've been up to. Think of the joy that would bring them.'

Alice smirked. 'What about Jem?'

'What about him?' Lily answered too quickly, and blushed.

Rolling her eyes, Alice continued. 'What does he want to do next?'

Lily shrugged. 'I'm not sure.'

'You mean you haven't planned the rest of your sickeningly happy life together yet then?' Alice nudged her, gently.

Lily didn't know how to respond. She was still so bowled over by her feelings for Jem, and even more bowled over by his apparent reciprocation of them, that she hadn't actually stopped to think about what would come next.

'I'm sorry, Lil. You'll be getting no pressure from me.' She held up her hands in surrender. 'But I am stupidly happy for you, by the way.'

Lily smiled at her friend. So much had changed recently, but the sight of Alice's smile was everything to her. If she could just keep that smile, just there where it was, she would be happy.

'Are you feeling all right?' Alice asked. 'I realised I haven't asked you. Since Alf, and then your injury, things must be hard. I'm sorry I've been so wrapped up in my own mess.' Alice rubbed her eyes, leaving deep red patches on her face that contrasted with her alabaster skin.

'Grief is a strange thing,' Lily responded. 'Minute by minute, it presents as a different creature. I can wake up and feel hopeful again, with the sun shining through my window and the birds singing outside. But by the time I've walked out of my door, I'm carrying a giant on my shoulders and being asked to function normally, as if he weren't there. Sometimes it's like I'm walking through knee-deep bog, without an end in sight, and other times it's just a little rocky underfoot. The pain is always there, it's just sometimes I feel strong enough to cope with it, and other times I feel like I might drown in the depths of it.'

Alice nodded knowingly. 'I understand.'

'But I guess there's no better distraction than imminent doom.' Lily tried to smile, but the statement came out a little more tense than she'd intended.

'We'll be fine,' Alice said quietly, but it was clear she didn't even believe herself.

A rumbling broke both friends from their conversation. The training fields fell into silence, until…

'THEY'RE HERE!'

Chapter Thirty-Six

Farlan's voice had echoed from a window at the top of the manor where he had a view of the entire stretch of moorland that surrounded them. 'THEY'RE HERE!'

Grace darted inside at the proclamation and marched straight up the stairs to the room she knew his voice had come from. She wanted to see for herself what they were dealing with. She had a mind, although she couldn't tell Alice, to just march her brother and the children out of the manor entirely, to march with them until they were so far away from danger that nothing could ever touch them. She knew, though, that not a single one of them would let her, and the thought made her so full of rage that she needed an outlet.

'Where?' she asked, barged into the room with her shoulder. 'Where are they?'

Farlan spun on his heel, terror etched across his features. He pointed out of the window, without speaking.

Grace stormed up to the window, resting her elbows on the windowsill so she could lean forward and squint into the distance. And there it was. A hazy line of shimmering gold in the middle distance. Some of them held tall flags adorned with the tree circled in light; others held golden shields. They moved in a wave. The closest thing she could compare it to was the murmurations of autumn, during which hundreds of starlings moved synchronously in the air. The Brotherhood, too, moved like that, in a strange, otherworldly flow. They lacked the mystical beauty of the autumn flock though. Instead, all Grace felt was an icy fear trickling down her spine.

'What's your plan?' Farlan asked, blinking away his watery eyes.

Grace frowned at him. She had no time for this simpering boy; he was yet to prove his usefulness, and she didn't understand why everyone else had just accepted his presence as if he weren't descended from the very people marching towards them on the horizon. 'Why do you care?'

'Because I want to help, for goodness' sake!' Farlan swore. 'Let me help.'

Grace rolled her eyes and stormed back out of the room, leaving Farlan to his thoughts. She didn't have time for him right now.

As she dashed down the corridor and down the stairs into the entrance hall, she had one focus: find Alice. But the task was going to be far more difficult than she had anticipated, as the panic of the Brotherhood's approach had seeped into every single person at the manor. It was chaos. People rushed from room to room – gathering supplies, stuffing bread rolls into their mouths, shuffling children into the safest rooms. There were shouts, screams, and crying that rolled like thunder from one end of the manor to the next. Spells were thrown like apple cores discarded from carriage windows and Grace couldn't tell if the atmosphere was one of determination and excitement or utter terror. Deep down, she knew it was probably a mixture of both.

The rumbling in the distance was growing in intensity. They didn't have much time.

'EVERYONE WHO CAN FIGHT, GET OUTSIDE! NOW!' Grace yelled.

Silence fell immediately, before the noise regained traction as those willing to fight filed outside.

'Everyone else, prep this area, and every downstairs room, to treat casualties. If you're in here, you're still being useful. Keep the smallest children away from the middle of it; keep them distracted.' The faces staring back at her looked frightened but determined. 'You've got this, everyone,' Grace said, nodding at them. 'Don't be scared. Use that energy to keep you moving. All right?'

'Yes, Grace,' they said, with varying degrees of confidence.

'If anything happens, anything really bad, come and get me. Lysa?' She pointed at a teenage girl she had trained with way back in Hecate's lair, before Alice arrived. 'You're in charge of keeping this place running. Understood?'

'Got it.' Lysa nodded.

'Find Morven and Cass. They'll be your seconds. If anything happens, send either of them.'

With a deep exhale, Grace turned on her heel, rolled up her shirt sleeves, and marched outside.

Grace found her companions exactly where she'd known they would be: at the front, ready to fight. Except, there were more of them than she had anticipated.

In a line, each poised to fight, were Alice, Lily, Jem, Morven, Cass, Brenna, *and* Maeve. They were all here. 'What's going on?'

'There you are, Grace.' Alice attempted a smile, holding out her hand, which Grace took.

'Here I am…' She didn't understand. Why was everyone here? They had agreed a strategy.

'Before you say it,' Jem chimed in, 'we couldn't wait behind. There are plenty of exceptional healers still inside the manor. They don't need us. *You* need us. We need to be here.'

'But that isn't what we agreed, Jem.' Grace lifted her face, looking down her nose at her brother with suspicion. 'What else is going on? And why, pray tell, are the twins here?' She gritted her teeth, lowering her voice. 'They're only *nine*.'

'Nine and three-quarters, actually.' Brenna replied, crossing her arms. 'You trained us. You should know that we're strong enough.'

'You're strong, yes, but that, over there, is a horde of fully grown adults, Brenna. You're a child.'

'You're hardly a fully grown adult yourself,' Maeve snapped back.

'This is irresponsible,' Grace growled. 'Why is no one acting like this is total madness?!' She could feel her cheeks going red with the frustration.

'Because they're chips off the old block, sister.' Jem squeezed her shoulder. 'We practically raised them. Why are you expecting anything less than sheer dim-witted arrogance and determination?'

'I'm not happy about this.' Grace ran a hand through her jaw-length hair. Her scar ached, as if it knew danger was marching towards them.

'Neither are we.' Alice slipped a hand into hers. 'But there's no sense in using all of our fighting energy on the twins. You're right; there's a whole host of very strong, very intimidating people coming towards us. We need our energy for that.'

'Where's Farlan?' Jem asked, changing the subject.

Ahead, the mirage of figures was closer still. A few more minutes and they would be overcome.

'I left him upstairs. I figured he'd come out and join in,

but perhaps I was too optimistic. He's probably hiding under a bed somewhere.'

'We can trust him though. Right?' Alice asked no one in particular.

Lily sighed and shrugged her shoulders slightly. 'He's related to them. We can trust the Farlan we know, but there's always a chance that he will be someone different when faced with the Brotherhood.'

The elongated cry of battle broke through the air. But it didn't come from in front, from where the Brotherhood were approaching. It came from behind. Grace whipped around and her heart dropped to the floor.

'Surrender to the Brotherhood.
Surrender to the Brotherhood.
Come into the light and
Surrender to the Brotherhood.'

Golden cloaks. Within the manor boundary. Running straight for them.

Chapter Thirty-Seven

Lily couldn't believe her eyes. How was this possible? How could they have found a way in? She gathered her strength to cast her most powerful spell, the destructive tornado, when she realised.

There was only one way the Brotherhood could have made their way inside the manor walls.

I'm such a fool.

'THE SECRET DOOR!' she yelled to the people surrounding her.

Jem turned to look at her with horror and understanding in his eyes.

'We need to contain them!' he shouted back.

Lily could only nod.

'I'll go!' he cried, squeezing the top of her arm. 'Stay alive, Lily Knight. That's all I ask. Stay alive.' He kissed her forehead and then he was running, and she thought her heart might give up beating. 'Morven, Cass,' Jem cried as he ran. 'With me!'

Lily watched as they sprinted away. She desperately hoped they would be able to work out what had happened, and how, but she didn't have time to think about it. She needed to act, and fast.

Alice and Grace were locked together, muttering their spells under their breath. Brenna and Maeve mirrored them, although with less intensity and much more fear. Lily didn't have a Protector. She was alone in this.

But something unexpected happened. Grace and Alice broke free from each other, and offered her a hand each. She took them, and the three of them faced the onslaught. 'I WILL PROTECT YOU BOTH!' Grace cried, and they dropped each other's hands.

Fire burst from Alice in an explosion of sparks and flames. She channelled it towards the front runners, and laughed with glee as they were set alight. Soon, the screams from both sides filled the air.

Creaking metal added to the noise, and Lily looked behind to see that the Brotherhood had broken through the gates and were approaching from all sides. The Shadow Sect were strong, but they couldn't match the sheer number of the Brotherhood. She swore. The five of them formed a pentacle, with their backs to each other and their power pointing towards a different mass of men. The others in their party did the same, so that every possible angle was covered. But they were being overwhelmed. There were already more unconscious witches on the floor than there were Brotherhood, and they continued to drop, and drop, and drop.

'There's too many of them!' Alice cried.

'No such thing,' Grace replied. Lily didn't know how she kept her voice so playful. 'Come on everyone, keep pushing!'

Lily conjured up her shield that she had practised so many times at the castle, and tried to focus on spreading its diameter out to cover more than just herself. She could feel Alice behind her, feel the heat of the flames she was throwing into the crowd. The strength of Grace's protection meant that Lily was able to focus, to feel the power flowing through her and out of her hands.

The witches of the Brotherhood were terrifying. In their golden cloaks, they shot daggers of magic into the Shadow Sect, picking off witches one by one.

'Fenn will kill you all in the end!' Grace shouted.

'You're nothing to him. Join us!' Alice continued.

Their words had no impact. The Brotherhood continued to push from all sides. Spells, daggers, arrows, all flew through the air.

They were outnumbered, outflanked, overpowered.

Lily deflected one spell, a pocket of fire thrown directly at her face, only to be struck across the arm by a spell from a water witch. A shard of impossibly hard ice sliced through the sleeve of her dress and caught her upper arm. Lily cried out in pain as she felt the warmth of blood as it trickled down her arm. Another shard broke around the side of the shield and sliced Alice across the cheek.

Shields were only useful for so long, Lily realised. She was wasting her time attempting to protect those around her. No, the best way to protect them was to attack, to wipe out the enemy.

The time for pacifism was gone. Alf was gone; Hecate was gone. Everything they knew and treasured was at risk of suffering the same fate.

Lily thought of the golden eagles she had seen hunting in the mountains behind Alder Vale when she was growing up, and the sea eagles she had watched from the lantern room of the lighthouse. All her life, she had dreamed of drifting up into the clouds to be amongst the birds, but she realised in that moment that she wanted to be up there not to sit and dream. She wanted to be up there because that was how birds of prey found their victims. How they hunted. The eagles would hover up there, before swooping down, claws extended, to catch their prey. If Lily wanted her friends to live, she realised, she had to spread her wings.

If there was ever a time to allow the darkness within her to escape, it was now.

Chapter Thirty-Eight

Jem, flanked by Morven and Cass, sprinted towards the secret door. How could they have been so stupid? All of them had used the door, all of them knew it existed, but no one had thought to guard it.

They were running, but keeping to the shadows and hiding behind trees. It would do them no good to be picked off by a rogue spell from a distance, before they had even had a chance to block any more of the Brotherhood swarming through the door.

All Jem could think about was how stupid he felt. How naïve he was to have believed that their secret door was actually secret. Without Hecate, they didn't have the protection they had taken for granted, and now the world was at risk of caving in upon them because they had been foolish enough not to consider every possible way they could be attacked.

Leaving Lily and Grace to patch up such a stupid mistake made it so much worse. If something happened to them whilst he was away, he would never forgive himself.

'Stop beating yourself up, mate!' Cass shouted as they ran, trying to keep to the shadows to avoid being seen by the onslaught of the Brotherhood. 'There's no way they could have found it on their own! Someone's betrayed us. We couldn't have known!'

Betrayal. Could it be possible?

'Cass is right, Jem. We need to be on our guard,' Morven shouted.

When had they grown up? He couldn't put his finger on the moment he had stopped seeing them as children he needed to protect and started seeing them as his friends. If he had to face whatever they were running towards, he was glad to have their company. Especially in the light of having come so close to losing Cass altogether.

His questions of betrayal were answered as they drew closer to the door, where the Brotherhood fighters were still filing through in droves. The figure standing by the door, *holding it open*, was Farlan Aelfdene.

'The traitor...' Jem said, mostly to himself, the venom slipping from his lips. 'TRAITOR!'

Jem slipped out of the shadows and ran full pelt towards the boy he knew they should never have trusted. He launched himself at Farlan, tackling the boy to the ground with every ounce of strength he had. He threw punch after punch after punch. Farlan barely had the chance to catch his breath, let alone fight back. But Jem didn't care; he needed retribution. Betrayal was one of the worst things a person could do, and he wanted nothing more than to make Farlan feel the pain that he had caused.

Why hadn't they seen this coming? He was one of them. Of course he was. And they had allowed him to swan in because Hecate Winter, of all people, had decided he could be trusted. How would he tell the others?

'Jem!' He could hear Morven shouting, but she sounded leagues away. 'Jem, stop! Stop!'

'Stop it, Jem!' Cass had joined in. Cass, of all people, he had thought would understand. 'Jem, stop it!'

He could feel them pulling at his arms, trying to drag him away, but he wasn't finished with Farlan. They pulled and pulled but he fought back. He had so much untapped rage inside him and in normal circumstances it would have frightened him. But here and now, with such high stakes and everything at risk, it felt like the most logical way to channel his grief and his fear. The punches just kept on rolling out of him, and he watched almost passively, from a distance, as Farlan's face became more and more bloody.

He could hear Morven and Cass shouting, but it didn't matter. They were far away, and he was here, making a difference. Avenging Glenn and the lighthouse and everything they had lost.

Out of nowhere, a slap across the face broke him out of

his all-consuming headspace, and Cass and Morven took advantage of the momentary lapse of concentration and overpowered him, dragging him several paces away from Farlan's unmoving body. 'I was handling it!' he cried, shaking their tight grip from his arms.

'Farlan didn't kill Glenn, Jem,' Morven said, proving once again that he was more transparent than he realised.

'And he didn't burn down our home,' Cass continued. 'You don't need to enact justice on him. That will come in its own time. But he's not the enemy now. He can barely stand up.'

Jem frowned and looked from his bloody fists to the boy in the velvet suit. He bent double and vomited. *What had he done?*

Farlan was a bloody pulp on the ground.

'Is he...?' Jem spluttered, not daring to end the sentence.

'No,' the boy managed through a mouthful of blood. 'I'm not.'

Morven rolled Farlan over until he was on his side, and could expel the blood from his mouth himself. 'You're not welcome here,' she said. 'And I'm not helping you for any other reason than I don't want your death on Jem's conscience. He's got enough to deal with.'

Jem swallowed and wiped his hands on his trousers. Cass helped him up, and Jem threw his arms around him. 'Thank you.'

'Now you've finished beating the living daylights out of Farlan, we really need to get that gate closed.'

Jem nodded, and the three of them ran over to where the Brotherhood warriors were flooding out through the hidden gap in the wall. All three of them charged, weapons drawn, relying on surprise as their biggest advantage. They overpowered the few stragglers who had just come through the door, and made enough commotion that they managed to heave the door closed and force the bolt into the locked position, trapping anyone still left in the tunnel beyond.

They turned around and saw several murderous faces looking back at them – those who hadn't already run towards the main battle, and had instead chosen to enact revenge on the three people who had just trapped the rest of their army.

'Stay alive, you two,' Jem said, before nodding at the pair of them, and receiving short, curt nods back. It was now or never.

Jem yelled, his sword drawn, and ran into the fray. The first few assailants fell quickly, but they were being replaced as quickly as he could take them down. His sword met the metal of the Brotherhood's weapons, and all he could do was continue to swing it over his head and bring it down onto whoever stood in his way. He didn't have the time or the energy to bother attempting defensive movements. He fought like his sister had always taught him to – heavy, fast, and without remorse.

'Jem!' he heard Cass shout. The fear in his voice sent chills down Jem's spine.

Cass was staring into the middle distance with a look of

horror on his face. Those around him had also ceased fighting and were also staring at whatever Cass had seen.

Jem turned slowly, dreading what his eyes would fall upon.

And then he saw it. *Them.*

Chapter Thirty-Nine

'Alice!' Lily cried above the incessant noise of battle, 'Alice, hold my hand!' She reached behind her until she found her best friend, and held on so tightly, trying to find the strength to trust in herself, in her ability to control whatever was about to be unleashed.

'Grace,' Lily heard Alice shout. 'Grace, you've got us, haven't you?'

'Always!' Grace shouted back. Lily watched as the woman Alice loved fought with every fibre of her being, whilst still keeping up her protection responsibilities. It was a remarkable feat, and Lily could have watched that intricate, powerful dance of sword and magic all day.

With a glance at Brenna and Maeve, who were blasting out shield spells to cover as many people as they could, Lily was content that the decision she was making was the right one. It was time to end this.

She took a deep breath, closed her eyes, and allowed the power to fill her up to the brim. She held the image of the eagle in her mind, focusing on its talons, its wings, its beak. Her magic rushed and flowed within her, until every inch of her body was fizzing with the might of her untapped potential. It had been waiting for this moment.

Lily felt her feet lift from the ground, but she didn't let go of Alice. Alice, too, began to ascend into the sky. She hoped Grace would still be able to protect them, but there was a quiet acceptance that to unleash her power was to accept that she, and only she, could control the outcome of what was about to happen. A peace settled over her as that realisation truly sunk in.

Lily opened her eyes and looked down at the battlefield. It was a sea of red and gold, but their sudden ascension seemed to have captured the attention of even the most determined of fighters. Pockets of smoke from fire spells made the air hazy and shadowy, and Lily could just about make out the healers carrying bodies into manor. So many bodies. So much death.

We're losing.

The crowd below paused and looked up at them in awe. It was time. Lily took her best friend and wrapped her arms around her. She clung to Alice with all that she had. She focused on every happy, strong memory they had together, and spoke them aloud so that Alice could see them in her mind, too.

'Nights by the fire in your cabin. Warm afternoons by the stream. Picking wildflowers. Foraging for mushrooms. Feeling the moss beneath our feet and the sun on our skin. Knitting blankets whilst you cook stew. All those times we lived in the moment whilst hoping for an even brighter future.' Lily felt Alice's power flowing within her, and her own power flowing into Alice. Together, they were stronger than the mightiest river. They could move mountains, fell entire forests, destroy everything... if they wished.

Instinctively, they both knew it was time.

They both pulled from their embrace, taking a simultaneous deep breath, turned to face the battlefield, and then let out a mighty, all-consuming cry.

Fire. Flames. Impossible heat. Lily captured Alice's magic in a multitude of swirling gusts, fanning the flames into a frenzy that rained down across the Brotherhood. The flames danced around their own army, catching only those in golden cloaks. *Flaming* golden cloaks, now. The sky was ablaze; the ground was ablaze. As far as the eye could see, Lily's air magic pushed Alice's flames across the landscape, turning it all to ash and dust.

Lily could sense Grace's power keeping them protected high in the sky, but she knew it was unnecessary. The few rogue spells that had made their way up to Lily's level had simply bounced off them, unable to touch power as strong as theirs. With Alice by her side, anything was possible. She could feel the warmth of magic flowing through her, instead of bursting from her. She sent spinning tornados of flames through the crowd, decimating everything in their path. There were no bodies where the tornados landed, only embers.

Chaos broke out on the ground. The Brotherhood fighters were screaming like children as they ran from the blaze, but all Lily could think about was how she was finally up in the air with the birds, exactly as she'd always wished.

'Focus, Lily!' Alice's voice cut through her imagination. 'Focus! I'm losing you!'

Alice was right. Lily was trembling, her focus entirely lost. She could feel the power slipping out of her fingers, and she waved her arms around, desperately trying to claw it back. As she looked over what she had done, her heart felt like a stone in her chest. The sky was black as midnight, even though it was the middle of the day, as though someone had thrown a shroud over the sun and coated the world in a premature blanket of dusk.

Not someone.

She had thrown that shroud over the sun. *She* had created every single pile of ash and dust on the battlefield. The cinders swirled in the air, catching in her throat, just like the tears that were threatening to burst from her eyes at any moment. And then she fell.

Out of the sky, Lily fell down, down, down.

She hit the ground with bone-rattling force, but she didn't – *couldn't* – care.

The fight wasn't over, but Lily couldn't think. Couldn't focus.

She had killed.

She was a murderer.

Chapter Forty

'Oh...!' Cass cried, pointing behind them.

Jem was staring into the sky along with Cass and Morven, all of them open-mouthed, no longer caring to look around at their attackers. Not a single person surrounding them was fighting anymore; they all just gazed, dumbstruck.

In the sky were two figures, their hair floating about them like it was no longer following the natural rules of the world. One had hair like a raven's wing, the other had masses of flaming locks. They were embracing, floating impossibly high above the ground. Lily and Alice. Sisters of Shadow – one light, one darkness – casting their great shadows down on the world below them. Except, it wasn't shadows they were casting. It was spells.

As Jem watched, he saw Lily break from her embrace. She started to move her arms in a strangely elegant way, like she was trying to ball up an invisible string of tangled yawn, and then the destruction began. He didn't need to watch to know what was going to happen. But he did need to get everyone else to safety.

He looked at the bloody pulp that had once been Farlan and was glad to see the rise and fall of his chest. He hadn't wanted him dead, but if Morven and Cass hadn't intervened when they did, he would have been in much deeper trouble. 'Get him inside!' he shouted to Cass, who just nodded. He knew they wouldn't recognise the man he was in that moment, but they didn't have time to mull over what he had done. 'Morven, go with him.'

'What are you going to do?' Cass shouted above the noise of flames raining down upon the Brotherhood.

'I'm going to help the others!' He set off at a run, right towards the middle of the frenzy.

As he left, he heard Morven cry, 'Be careful!'

He couldn't promise that he would be, so he carried on charging forwards. He had to get to Grace. With Lily and Alice way up there, he knew she would be unguarded, using all of her energy protecting them.

Just before he reached his sister, a hooded figure stepped out in front of him. Jem dug his heels into the ground to stop him from ploughing the person down. He could hear a sinister chuckling, and then the figure removed its hood.

He knew the face instantly. And the figure knew his. The last time he'd seen him was in a great grey building. When Lily had almost died.

Fenn Crydlund.

'Jameson Rafferty. We meet once more.' His voice was more serpentine than ever, and his awful face was creased with a smug confidence.

Over Fenn's shoulder, he watched Lily, *his* Lily, fall out of the sky like a shooting star. This was the worst possible timing to be face to face with the leader of the Brotherhood. All he wanted was to run to his sister and to Lily, and after his attack on Farlan, he didn't know what else he had left.

Fenn continued. 'I see you've met my little spy.'

'What?' Jem blinked, frowning.

'Farlan Aelfdene. I trained him well, don't you think? All that time convincing people he was useless, all that time, working for me.' He was so slithery it made Jem want to retch.

Jem scoffed. 'You can hardly take credit for him. He had to be rescued. He's done nothing around here except wander about, getting in the way.'

'That's not true.' It wasn't Fenn who spoke this time, but Lily. She, held up by Alice and Grace, had picked her way through the smouldering crowd and the three of them flanked Jem on either side. Alice kept Lily upright, and Grace fell into step beside her brother. Lily looked like death warmed up, with a heavily bleeding arm and bruises covering her head-to-toe. But she was still the most breathtaking person he had ever seen. 'He was the one who saved me, Jem, remember? He was the one who knew how to help me recover.'

Blast. She was right. Without Farlan, Lily would still be unconscious, or worse.

'Yes, well, it can't be denied that the boy does have rather a sentimental streak, but he certainly doesn't get that from me.' Fenn looked full of bravado, but underneath it all, Jem sensed fear.

'You can't have trained him very well,' Grace piped up, 'if he's saving the very person you want to see dead.'

'Hang on...' Lily said suspiciously. 'How would he get anything from you? You can't *teach* sentimentality.'

'You are Alfryd's niece. You've got his brains.'

Brenna and Maeve joined them, clutching on Jem's cloak like they were toddlers. A glance down proved to him what he already knew; they were bruised, badly, and broken-spirited. They should never have been on this battlefield.

'Farlan's your son. Not your nephew.' As Lily said it, realisation passed over him.

Of course.

'Yes. I orchestrated every little tragic moment of his tragic life. His mother was my brother's darling wife, that's true. But it wasn't my brother who created him. When he found out the truth, I proved to him, to everyone, that Farlan was just a pawn in our greater game. I broke his legs; I took his eye. I planted him where I needed him to be, led Hecate on a wild goose chase to ensure finding him would feel like entirely her idea, and he's been sending me intelligence on you, your plans, and the whole map of this place for weeks.' The self-satisfaction in his face was so great now that Jem was losing his newly gained aversion to violence very quickly.

'That doesn't make any sense,' Grace snapped. 'You think you're so clever, but Farlan's not a bad person.' Jem was surprised to hear his sister defend the boy she had been consistently impatient with since she had met him, but that was Grace, he supposed. A fierce defender.

'Inherently, yes. I suppose it doesn't matter how much you try and suppress someone's nature, so I resorted to good old-fashioned blackmail.'

'I'm done with talking,' Alice snapped. 'You've taken away everything, but now where's your army, Crydlund?' She waved her arms around at the few pockets of men, covered with burns, that surrounded them. 'Where are your protectors?'

'Now, now...' Fenn's eyes darkened. 'Who said I needed them?'

He flicked his arm out and before any of them could react, he held Brenna by the throat.

'SURRENDER!' he cried. 'Surrender to me, or she is the first of you to die.'

Chapter Forty-One

Smoke obscured the faint sunlight, casting dark shadows across Midnight Manor. Alice watched Fenn Crydlund – murderer, leader of the Brotherhood – take the child in his arms and press his knife to her throat.

Threatening to harm a child was bad enough, but this child in particular was so precious to Grace that Alice would have thrown herself from a cliff if it meant saving her from experiencing any more pain. She glanced around, trying to figure out her next move. She needed to be tactical; she needed to resist succumbing to her emotions. To her horror, she saw that they were surrounded.

'*Surrender to the Brotherhood.*
Surrender to the Brotherhood.
Come into the light and
Surrender to the Brotherhood.'

Fenn's downtrodden arm had circled them, and were

pressing in with ferocious intensity. They had suffered heavy losses, largely thanks to Lily, but they weren't entirely defeated. Most of the Midnight Manor witches were injured, limping their way towards treatment and healing, but those left had joined the throng.

Alice closed her eyes. Hecate had taught her one particular spell that she hoped would be useful, if she could actually pull it off.

She inhaled deeply, closed her eyes and tried to embody Hecate. She channelled her power, her strength, her confidence, and then sent her mind outwards, towards every witch in the surrounding area.

Surround them. Protectors, focus on your witches. Witches, focus on the Brotherhood. I will handle Crydlund.

If you value your life here at Midnight Manor, if you value your freedom as a witch in the Shadow Lands, show no mercy.

Alice could barely believe that she had the confidence to give such an order, but she could feel Hecate within her. She knew what Hecate would say, and how she would say it. But Alice channelled herself, too. There would be no punishment for those who would not – or could not – do as she asked. Wars were not won on blackmail and threats, as Fenn himself would soon learn.

'You have two choices, Crydlund.' Alice spoke, barely recognising her own voice. It was rich and thick like treacle, but also sharp as red wine. '*You* surrender, and we let you leave this place on the condition that you and your supporters never set foot in the Shadow Lands again. Or every single one of you dies, right here, right now. Your choice.'

She could feel Lily and Grace's eyes on her; they burned into her like hot coals.

But she could also feel the amassing power of the witches and Protectors who had circled the remaining members of the Brotherhood. They were surrounded, just as Alice and her companions were surrounded.

'What are you waiting for?' A shout came from one of Crydlund's hooded men. 'Kill her and get this over with!'

'Come on Alice!' Another shout, from what sounded like Ailsa Merryck, cut through the air. 'End this!'

'I've come all this way, Alice,' Crydlund hissed. 'We're hardly going to walk away.'

Alice wanted total clarity. 'So you won't surrender?'

Fenn Crydlund smirked. 'Over my dead body.'

Alice felt a hand slip into hers, and a glance to the left confirmed that Lily was standing by her side.

'So be it,' Lily and Alice said synchronously. 'NOW!'

They sprinted straight at Fenn, knocking him to the ground and pulling Brenna from his grip. At the same time, the witches in the outer circle unleashed the very best of their magic: the fire witches sent flames billowing into the already shrunken crowd of golden-cloaked men; the water witches manipulated their power to send gallons of water flowing at head height, so the men couldn't breathe; the earth witches uprooted trees, using them to swipe through the crowd like they were toy soldiers; and the air witches sent their hurricanes to devastate whatever was left behind.

The Brotherhood tried to fight back. Swords swung in all directions, magic pushing against magic, doing far more damage than Alice was comfortable with, but all she could do was channel her power into the invisible hold she had on Fenn. She held him by the throat with her mind, so that he couldn't get up, fight back, or deliver orders from his pathetic heap on the ground. He struggled beneath her grip, kicking his legs, flailing his arms, all to no avail.

The witches continued their onslaught, through many and increasing injuries. It seemed that they, too, were channelling some strange power from the loss of Hecate; it was what she would have wanted.

The last few stragglers of Fenn's army bolted when they saw there was no hope. Alice watched with smug pride as fully grown men ran away screaming like frightened deer through a forest. Not a single one looked back over their shoulder. They all but left him for dead, and Alice gave the command to let them go. They were no danger to the Shadow Sect now; they knew what the coven was capable of.

Shouts of jubilation rippled through the witches. All that fear, all that build-up, all for them to run away with their tails between their legs. They had annihilated the Brotherhood's ranks, and now all that was left was their pitiful leader.

Alice loosened her grip on his throat and allowed him to

rise to his feet. He snarled, an expression she mirrored back to him, before speaking her mind.

'You will not return here, Fenn Crydlund, and you will leave the Shadow Lands for ever.'

Fenn laughed, looking around at Alice, Lily, Jem, Grace, and the children. 'I told you,' he said with a grimace. 'Over my dead body. Or,' he licked his lips cruelly, *'over hers.'*

Before Alice could stop him, Fenn drew his sword in one smooth movement and plunged it deep, deep into Grace's upper torso.

There were a few silent moments of abject horror, as the group took in the scene before them: Fenn's smile, the blood pooling on the outside of Grace's shirt, the paleness of her face, the shock in her eyes.

Jem responded almost instantly, grabbing Fenn's head in his hands, and twisting it grotesquely. It snapped, and he fell lifeless to the floor.

Fenn Crydlund was dead.

Chapter Forty-Two

'Come on, Lily,' she said to herself, over and over again. 'Now is the time to use this forsaken magic for good. This is your one chance at redemption. Come on, come on…'

She was in the kitchen. They had rushed Grace from the manor grounds to the large kitchen table, and then looked around for a solution. Grace was still breathing, although it was laboured, and all the colour had left her face. Her skin looked mottled and ashen, lacking her usual rosy cheeks and glowing complexion.

Lily had started firing out orders, and Jem, Morven, and Cass had followed her guidance blindly, all of them silent and wide-eyed with shock. Alice could do nothing but watch, with horror, as Lily and her companions got to work on the wound that bled profusely from Grace's collarbone. All Lily could think about was how lucky Grace had been, which was a strange thought considering the situation she was in. But a stab any lower on her torso and there would have been nothing Lily could have done. At least with this wound there was hope.

With Jem's help, Morven and Cass cleaned the wound whilst Lily made up a poultice. She used a pestle and mortar to grind up the ingredients, and then dampened a clean cloth.

'Out of the way!' she ordered, as she noticed they were dithering over the wound. She didn't want Jem to start panicking. 'Hold this.' She passed the cloth to Morven and began to pack the wound. The poultice covered the wound nicely, and soon there was no more blood pouring from the puncture. She took the cloth back from Morven and placed it on the poultice, before wrapping more bandages around Grace's chest.

Once the poultice was applied and Lily was happy with the result so far, she ushered everyone out of the room, with clear instructions on what she needed. But the truth was, there was nothing she really needed except for them all to go and get some fresh air. All three of them were descending into a hysteria that could only end badly, so she sent Jem in search of Brenna and Maeve, and Morven and Cass in search of a very specific flower which Lily knew didn't grow in this part of the Shadow Lands. The search for it would keep them busy for as long as she needed them out of the room.

'Ali,' she said, taking a few steps away from Grace now

that she was almost sure she wasn't about to die. Almost. 'Ali, I need your help.'

Her best friend stood in the corner with her back pressed against the wooden-clad wall. Tears streamed down her face in one continuous barrage. She didn't respond.

'Alice Blackwell, I need your help if we are going to save Grace's life. Help me. Please.'

Alice blinked, sniffled, and wiped her face with the sleeve of her tunic dress. The tears were still rolling, but she looked Lily straight in the eye. 'What do I need to do?'

Lily nodded, reaching out a hand to encourage Alice to come closer. 'I read about a spell in a book back in the castle. I remember it because I liked the idea of magic being used to heal, not hurt. The word was *cridhleighis*. It means 'to heal the heart' in the ancient language, so the book says, but I interpreted its meaning as a healing spell for all matters of the body, because it is the heart that keeps us alive. For it to work, properly work, one of the witches casting has to have some sort of bond with the injured party, be that acquaintance, friend, or lover. I thought, between the two of us, we could really amplify this. We could heal her entirely.'

'*Cridhleighis*...' Alice repeated. 'C*ridhleighis, cridhleighis*. Will it work?'

'I don't know. But there's no harm in trying, is there?' Lily tried to instil a sense of hopefulness in her friend by being hopeful herself. Alice didn't need pity or pandering to; she needed a friend with a plan.

'What do I need to do?' Alice asked, stepping closer to

Grace for the first time since she'd been placed on the table. Alice leaned down and gently kissed Grace on the forehead, before looking to Lily for the next instruction.

'Place a hand on her heart, and I will place mine on the wound. With your other hand, take mine, and we will channel our energy into her. It might not work, Alice,' Lily reminded her.

Alice nodded. 'I know.'

Holding her best friend's hand, Lily placed her other hand on the wound on Grace's collarbone and closed her eyes. Together, they repeated the word.

'*Cridhleighis, cridhleighis, cridhleighis.*'

After a few, painful moments, Lily opened her eyes. She looked across Grace to her best friend, who still had her eyes screwed shut, blocking out the world. Lily looked down at her patient, at the pallid face, the damp brow, the shadows beneath her eyes. She removed her hand from the wound and picked up Grace's limp arm, where she felt the wrist for a heartbeat.

She felt nothing. Lily felt her throat constrict. Alice had lost too much already; she was too fragile. And Jem... He would never recover, never forgive himself, if the worst happened. A world without Grace would be catastrophic. For all of them.

The silence and the stillness were agonising. All Lily could think about was how, in a few moments, Alice would realise that Grace wasn't coming back. She couldn't bear it. Grace had to live.

Lily held her hand on the wound, pressing into it so hard that, had Grace been awake, she would have been swearing and threatening Lily, of that she had no doubt.

Come on, Grace. Come on.

Lily started to count, letting the rhythm of the numbers keep her present, hoping against hope that soon, soon she would feel something.

One, two, three, four, five...

'Lily, Lily she's not waking up, is she?' Alice stuttered. 'Lily, please help her! Please, Lily, I can't...' The tears were streaming uncontrollably down her cheeks, but Lily couldn't look at her best friend any longer. It was too difficult. She just kept counting, trying to force as much magic into Grace as she could.

'Focus, Alice,' she said, without looking up.

Alice sniffled and Lily saw her nod out of the corner of her eye.

Cridhleighis, cridhleighis, cridhleighis. They kept repeating it, over and over.

Six, seven, eight, nine, t—

'Shit!' Grace shot upright on the table, clutching her shoulder. 'Bloody hell, that hurts. What happened?'

Lily and Alice looked at each other, before simultaneously bursting into tears. Alice embraced Grace with a little too much gusto, causing the young woman to flinch and swear a little more. At the same moment, Jem burst back through the kitchen door with Brenna and Maeve hot on his heels.

'Grace!' he cried, running over. 'My goodness, you're alive! You're alive!' Now Jem was crying, and for the first time since Lily had known him, he didn't seem in a hurry to hide the tears.

'Of course I'm alive, you dimwit,' Grace grinned. 'Who else is going to drive you insane? I can hardly ask the twins – they're far too unreliable.'

'Hey!' Brenna and Maeve said, but they were grinning too.

Alice sat on the table by Grace and wrapped a protective arm around her. The two of them shared a small moment of affection, forehead to forehead.

Jem wiped his tears on his sleeve, before pulling Lily into the tightest embrace. 'Whatever you did, thank you.'

'It's nothing,' Lily said, burying her face in his neck.

'No, it was everything. You saved us.' He pulled out of the embrace and held her face in his hands. 'You saved every single one of us, Lily Knight.'

'The real question is,' Cass piped up, breaking the atmosphere. 'Where is Farlan, and what are we going to do about him?'

'I'm here.' Farlan appeared in the doorway with his hands held up in surrender, his stick held tightly in his right hand. 'I get it if you all want to kill me.' His face and hands were swollen, he was covered in dried blood, and the skin that wasn't bloody was black and blue. One look at Jem confirmed what she suspected to be true.

'I don't think we need any more death today,' Lily

responded before anyone had the chance to threaten him. 'I'm sure you have a perfectly reasonable explanation for why you betrayed us all for the Brotherhood. Right, Farlan?' Her voice sounded more venomous than she had intended, but it seemed to do the trick.

He sighed, eyes swimming with tears. 'I do. I do have an explanation. Whether you think it's reasonable is—'

'Stop yammering before I make you,' Cass threatened. His fists were balled up so tightly that his knuckles had turned white.

'He's been blackmailing me,' Farlan began. 'I fell in love with someone a while ago, someone I wasn't supposed to love, and Fenn found out. I didn't know I was allowed to be in love, and Fenn used that weakness to his advantage. He realised that he could use that person against me, to manipulate me into doing his bidding. But Wylf wouldn't allow himself to be used. We hid together in my manor for weeks, until one day I woke up and he was gone. Crydlund had taken him, and ever since, he's been threatening Wylf's life to get me to do as he asks. This was the final task, he said, before he would release Wylf and allow us to be happy.'

Lily's heart ached for him. She believed him without a second thought. She could see Jem and Morven were having trouble, but even Cass had softened.

'Where is he now? Wylf, I mean.' Grace asked.

Farlan shrugged.

'Fenn's dead, Farlan. You're free. You're free to go and

find Wylf and live your lives away from that man's influence,' Lily said, wandering over to take his hand. 'You don't have to do anything you don't want to do, ever again.'

Farlan broke down, so Lily enveloped him in a hug. She knew, even in his betrayal, that he had acted out of desperation, out of love, even if it had been misplaced.

His crime had been to love, and Fenn had manipulated that. He wasn't a bad person, just a tortured one.

Chapter Forty-Three

'All right, everyone. I'd like to say a few words.' Jem's voice echoed through the dusk.

The sky above him was laced with the kind of pinks, purples, and blues you only see in the depths of winter. The stars had already crept from their hiding places and twinkled above them like distant lanterns.

Everyone from Midnight Manor stood in the furthest field, the last area of flat ground before the forest. They had spent the days after the battle with their heads down, working on restoring the manor and its grounds to their former glory. The first job had been to honour those who had given their lives. Those with magic and those without had worked together to dig a series of graves. Headstones were carved using delicate spells, and the bodies had been lowered one by one into their burial places. There were no exceptions made for Shadow Sect or Brotherhood; each got their own special place in the ground, their own headstone, their own posy of snowdrops, their own candle.

Lily could see the pain and anguish in Jem's face as he stood on the little grassy knoll that elevated him high enough so that everyone could see him. He stood alone, and she couldn't bear it, so she picked up the hem of her dress and tiptoed around the graves and the mourners until she found herself by his side. She slipped her hand into his and gave him a half-smile. Grace and Alice joined them, and then so did Morven, Cass, Brenna, and Maeve. He didn't have to do this alone.

'What you have faced in the last few weeks is nothing short of horrific. You have lost your leader; I know she was like a mother for so many of you. Hecate Winter was a complex person, and she did awful, terrible things. But she also gave every single one of you a home, and built a community. And that has to be applauded.

'You've dealt with pain, murder, death... so much death.' His voice caught in his throat, and Lily squeezed his hand for strength. He swallowed, then continued. 'It's going to take a long time to recover from everything that's happened. It may even take a lifetime. People, especially young people, aren't supposed to face this much pain. But you can find strength in each other and within yourselves. You will never be alone in this struggle. You will always have a home, something to eat, somewhere to sleep, books to read, people to love you. No matter how old you get, no matter where life takes you, you will always have a home here.

'The people who died, died for the promise of a better life, one in which they would no longer be persecuted for who they are. We need to build a world of love and acceptance, for them, in their honour. Every single grave you see around you houses a person who believed in something *better*.

'I know you'll be experiencing every feeling under the sun right now. I feel it too. I've been there, more times that I want to admit. Healing from something like this takes time and effort and dedication, and I promise you, I will be here healing too. You don't have to face these feelings alone.' Jem exhaled, and then continued.

'We are here, as the sun sets, to celebrate the lives of those who have passed. Please, now is the time to light your candles, say a few words to each other, to those we have lost. Acknowledge their sacrifice, acknowledge your pain, and allow the light of the candle to bring you hope. Once you're done, make your way back to the manor in your own time. Dinner will be waiting for you.' Jem exhaled a deep breath, and turned to those who surrounded him.

Lily pushed up onto her tiptoes to kiss his cheek. 'That was beautiful.'

'It really was, Jemmie,' Brenna agreed.

He didn't speak – or perhaps he couldn't. Lily wasn't

sure which. But as a group, they lit their own candles and placed them down on the graves below them.

'I'd like to plant some trees and flowers here, if that's all right with you all,' Lily began. 'I'd like to turn his field into a place of peace and reflection, where we can all come to take a few moments, and a few breaths, to remember those we've lost. It shouldn't be a place we all avoid coming to; it should be a fine place to be, filled with peace and humming with the life of bees and butterflies.'

'I think that sounds perfect, Lil,' Grace said, smiling at her. She then pulled out a hipflask from her trouser pocket with her good arm and lifted it. 'To Glenn. To the lighthouse. To Hecate. To everyone we have ever lost, and will ever lose.' She took a swig, and then passed it around.

Lily glanced up at Jem with Grace's mention of Glenn, and saw a lone tear roll down his cheek. Quietly, she wrapped her arms around his waist and held him. She wanted him to know he'd never be alone in this either.

The group of friends stood just outside the great wooden doors of Midnight Manor.

The clean-up of the manor after the burial had been a long and arduous task, but everyone had mucked in, and the place almost felt like a sanctuary again.

On the back of a large chestnut horse sat Farlan, in his travelling clothes, his saddlebags filled with food and his belongings strapped to the saddle. He had decided, after helping with the clean-up and apologising every few minutes, that it was time to go and reclaim what he had lost. Lily knew he was nervous. She walked over to his horse to say goodbye, but Jem got there first.

'Easy does it, old boy,' Jem said, stroking the nose of the horse, before looking up to Farlan. 'I'm sorry... about everything.'

'You have nothing to be sorry for, Jem,' Farlan assured him. 'The fault is, and always will be, mine.'

'Well, let's all agree to disagree,' Lily chimed in, 'shall we?'

The young men smiled at her.

'You'll write and let us know you're back safely, won't you?' Morven asked, smiling sweetly. Jem and Lily exchanged glances, and then Lily had to look away to avoid laughing.

With a smile and a wave, Farlan kicked his heels and rode away down the stony driveway and out of the heavy cast-iron gates.

'I can't say I'm jealous of him heading back towards Hythlund. What an awful place,' Cass said, shivering.

'Yeah,' Morven agreed. 'I'm glad my need to explore is firmly out of my system. I never want to leave this place again.'

'Well, you don't have to,' Maeve said cheerfully, 'and at least I know not to bother getting any explorer ideas now too!' She grinned.

'What now, then?' Grace asked. Her arm was still in a sling from the injury to her collarbone, but she was using it to its full advantage as part of her swashbuckling highwaywoman look. She knew Alice thought she was the most handsome soul in the whole of the Shadow Lands, and she intended to keep it that way. 'There must be some mischief that needs making?'

'Mischief? Honestly, Grace, I just want a long bath and a couple of nights of uninterrupted sleep before I even consider what comes next,' Jem remarked.

'I agree,' Lily said. 'A bath sounds great.'

'I'm not sure we've got one big enough for both of you,' Grace sniggered.

Lily blushed and Jem stuttered, which made Cass and Morven laugh heartily.

'Oh, Grace, leave them alone,' Alice said, smiling.

They all stood in front of the manor, waving until Farlan was long out of sight.

'Jem?' Brenna's voice sounded nervous. 'Can we stay here at Midnight Manor for ever?'

'Yes,' Maeve agreed, 'for ever and ever. Please, Lily, please!'

'Well...' Jem looked around at his found family. He wrapped an arm around Lily's waist and flung the other over his sister's shoulder. He saw Alice take Grace's hand, and Morven and Cass each invited Brenna and Maeve to piggyback on their backs. 'It would be rather a shame to waste such a beautiful place.'

'We could continue Hecate's work, in a way,' Lily said, smiling at Alice. 'In a kinder way.'

A ripple of agreement passed through the friends.

Alice smiled back at Lily. '"Midnight Manor School" has rather a ring to it, doesn't it?'

'Midnight Manor School, it is.'

Epilogue

Trailing roses climbed the dark stone walls of the manor, breaking up the once miserable exterior with flashes of peach and pale-pink blooms. Outside the great gates, a couple of signs had been erected, allowing visitors to know they'd come to the right place.

The first read, *Midnight Manor School: a home for children in need of education, both magical and ordinary.*

The second, *Blackwell & Knight's Apothecary.*

The sound of laughter broke through the still morning air. A long table had been assembled in the rose garden, and Lily Knight and Alice Blackwell were already hard at work, organising the place settings. It was midsummer, and Lily had promised the whole school that it would be a day for celebration, a day to rid themselves of the weight of everything that had come before, a day to step forwards into the future with hopefulness. Alice had heartily agreed to help, and the two of them had planned a day of celebrations. There were vegetables from the vegetable patch Lily and Jem tended together, Grace had learned how to bake in a hilarious attempt to impress Alice, and Morven and Cass had planned out the day, hour by hour, with things like ribbon dancing, flower crown making, feasting, and a bonfire in the evening.

Brenna and Maeve were chasing each other through the garden, playing tag. Lily watched them with sparkling eyes as they played, their brightly coloured silk cloaks flapping about in the breeze. Since they had established a more formal school and home for children, the girls had been so much more settled. So had everybody. Even Alice, who had long been prickly and buried in her grief, was now flourishing. Her cheeks glowed pink and her eyes were sparkling emeralds in her alabaster face; her dark velvet dresses had made way for looser, less buttoned-up linens – still dark in colour but so much lovelier.

It was nice too, Lily thought, that Jem and Grace were able to take in lost souls without feeling guilty or like they had to hide anymore. They could teach pupils, some of which had parents who happily paid for their children to be taught ancient skills, alongside literacy and numeracy and, of course, magic for those with a flair for it. The older witches of the Shadow Sect had taken to teaching too, and they had all fallen into a natural rhythm of learning and teaching. There was no exclusionary behaviour at Midnight Manor. Everyone was welcome; everyone had a place. There were no restrictions, no uniforms, no pointless rules: all students could wear what they wanted, so long as it allowed them to freely move their bodies; all students could read whichever books they liked from the library without justification; and all students could approach all teachers with whatever problems they had. Lily hoped it was a place where everyone would feel at home, even long after they grew up and flew away.

With help from Alice, Lily lined the table with glass bottles filled with posies of wildflowers that she'd collected on her early morning walk with Jem. They walked every morning, sometimes for miles, always hand in hand, discussing the future of the manor. They both had dreams and plans that were overflowing, and Lily found it a relief to have someone to vent to.

The apothecary had been his idea, thought up on one of their walks. He had suggested that she and Alice make the trip back to Alder Vale to gather ingredients and heal their connections with the village folk. Also, to thank them for saving her life. He thought they would be more than happy to help her, and he had been right. Lily and Alice made the trip not long after Farlan sent his first letter, informing them that he had been reunited with Wylf, and that they both would reside in the Aelfdene Manor until they found somewhere smaller and more suited to the pair of them.

Alder Vale had been exactly as Lily had remembered, except she had a new appreciation for it upon her return. Jemima and Orla had embraced both of them and apologised to Alice so many times that they both became quite embarrassed. They helped the young women to source an old wooden cart to be pulled by one of their horses, which they then filled with all of the books and remedies that filled Alder Vale Apothecary. Lily knew she could never make that building feel like home again; it reminded her too much of everything she had lost. But between her and Alice, they collected everything they could possibly need, before setting up shop in a little cabin on the edge of the manor's land, built whilst they were away by hand by Jem and Grace.

Jem and Grace were always building. It was something cathartic they could do together, he had told Lily one evening when they were lying wrapped up in their duvet in the room they shared. He and Grace had plenty of plans for the place, but mainly they wanted to build a little settlement at the very back of the manor's boundary line, a little way into the forest.

On another of their walks, Jem had taken her by the hand and asked her if she would like him to build them their own tiny cottage, next door to Alice and Grace, who would be next door to Morven, Cass, Brenna, and Maeve. Lily had burst into tears at the idea, but now the thought only filled her with a rich warmth. They would lead a quiet life, she knew that. Each of them would have their own purpose, their own plans, but they would always return to their little cottages, next to their awfully big manor, and share their hopes and dreams with one another, as they had done for so long.

Sisters of Midnight: The Playlist

- *Ferryman* by Johnny Flynn and Robert Macfarlane
- *Which Witch* by Florence + the Machine
- *In Dreams* by Ben Howard
- *O Sleeper* by The Oh Hellos
- *Lady of the Lake* by Enaid, David Arkenstone
- *The Raven's Rock* by Lúnasa
- *Under Giant Trees* by Agnes Obel
- *Shrike* by Hozier
- *Sound the Trumpet (Instrumental)* by Celtic Expressions Band
- *Wildflower Jigs* by The Gothard Sisters

Acknowledgments

Holy moly, I can't believe that we're here already. After three books, there are so many people I'm indebted to, and I can barely think of a way to put that into words, but I'll go ahead and try.

To the whole One More Chapter team, you are such a hardworking, kind bunch and I will forever be blown away that you wanted to take a chance on this story, my story. It is a delight and an honour to be one of your authors, in amongst some of the most talented writers I've ever known.

To Bethan Morgan, your vision for Lily, Alice and the lighthouse kids has taken this trilogy to places I couldn't even have dreamed of. Your enthusiasm for these books, and the patience, kindness and dedication you've shown me over the past couple of years have been totally mind-blowing. You are a Super Editor and I'm so lucky to have had the chance to work with you. Thank you for everything.

To all of my dearest friends: Beth Davidson, Beth Cocking, Chelsea Coyne, Jessica Blake, Rosie Cunniffe, Lydia Crook, Stig Svendsen, Jen Rossall, Ryan Cooper and everyone else I know and love. Sorry for becoming a hermit for the past two years! I am surrounded by the most loving bunch of people, and I honestly couldn't feel luckier to know and love you all.

To the most wonderful bunch of inspiring women I met last year who have not only been so supportive of my writing, but also have encouraged me out of the door and into the hills and lakes of the Lake District around deadlines and stress, I'm so glad to know you all. Jess Shipley-Burgess, Hannah Shaw, Kim Teale, Claire Bryce, Cat Parkinson, Nida Bee. More adventures in 2023 please!

To my parents for the endless support, love, care, pep talks and hugs. I honestly won the parent lottery with you guys and I can't thank you enough for all you have done, and continue to do to support me in reaching my dreams. None of this would have been possible without you and I will be forever in awe of your ability to make me smile!

To my husband, Arron. You are my rock. You are the brightest, shiniest soul and have kept me upbeat and positive when it felt like the world might cave in. These past few years have been so unpredictable, and you've been one step ahead the whole time, holding me up, cheering me on. You are quite literally the greatest of all time.

And finally, to you, dear reader. Thank you for picking this book up, and picking up its two predecessors. This story lived in my heart and my mind for so many years, and now it's yours. I hope it brings you comfort and happiness in the years to come, and I hope you'll be able to return to the Shadow Lands with Lily, Alice, Jem and Grace whenever you need a little cosy fantasy pick-me-up. Knowing my words and my characters have found their way to your heart makes every single sleepless night and frustrated tear worth it. What a joy it is to create.

Thank you.

ONE MORE CHAPTER

YOUR NUMBER ONE STOP FOR PAGETURNING BOOKS

One More Chapter is an award-winning global division of HarperCollins.

Sign up to our newsletter to get our latest eBook deals and stay up to date with our weekly Book Club!
Subscribe here.

Meet the team at
www.onemorechapter.com

Follow us!
@OneMoreChapter_
@OneMoreChapter
@onemorechapterhc

Do you write unputdownable fiction?
We love to hear from new voices.
Find out how to submit your novel at
www.onemorechapter.com/submissions